Madeline Oxley could not comletely fault Adam Coates. Her father had hoodwinked them both...but now that she stood at last before him, how could she ever walk away?

"Your father sent me the wrong bride!"

Madeline gritted her teeth. "Sir, you are not the only one who has been *inconvenienced* by this. I just spent forty-six days on a damp, creaky ship, and now you tell me in front of everyone that I'm not the one you ordered, and I shouldn't have bothered. I believe I've had quite enough insults for one day. My father assured me you had asked for my hand. I had no reason to question the truth of it."

Adam's chest heaved with a sigh. "No reason to question it? Do you not have a mind of your own?"

Oh, this was too much. "To tell you the truth, Mr. Coates, I do have a mind of my own—a mind to poke my father with a knitting needle, and if I may say so, you could use a poke yourself!"

* * *

Adam's Promise
Harlequin Historical #653—April 2003

Acclaim for Julianne MacLean's work

Prairie Bride
"A promising debut!"
—*Affaire de Coeur*

"Vivid and perceptive, Julianne MacLean is a
powerful storyteller. I felt like I was right there!"
—Bestselling author Pamela Morsi

"...a tender triumph..."
—*Halifax Chronicle Herald*

"...an exceptional uplifting romance guaranteed
to bring a smile to the face of any reader!"
—*Old Book Barn Gazette*

JULIANNE MACLEAN

Adam's Promise

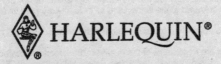

HARLEQUIN®

TORONTO • NEW YORK • LONDON
AMSTERDAM • PARIS • SYDNEY • HAMBURG
STOCKHOLM • ATHENS • TOKYO • MILAN • MADRID
PRAGUE • WARSAW • BUDAPEST • AUCKLAND

ISBN 0-373-29253-8

ADAM'S PROMISE

Copyright © 2003 by Julianne MacLean

This edition published by arrangement with Harlequin Books S.A.

® and TM are trademarks of the publisher. Trademarks indicated with
® are registered in the United States Patent and Trademark Office, the
Canadian Trade Marks Office and in other countries.

Visit us at www.eHarlequin.com

Printed in U.S.A.

Please address questions and book requests to:
Harlequin Reader Service
U.S.: 3010 Walden Ave., P.O. Box 1325, Buffalo, NY 14269
Canadian: P.O. Box 609, Fort Erie, Ont. L2A 5X3

Dedication:

For you, Stephen.

Acknowledgments:

To the town of Sackville, New Brunswick, Canada,
in particular the Tantramar Heritage Trust, for hosting
Yorkshire 2000—an event to celebrate the Yorkshire
settlers who immigrated from England to Nova Scotia
between 1772 and 1775—and to all the volunteers and
organizers who inititated and contributed to the
extraordinary event. To the Mount Allison University
Canadian Studies Program for sponsoring the academic
conference during the festival, which started me on the
research path to writing this book. And to the Mount
Allison University Library, the Cumberland County
Museum and the Nova Scotia Public Archives, for being
so dedicated in maintaining their collections.
Any historical inaccuracies are entirely my own.

Also, to my agent, Paige Wheeler,
editors Melissa Endlich and Tracy Farrell,
and my friends and helpful readers Deborah Hale,
Tory Leblanc, Ruth MacLean, Georgie Phillips and
Tammy Sisk. Thank you also Mom and Dad,
for being such amazing grandparents.

Finally, to my cousin Michelle,
for your unwavering love and friendship.

Author's Note:

Anyone who has ever had the pleasure of taking a walk
on a damp day on the Tantramar Marsh will forgive me
for the artistic license I took with the mosquitoes.
I wouldn't have been able to tell much of the story
the way I did if I had given them their due.

Prologue

Yorkshire, England, 1775

Madeline Oxley gathered her cloak about her and picked her way over the damp, foggy moor toward home. She peered through the mist shrouding her little stone house, nestled in the valley alongside the stone piggery and the other buildings, then came to a halt.

Oh, she wished she did not see what she thought she saw. She blinked slowly and looked again. Yes, it was still there. Her father's carriage. He had returned.

A nervous little breath puffed out of her lungs. She did not like surprises. The past few days, with her father gone, she'd tasted freedom. Not freedom to come and go, mind you—she was always free to do that as she pleased—but freedom in a more mindful sense. She didn't have to look upon that expression of disappointment and disapproval, the look that never failed to sit like a wet stone in her belly at every meal.

With a resigned sigh, she walked down the hill and across the cobbled yard, past the chicken coop and stable and around the empty carriage to the front door. She unhooked the clasp on her cloak and stepped inside. Warmth from a strong fire crackling in the parlor touched her chilly, red cheeks.

The door clicked shut behind her. She removed her cloak and carried it into the room where her father sat in a chair in front of the flames. "Hello, Papa. How was Thirsk?"

He folded a letter, slipped it into the breast pocket of his waistcoat and gazed up at her over the rims of his gold spectacles. "Thirsk was most pleasant, indeed. More gainful than I expected."

Madeline tried to keep her tone light and cheerful. "Oh? How?"

"It seems a burden has lifted. I received a most generous offer from a man I haven't seen in a number of years."

Madeline swallowed uneasily. "What kind of offer?"

Her father raised his chin as if contemplating how best to phrase whatever he was going to tell her. "Sit down, Madeline. We must have a word."

A word? She had a constricting feeling around her ribs—the feeling she always got whenever her father wanted to have "a word" with her.

Still holding her cloak over her arms, Madeline sat down in the chair opposite him.

"It's good news for both of us." He leaned back and crossed his legs. "It seems you'll be married after all."

Madeline's body went stiff. She wet her lips and tried to speak in a steady voice. "May I ask—to whom?"

Her father cleared his throat and shifted in his chair. "Well, he's a bit older and you probably won't remember him. It's been a number of years since he's been here."

"I've met him?"

"Yes."

"It's not Mr. Siddall, is it?" she asked, unable to conceal a fiery panic she hated to hear in her own voice. But how could she help it? Mr. Siddall was three times her age, and the last time she'd seen him, his teeth were black and rotting and it was all she could do now to hope that, for the love of God, they'd fallen out.....

"No, it's not Mr. Siddall," her father replied. "Mr. Siddall is a local gentleman. He would never offer for you—not after what happened at Stanley Hall, and how you behaved so impertinently afterward."

The words struck Madeline like a slap, for her father had not defended her in the scandal that had ruined any chance she'd had at marriage with a decent man. Her father had even made it worse, by turning against her and blaming her publicly.

Determined not to let her father see that her wounds still burned, she raised her chin to speak with as much dignity as she could muster. "Who, then? If I'm not good enough for Mr. Siddall, what manner of man have you agreed to ship me off to?"

He sighed deeply, as if he could not understand why he'd been cursed with such an impertinent disgrace of a daughter. "As I said, you probably won't remember him. It's been almost fifteen years since he's been here. You couldn't have been more than an infant."

"Fifteen years ago, I was seven, Father."

He waved a hand at her. "Yes, yes, whatever."

Madeline felt the familiar sting of her father's antipathy toward her, and squeezed her hands together on her lap to harden herself against it.

Her father tugged at his linen cuffs. "It seems he's not aware of your scandal, which is a miracle in itself, wouldn't you say?"

Madeline simply gazed indifferently upon her father, who continued his account.

"The gentleman I'm speaking of left Yorkshire four years ago for Nova Scotia. According to his description of things, there are very few women there. He would like to be married again, and it appears that he remembers you fondly. Though why, I cannot imagine. You never sat still long enough for any man to get a look at you." He turned his gaze toward the fireplace. "Regardless of that, he's asked for your hand."

Madeline steeled herself. "And you said yes?"

"Of course. I already sent my reply. You'll be leaving on the next ship out of Scarborough in five days. I've arranged for you to travel with a family from Helmsley."

Nausea welled up inside Madeline. *Five days?* She would be leaving Yorkshire forever and crossing an ocean in *five days?*

She tried to focus on the shock of that and only

that, rather than the fact that her father could be so cavalier about never seeing her again.

She swallowed hard and sat up straighter. "You still haven't told me his name."

"His name?" Her father cleared his throat as if he were nervous about revealing it. She wished he would just spit it out and end this debilitating dread. "His name is Adam Coates."

Adam Coates?

Madeline's heart stumbled and took a high-flying leap.

"But as I said," her father continued, "you probably don't remember him. It's been a long time."

Remember him? How could she not? She'd been overwhelmed by the sight of him the first moment he rode into their yard fifteen years ago on his big black horse, to call on her older sister, Diana. Diana had been eighteen and devastatingly beautiful, while Madeline had been a rather willful child of seven who refused to go to her room when her sister's suitor came calling.

It had been the first time Madeline had ever seen a man so handsome he'd sent the clouds dashing right out of the sky. He'd hopped down from his horse, made a great sweeping bow in front of her and said, "Who is this beautiful young lass? A princess, surely!"

Years later, when she began to think about men in a romantic way, her dream suitor always seemed to have Adam Coates's handsome features. For he had been the prince charming of her dreams, the gallant hero who had come to rescue a little princess locked in a tower.

All the sounds in the room retreated into some kind of garbled bubble while Madeline sat there in disbelief, staring blankly at her mumbling father.

She interrupted him. "But what about Diana? Why didn't Mr. Coates ask for *her* hand? He loved her once, and she's a widow now." Good God, her voice was shaking.

Her father removed his spectacles and set them on his lap. "He didn't mention Diana. I suspect he doesn't know she's been widowed. Besides, Diana is better off here with me."

You mean her inheritance is better off here with you.

Madeline's foot began to tap beneath her skirts as if it had a will of its own. *Adam Coates?*

"I thought he was married," she said as casually as possible. "He had four children, if I recall."

"Ah, so you do remember him."

Vividly, she thought.

"Vaguely," she replied.

Her father put his spectacles back on. "Well, yes, he did marry someone, quite soon after Diana married Sir Edward. Too soon, I think. A young woman from York, who already had a son. I don't believe she gave him an easy time, but that's all in the past now. She passed away before Mr. Coates left for Nova Scotia."

"I'm sorry to hear that," Madeline said softly.

Her father stood and gestured for her to stand also. "I know, my dear, that after what happened at Stanley Hall, you'd resigned yourself to spinsterhood, but you can not afford to pass up on this offer. The man has made a success of himself. He's as wealthy now as any aristocrat and he knows nothing about the scandal. With any luck, he won't find out until after he's wed you. Lord knows you'd never get such an offer from anyone here, so mind what I say and go without kicking up a fuss and try to make the best of it, will you? From what I hear, it's a different world over there. Perhaps you can make a fresh start and live a respectable life.''

She nodded politely. "Yes, Father.''

He took a step back. *"Yes, Father?* That's all you're going to say? Heavens above, I expected a full-blown battle over this. I don't think you've ever said *yes, Father* to me about anything in your entire life!''

She lowered her gaze, careful not to give away any of what she truly felt. "If I'm to leave here in five days, I would very much like our time together to be agreeable.''

His shoulders slumped visibly. "Well, that's long overdue. Now off you go, and think carefully about what you want to take with you. I can only spare two trunks.'' He sat down again, waving her off. "And Mr. Coates requested that you bring a bushel of wheat for seed—yellow Kent and Hampshire brown—and that you lay it under your head like a pillow during the crossing, to prevent it from getting wet.''

That last request sailed over her head, pushed aside by all the other thoughts and dreams that were circling around her like a hurricane. Adam Coates. It hardly seemed possible.

* * *

After Madeline left the room, her father rested his head against the high back of the chair and drummed his fingers upon the armrest. What should he do with the letter still in his waistcoat pocket? he wondered.

Promptly he decided to lock it away in the secret compartment in his desk drawer. Knowing Madeline's inquisitive nature, she might wish to see it, and that was out of the question. She would never agree to leave Yorkshire if she knew the truth—that the woman Coates was expecting to wed was her sister, Diana.

Chapter One

The British Colony of Nova Scotia
Seven weeks later

Charlie Coates nearly skidded sideways into the large cherry oak table in the dining room. "The ship's in the Basin!"

His father, Adam, seated at the table, looked up from his book and calmly removed his spectacles. He set them down beside the sterling silver candelabra.

"Calm down, son, and catch your breath. It's just a ship."

"But it's *her* ship, Father!"

"Yes, that it is." Adam couldn't deny the tremor of anticipation that moved through him at his son's reminder. "I suppose I should go and greet her, shouldn't I?"

He gave his youngest son a smile and rose to stand.

"I'll hitch up the buggy!" Charlie offered. The boy spun on his heel and dashed out of the house.

Adam stood at the dining room table for a moment and listened to the mantel clock ticking.

How many years had it been? Twenty? No, not twenty. Fifteen. He couldn't pretend, not even to himself, not to remember the exact day Diana had jilted him to marry another.

Nor could he forget how long he had been married to Jane, God rest her soul, for her violent outbursts had taken their toll on him, to be sure. He was not the idealistic man he used to be....

Glancing down at his simple clothing—his plain white shirt and tawny breeches—Adam wondered what Diana would think when she first saw him. Would she recognize him?

His appearance hadn't changed that much over the years, except for perhaps a few gray patches in his hair and the lines around his eyes. He was forty-three now, but he was as strong and vigorous as any man half his age. Stronger, even. He held out his rough, callused hands and looked them over. Most of the changes, he supposed, she would not be able to see. At least not right away.

Good Lord, what would *she* look like? How had the years treated her? Had they darkened her exquisite golden hair or tarnished the clean, pale complexion he remembered?

Not that it mattered, he decided. She would still be Diana—*his* Diana—and he would adore the changes, whatever they were.

With a mingling of euphoria and nervous anticipation, he walked out of the dining room and went upstairs to quickly change his clothes.

Madeline stood with her hands tight on the rail, her feet braced apart on the rolling deck of the *Liberty*.

The glorious wind whipped her skirts and cloak, and a salty spray cooled her cheeks. She closed her eyes to breathe in the moist, clean scent of the sea and listen to the schooner's heavy keel slice through the frothy waves below.

It wouldn't be long now, she thought dreamily. Then there would be no more waiting, no more imagining what it would be like to see Adam again after all these years.

Adam. Should she call him that when she first saw him? How strange to use his Christian name, when he'd always been Mr. Coates to her. She wasn't sure she'd be able to force the word past her lips with any measure of casual dignity and sound like a wife.

Well, she wasn't his wife yet, but she would be soon. Very soon.

Her heart did a little dance inside her chest at the thought of marrying her ideal, even though she had been just a child when she'd last seen him.

Anxious gulls squawked against the blue sky overhead, swooping over the billowing sails as the boat neared the dock at the mouth of Cumberland Creek. The schooner docked smoothly and surely. Soon Madeline was stepping down the gangplank to the wharf below and gazing eagerly up at Fort Cumberland on the hill in the distance.

Madeline paused there a moment to take in her surroundings while the crewmen unloaded her trunks. The salty tang of the sea whisked by on a fast wind, whipping her skirts around her ankles and tugging at her dainty bergère hat. She reached a hand up to keep it from flying off, while the ribbons flew wildly beneath her chin. She squinted toward the rolling, windswept expanse of grass that stretched for acres and acres into the distance, flanked on either side by ridges of wooded upland.

This land—this magnificent land—it would be her home. It hardly seemed possible!

"Come along! This way!" Mr. Ripley called out, waving toward his family. He and his wife had been Madeline's guardians and companions during the crossing. Madeline hoped the kind family, who knew nothing of her scandal, would find land nearby and become her neighbors here.

"You, too, Madeline!" Mr. Ripley called to her. "Follow us this way to the fort. We had your trunks put in the wagon with ours." Madeline picked up her skirts and began the long trek along the cart road, stepping carefully over the loose stones. They reached the top of the hill and made their way to the fort's entrance.

While Mr. Ripley located an empty room for his family in one of the barracks, Madeline glanced around the courtyard. Wondering if Adam was already there waiting, she searched the faces of the tradesmen and farmers.

Good heavens, her heart was beating like a wild thing in her chest. It had been a lifetime since she'd last seen Adam, but there was no way on God's green earth she would not recognize him. She would know his eyes the moment she caught them in her eager gaze. They were the bluest eyes she'd ever seen in her life. Unforgettable.

Doris Ripley appeared beside her. "Is he here yet?"

"I don't see him," Madeline said. "Perhaps he doesn't know the schooner has arrived. I should send a message to him."

"I'll find someone," Mrs. Ripley quickly offered. She looked around, anxious to help.

At that moment, a tall man walked into the courtyard. He wore a finely made black coat, the ruffles of a clean white shirt visible at his collar, and a black tricorn hat. He carried himself with a grace and confidence that made most heads in the yard turn and stare.

Even from a distance, Madeline knew. It was Adam.

Her blood rushed to her head, and her knees came dangerously close to buckling beneath her skirts.

She grabbed blindly for Mrs. Ripley's sleeve before the woman walked away. "He's here!"

Mrs. Ripley looked toward the fort's entrance. "My word, Madeline" was all she said, in a breathy voice.

Fighting the crippling sensation that had taken over her legs, Madeline watched him. Dear God, he was a magnificent man, even more handsome than she remembered, if that was possible. The years had been good to him. There was a confident manliness in him now. A maturity.

Madeline quickly straightened her fichu, ran her hands over her tight, boned bodice and down her striped cotton skirt.

Adam walked toward a man just inside the entrance, and spoke to him. The man pointed a powder horn toward Madeline and the other passengers from the *Liberty,* who were all standing in a crowd outside the barracks. The next moment, Adam was walking toward them, his long strides full of purpose, his gaze searching over everyone. There was anticipation in his eyes.

Could it be he was as ardent in his yearning as she?

Mrs. Ripley nudged Madeline a few times in the arm, and she heard someone behind her whisper with interest, "Is that Miss Oxley's fellow? Goodness..."

What was said after that, she had no idea. It was all Madeline could do to keep a calm, composed expression on her face and prepare herself to say hello.

Adam stopped in front of Mrs. Ripley, removed his hat and slid it under his arm. His dark hair—lightened with a hint of gray here and there—was tied back with a ribbon. His eyes were still as blue as an autumn sky, framed with black brows and black lashes, and he wore a polite yet confident expression.

Madeline's heart warmed at the sight of him. Though she knew he was a stranger to her now, she felt as if she'd known him all her life, which, in a way, she had. The idea of him was a part of who she was, a part of her identity.

He glanced once at Madeline—rather indifferently—then turned his attention back to Mrs. Ripley again. "Good afternoon, madam. I'm here to meet someone, and I wonder if you could tell me—"

Before he had a chance to finish, Mrs. Ripley put her arm around Madeline's waist, pushed her forward and said with a warm smile, "Yes, Mr. Coates, she's right here."

Adam's gaze fell upon Madeline again, a little more attentively this time. For a long moment, he studied her face.

Madeline felt suddenly self-conscious in front of all these onlookers.

She cleared her throat to say *How do you do, Mr. Coates,* but before she had the chance, his dark brows drew together with a look of concern.

"No, it's someone else I'm looking for. We're to be married. Her name is Lady Thurston."

Chapter Two

Madeline felt the color drain from her face like a slow, painful torture. No one spoke. There was only the uncomfortable rustle of skirts behind her, the sound of a knife whittling somewhere off to the side, then a woman cleared her throat.

"Is she here?" Adam finally asked, looking hopeful.

Madeline's whole body went numb.

Mrs. Ripley struggled for a reply. She knew that Madeline had first met Adam when he was courting her older sister, Diana, so Mrs. Ripley must have understood that a mistake had been made.

"I'm afraid Madeline's sister did not accompany her." It was a tactful, clever response, and Madeline was thankful for it.

Adam turned his gaze toward her again and she knew the precise instant he understood who she was. His disappointment was clear in the depths of his eyes and in the set of his shoulders. The color drained from his face, too.

"I'm sorry, I—" He stumbled over his words.

"You're Diana's *sister?* What was your name again?"

Madeline squared her shoulders against the stinging humiliation and labored to speak in a steady, dignified voice. "My name is Madeline."

Adam stared at her for another few seconds. "Yes, I think I remember you now." He paused again. It was the most acrid silence she'd ever experienced. "Was there some kind of problem? Why did *you* come?"

This couldn't be happening....

Dear God, she felt as if she were going to be ill. "I...I was told you wished it."

"No." He paused. "Well, this is awkward, indeed."

"Awkward for whom, sir?" Madeline replied sternly. "For you? Or for these people standing behind me?"

Thankfully, the others recognized the hint and casually dispersed, including Mrs. Ripley, who gave Madeline a sympathetic pat on the arm before turning away.

She was now standing alone, face-to-face with Adam Coates, not knowing what in the world to say to him—to this man who only a moment ago she had thought was her husband-to-be.

"Who told you I wished for you to come?" he asked directly.

"My father. He said you wrote him a letter."

Adam's mouth tightened into a hard line. "I did write to him, and to Diana, as well. Did he not deliver my note to her?"

"Not to my knowledge. She was away in London when your proposal arrived. I never saw the letter and I never even said goodbye to her. I barely had time to write and tell her where I was going."

The muscles in Adam's jaw clenched visibly as his anger took root and burst forth. He began to pace in front of Madeline. "I was more than clear about wanting to marry *Diana*. He had no right to send you instead. What was he thinking of?"

Madeline had to work hard to maintain her dignity, when her whole being was winding tight with rage at her father.

At Adam, as well, for humiliating her like this in front of everyone. Not to mention for crushing her dreams without even noticing, or taking the time to consider the fact that she, too, might be disappointed.

"My apologies for the misunderstanding, sir. My father has a tendency to manipulate things to his liking."

"Manipulate? He sent me the wrong bride!"

Madeline gritted her teeth together, unable to hide her fury any longer. "Sir, you are not the only one who has been inconvenienced by this. I just spent forty-six days on a damp, creaky ship eating dry oatmeal and drinking stale water, and now you tell me in front of everyone that I'm not the one you ordered, and I shouldn't have bothered. I believe I've had quite enough insults and frustrations for one day."

He stopped pacing and looked at her—*really* looked at her—as if for the first time. "Didn't you think it strange that I would ask for your hand? Didn't you question what your father was telling you? Diana and I have a history together, a past, and you were just a child then. You're still a child now.''

"I'm twenty-two, sir.'' She was quite unable at this point to keep the ire out of her tone.

"Ah, I see. Twenty-two, and wanting marriage so badly you were willing to deceive a man to get it.''

"It was my father who deceived you, not I!''

He did not accept her declaration of innocence; he merely continued to pace back and forth in front of her. "Whether you knew the truth or not, you played a part in it. Diana was the obvious choice. Lord in heaven, what were *you* thinking?''

What was she to tell him? That she had been thinking with her foolish, lovesick heart? That she had dreamed of marrying him since she was a child and had spent the past six weeks fantasizing about a wedding night in his arms? A lifetime in his heart? That she'd believed he wanted to marry her, too, because she'd *wanted* to believe it?

What a fantasy it had been! The man in her dreams had been full of mirth and adoration. This bitter, belligerent man was nothing like the young man she remembered.

"My father assured me you had asked for my hand. I had no reason to question the truth of it.''

Someone nearby split a log with an ax. The sharp *crack* made Madeline jump. She felt as if someone were taking an ax to her heart as well.

Adam's chest heaved with a sigh. "No reason to question it? Do you not have a mind of your own?''

Oh, this was too much. "To tell you the truth, Mr. Coates, I do have a mind of my own—a mind to poke my father with a knitting needle, and if I may say so, you could use a poke yourself.''

His dark eyes narrowed. She wasn't certain if he was furious with her, or just plain shocked out of his shiny black boots.

The man with the ax swung again and the sound of splitting wood cut through the silence. Madeline kept her eyes on Adam.

''What are we to do, then?'' he asked, his tone finally softening a bit.

''I don't know, Mr. Coates. As you said earlier, this is indeed awkward.''

''Well, I can't just leave you here.''

Good God, if he thought he was going to make her feel like a helpless orphan who had been flung upon him against his will, he was mistaken. She was a grown woman and she was innocent in all this. She had not asked him to write that letter to her father and she would find her own way out of this. With or without his help.

''Your father trusted me with your safety,'' he added, ''and I know for a fact that this schooner isn't returning to England. It's going to Boston, and God knows when the next ship will arrive.'' She heard him whisper, ''What a bloody mess.''

Madeline took a deep breath and counted to ten, fighting the urge to poke Adam not just with a knitting needle, but with anything she could get her hands on.

''You needn't worry about me, Mr. Coates. I'm sure the Ripleys would be pleased to have me stay with them. I've been teaching their children to read the past few weeks.''

He considered that a moment. ''Do they have land yet?''

''No, but Mr. Ripley plans to purchase something as soon as he finds a—''

''It'll take the man some time to familiarize himself with the area. A few weeks at least before he finds what he's looking for.''

A tattered-looking tradesman walked by, the barrel of his musket resting on his shoulder. He tipped his hat and smiled admiringly at Madeline. Adam watched the man's back as he crossed the courtyard.

''Well, you can't stay here,'' he said flatly, turning to face her again.

''Why not?''

''Because you're practically a child and you're alone and it would be unthinkable for me to leave you here.''

''I'm not a child,'' she reminded him again.

He sighed and shook his head at her argument, and once more, she felt like a burden. An insolent one, too, this time around. She had thought, when she'd said goodbye to her father, that she was finally escaping those wretched feelings.

''You'll stay in my home until we decide what to do. You'll be good company for my daughter-in-law. She's nearing the end of her confinement.''

All this was happening too fast—the confusion, the humiliation, the collapse of Madeline's dreams. She wasn't about to be shuffled off anywhere before she had a chance to think about what *she* wanted. "I will *not* come and stay with you, Mr. Coates."

"Why not?" he asked, as if her refusal were completely inconceivable.

"Because…because I don't want to." Oh, why couldn't she come up with something better than that? She sounded like the child he believed her to be.

"What we want isn't always what's best for us," he told her. "Or what we get."

Madeline bristled at his paternal tone. He sounded like her father—lecturing her, pointing out her constant rebellion. She hadn't liked hearing it from her father and she certainly didn't wish to hear it from the man who had just publicly rejected her.

Then she wondered if there was a double meaning to Adam's words. Perhaps he was referring to Diana breaking *his* heart all those years ago to marry a baronet.

Madeline wet her parched lips. "As I said before, I'll stay with the Ripleys."

"You will do no such thing. You're my responsibility now. You're Diana's sister, for pity's sake, and I will not leave you here."

Madeline could feel the frustration building up inside of her like a rising tide about to overflow.

All at once, an image of Adam's first visit to her home in Yorkshire years ago flooded back. She remembered how he had ruffled her hair like a puppy and shown her a magic trick. Good God, what had she been dreaming of? He was four times her age then, and he was twice her age now. She'd been so foolish!

She squeezed her eyes shut, feeling rankled all over again. She didn't want to spend any more time with Adam Coates. She didn't want to look at his irritatingly handsome face and relive this embarrassing stupidity over and over in her mind.

"Where are your belongings?"

"My belongings?" she asked, caught off guard.

"Yes, your trunks. I'll have them delivered to my home."

She tried to say no, but he was already going to find someone to do it. She followed him. "I told you I don't want to go with you."

"I'm not giving you a choice. You're Diana's sister and I mean to look after you."

"I don't need looking after!"

He stopped at that and turned to glare at her. She saw an unyielding conviction in his eyes and noted the lines around his mouth. The lines gave him the appearance of a man stuck in a permanent frown.

Those lines had not existed fifteen years ago—at least she didn't remember them—nor had they existed in her dreams of him. She did her best to appear unperturbed by all that had happened, and began to think that maybe she should count herself lucky to be spared having to marry him today.

"I see you're still as headstrong as ever," he said sharply.

His comment struck her hard. She hadn't thought Adam had remembered anything about her, or known that she was headstrong in the first place.

Then she recalled all the times Diana and Adam had gone for walks across the moors, wanting to be alone. Diana would beg Madeline to go home, but she was too young to understand why, so she'd argued with Diana and followed them anyway.

So that's what Adam remembered—the troublesome little sister.

Madeline stood there, saying nothing, waiting for him to give in.

He didn't. He simply rephrased his intentions. "I genuinely wish for you to come and be my guest. As I said, my daughter-in-law is confined to her room and she'll be disappointed if you do not come. In addition, both my daughter and my youngest son could use some instruction in reading and arithmetic. You have experience, you say?"

"Yes," she replied, before she had a chance to think about it.

"It will work out well, then." He started off again to fetch a driver to deliver the trunks, and Madeline stood there in the middle of the courtyard, feeling depleted and exhausted, and as if she'd just been manipulated all over again.

Sitting in the buggy beside Madeline, Adam flicked the lines and began the trip home along Cumberland Ridge, laboring to block out everything he had expected and hoped for today.

Of course, he couldn't. Inside he was reeling with a mixture of disappointment and rage. Over the past few weeks, since the letter had arrived saying his "bride" was on her way, crossing an ocean to be with him, Adam had somehow managed to fall in love with Diana all over again. He'd spent too many hours remembering how she'd made him feel years ago, how the sight of her lovely face had brought him to his knees. She was the first woman he had ever loved; they had been young and desperate for each other and had wanted to be together every minute of every day for the rest of their lives.

God, how he'd loved her—with all the fiery, intense passion of his youth. No one had known him like she had, and he'd thought he'd known her deeply, too. He *had*. All these years later, he still believed it. They had once told each other everything, expressed every feeling and desire. He'd held her in his arms and wanted to be with her forever.

Unfortunately, forever hadn't lasted very long. There had been no warning that the end was coming. No disagreements or falling out of love. No natural conclusion. She'd told him she was leaving him— crying her heart out on his shoulder—making him love her more than ever.

Of course, through the years, he'd come to understand why she'd made that choice. How could she not? Adam was the third son of a tenant farmer—a prosperous one, yes, but by no means anything close to gentry, and with no hope of ever becoming a landowner. Diana had married a baronet. She'd chosen wisely, as any prudent young woman would have.

The memories these past few weeks, thinking she wanted him back, had stirred his blood and made him feel young again, as if their lifetime apart were a mere heartbeat. Ever since he'd learned of her husband's death and known she was free, he hadn't been able to stop thinking of her, and when he let his mind return to those intimate, glorious moments they'd shared in their youth, it seemed like yesterday.

Now, sitting next to Diana's younger sister, who had been a child the last time he'd seen her, he felt more ancient than ever, and more pathetic to have been foolishly dreaming about Diana, the one who always seemed to slip through his fingers.

Strange, how Adam had thought after all these years, their coming together again was some kind of romantic destiny.

A ridiculous fantasy, indeed.

"Where is your home?" Madeline asked, jolting him out of his thoughts. "Is it far?"

He pointed straight ahead. "Farther along this ridge, hidden in the trees."

She sat up straighter to see as far as she could, and he sensed she was fighting the urge to stand up in the moving buggy.

He tried not to think of Diana, when there was no point torturing himself. Instead, he gazed at the landscape in all directions. "Quite a view from here, don't you think?"

Madeline gave him a cool, brief glance that told him she was going to reply only because it was the polite thing to do. Obviously, she was still upset over what had happened, and rightly so, he supposed. It had been an awkward scene in front of her traveling companions. Awkward for both of them, for if he was honest about it, he had been an ogre.

Lord, when had he become this ill-natured? It had happened so gradually over the years, he hadn't really noticed it until he was here, face-to-face with someone from his past. Someone who had known the man he once was.

"Is that farmland down there?" she asked.

At least she was willing to make an effort. He supposed he should do the same.

"They're salt marshes. Everything down there is dyked."

She stared in silence at the velvet green vistas below and the dark spruce forests on the uplands. Above them, white clouds sailed quickly across the vast blue sky.

"Your sons must be a help to you," she said.

"I couldn't do it without them."

He turned his gaze to her feminine profile and stared at her for a long moment. Her cheeks were delicately carved, her lips full. Her eyes had the look of girlish fascination at the unfamiliar world around her. She was such a child, yet she had left her home and crossed an ocean with the expectation of becoming his wife. His wife! Diana's baby sister. She had thought she would meet his sons as their future stepmother.

Good Lord. Did she know that Jacob, his stepson, was only four years younger than she?

With that thought, a tremor of uneasiness coursed through him. She couldn't actually be brokenhearted, could she? In a sense, he had rejected her romantically, and told everyone within hearing range that she was not the one he'd wanted. He considered saying something about it—offering an apology perhaps?— then he decided that it would just be rubbing salt in both of their wounds, and he should leave it be. There was no point dwelling on it. He would let her enjoy the view.

At least there had been no true, deep-rooted romance between them. In fact, she was probably relieved to be spared marrying a man she hardly knew. A man almost twice her age.

Yes, what was done was done, and there was no sense dragging the uncomfortable circumstances on any longer. All this would be straightened out soon enough, for he was not yet ready to give up on Diana.

Madeline sat back in the rolling carriage, gazing in a detached way at the windswept landscape she had thought would be her home. It was everything she had dreamed of, ripe for an adventure, and the reality of that only made her feel worse—as if her dreams had been mangled and mashed in front of her eyes and now all she could do was accept it.

Adam drove the carriage down the slope of the ridge and into the thick spruce forest where all was shaded and quiet and sheltered from the wind. Little more than a narrow bridle path was all they had for a road, and only the sounds of the horse's hooves thumping and the carriage wheels rolling over the ground, snapping twigs, filled the silence.

An uneasy feeling closed in around Madeline. What would become of her? She was an ocean away from her familiar world of moors and dales and meandering stone walls, and she knew no one here except for Adam and the people from the ship. She had no family.

Not that she'd had any family that she could depend upon back in Yorkshire, either, but at least she knew the country. Here, she could get lost in these deep, unfathomable forests or swallowed by a bear, God forbid. She squeezed her pink-and-silver guinea purse into a ball in her hands. Partly in fear, partly in fury.

"Are you all right, Miss Oxley?" Adam asked, surprising her.

She'd thought she was more proficient at hiding her feelings. She would have to do better.

"I'm fine, Mr. Coates."

"You don't look fine."

She took a deep breath, not sure how to reply. "I was just thinking about my future and where I will go after this." *And I've never felt more alone in my life.*

"I think the best thing is for you to return to your father in Yorkshire."

"I would rather not."

He was quiet a moment. "Do you think that's wise?"

How was she to explain that she'd left Yorkshire because she'd been ruined by an outrageous, unfounded sham of a scandal, and her father had never made any effort to defend her?

After this little debacle, she realized he had been more determined to get rid of her than she'd thought.

And more determined to keep Diana at his side.

"I'll be frank with you," Adam said. "There isn't much here for a young, unmarried woman. Very few settlers can afford a live-in governess and the chances of finding work, outside of keeping house for someone, are slim. The winters are long and severe—the icy winds over the marsh can take a bite out of your skin if you're not careful. And the mosquitoes…well, I guarantee they'll come close to driving you mad. Their bite feels like a hot needle prick in your skin and it swells up like a big boil for days afterward and itches insufferably."

"You're exaggerating."

He tilted his head at her. "Just wait and see. In a month, you'll be jumping into the muddy Tantramar just to escape them. Sometimes, they're worse than a black cloud around your head and—"

"You've made your point, Mr. Coates, but I'm not going home. I don't know what I'll do, but don't worry, I'll find some means to make my way. If not here, then perhaps in Halifax."

"There's no road to Halifax. It's all Indian trails and bridle paths."

She huffed in frustration. "What would you have me do, then? Go home on the next ship? Go home to a father who wanted me gone so badly that he deceived both of us to get rid of me?"

Adam removed his hat and ran a hand over his dark, backswept hair. "You don't know that."

"You said you asked him for Diana's hand. The man could read."

The horses snorted and tossed their heads. "Well, perhaps he simply thought it should be your turn. Diana had already been married. I doubt he was that determined to get *rid* of you."

Madeline chose not to correct him on that point.

He didn't need to know the truth, and at least he was no longer insinuating that this scheme was her doing.

"I still think it would be in your best interest to return to Yorkshire and be with your father," he told her. "Cumberland is no place for a young woman alone."

"I'll consider it," she replied, just to end the discussion.

A few minutes later, she watched a brown squirrel shimmy across an evergreen bough overhead and leap onto a taller tree. "How did you learn about Diana's widowhood?" she asked, curious about how this deplorable situation had come to pass.

"News makes its way over here eventually. And I may have made inquiries about her over the years."

Inquiries. Beautiful Diana. Men were always making inquiries....

Madeline gazed at Adam's mature face beside her, and even now, after all that had happened, her childish heart found it difficult to believe that she was actually sitting beside him, alone here in the forest, their thighs bumping every so often. She felt an unwelcome, impetuous thrill over it, and a twinge of hope that perhaps one day, he might forget about Diana and see Madeline differently.

Her skin tingled beneath her dress, and she wished she could throttle the sensation. She didn't want to start fantasizing again about this man who was not what she remembered. She would only wind up getting hurt, for she had yet in her life to experience otherwise.

"Did you love her that much, then?" She hoped

her tone hadn't revealed how hurt she'd been over all this, but she wanted to hear how he felt.

No. After that thigh-bumping thrill, she *needed* to hear it.

He clicked his tongue at the horses. "Yes, I did."

Madeline tried to crush the unwise pang of jealousy she did not want to feel.

Adam continued. "And I still wish to marry her. Perhaps you could help me?"

Help you? She tried to keep her voice light, to sound obliging. "How?"

"You could give me her address in London. I plan to notify my solicitor there, and if Diana agrees, have him arrange a proxy marriage. I want no mistakes this time."

Feeling very tired all of a sudden, Madeline nodded. She knew that Diana had been lonely since her husband died. If it was her whim, she would be sailing into the muddy waters of Cumberland Basin on the very next ship from England—as Adam's wife— and there was no sense harboring any secret hopes to the contrary.

Chapter Three

Madeline and Adam drove out of the woods and down a gentle slope onto the low, windy grasslands. A herd of black-and-white cattle grazed nearby, and they lifted their heads and stared, as if they were perplexed to see Madeline, who was not the woman they had been expecting. Knowing it was a ridiculous notion, she turned her face away from them and looked the other way.

In the distance, up on another hill overlooking the marsh, stood a large, majestic-looking red brick house. Madeline wondered if this was the place she had dreamed about, and wondered further how close her fantasies had been to reality. Judging by the look of the place, her fantasies had been eerily accurate indeed.

They turned into the tree-lined driveway that led up to the house, and barely made it to the door before a young boy came racing out of it to greet them.

Adam obviously wasn't the only one who had been looking forward to Diana's arrival.

"My youngest son," Adam explained with an apologetic tone.

The boy bolted across the front yard. Madeline shifted uncomfortably in her seat, dreading the matter of explaining the mistake and telling him that the woman his father had planned to marry hadn't even known he'd proposed.

They rolled to a gentle stop in front of the house. The boy approached and took hold of the harness. "Hello, Father!" He gazed timidly at Madeline as he waited for an introduction.

Adam stepped down from the buggy and came around to help Madeline. "Miss Oxley, this is my son, Charles."

The boy suddenly lost his enthusiasm. "Miss Oxley? But where's Lady Thurston?"

"She didn't come. There was a misunderstanding, and Lady Thurston's sister came to visit instead."

"Her sister?" Charlie gazed uncertainly at Madeline. "Will *you* be marrying my father?"

Madeline was thankful that Adam answered the question before she had to. "No, Charles. She's just visiting. I'll be sending another letter to Lady Thurston to clear everything up."

While the boy led the horse and buggy into the barn, Adam escorted Madeline into the house, the wide center hall decorated with teal wallpaper and dark cherry columns. An older woman wearing gold spectacles appeared from the back kitchen. She smoothed her skirt with her hands. "Mr. Coates, you've returned."

"Hello, Agnes. This is Madeline Oxley. Diana's *sister.*"

Looking bewildered, the woman stared at Madeline.

Madeline saw the situation work itself through the woman's mind, until finally she nodded in understanding. Madeline forced herself to smile. She would be glad to get these awkward introductions over and done with.

"Madeline, this is my housekeeper, Mrs. Agnes Dalton."

"It's a pleasure to meet you."

At that instant, a dark-haired girl came running from the kitchen. "Father!"

She flew into Adam's arms. He scooped her up and squeezed her before setting her back down. "Miss Oxley, this is my daughter, Penelope. Penelope, this is Miss Madeline Oxley."

"Are you Lady Thurston's maid?" the little girl asked. "Father said she might bring one."

Could this possibly be any more humiliating?

Adam quickly interrupted. "No, Penelope. This is Lady Thurston's *sister.* There was a misunderstanding about my marriage proposal, but it will all be cleared up soon enough."

If Madeline heard him say *sister* with that overly explanative tone one more time, she might decide to swim back to Yorkshire!

"So, you'll be my aunt, then?" Penelope said.

Despite the setbacks, Madeline couldn't help smiling at the girl. "I suppose I will be."

"Will you be living with us, too?"

Madeline tried to imagine living here after Diana arrived, married Adam and became stepmother to these children.

Could she live here, too? As the spinster aunt?

She glanced up at Adam's handsome face, noticed the line of his strong jaw, caught the scent of his shaving soap.

No, definitely not.

"I'm just visiting," she replied.

"For how long?"

"Very briefly."

"How briefly?"

Thank goodness the housekeeper stepped forward and cut off the interrogation. "You must be exhausted after your journey, Miss Oxley. The crossing wasn't too unpleasant, I hope?"

She was the first person not to make Madeline feel like a huge human blunder. "As smooth as can be expected."

"Let me show you to your room. You can freshen up and rest a while, then you can meet Mary."

"My daughter-in-law," Adam offered.

He gave Madeline a melancholy look that she wished she could read. Was it an apology for their awkward beginning? Or was it simply disappointment that Diana had not arrived?

He nodded at her, and she knew he was passing his duty over to the others. He was finished with her.

Madeline followed Mrs. Dalton to the staircase, peered surreptitiously over her shoulder at her once future husband.

Without a backward glance, he walked out the door.

* * *

The afternoon sun moved across the sky and glistened outside Madeline's lace-covered window, shining in her eyes and waking her from her nap.

She stared dazedly at the dappled light upon her quilt. It was a muted, golden glow, unlike anything she'd ever seen in Yorkshire, and she wondered how in the world the sun could be different here, when it was exactly the same sun.

Sitting up, she yawned and realized how exhausted she was after the long journey and the horrible, mortifying end to everything. She hadn't taken any lunch; she just hadn't felt like eating. Not that she was pouting. She was never one to wallow in self-pity. All she'd wanted to do was drift into a deep, rehabilitating sleep, then wake up and feel ready to begin again.

But as she looked around the bedchamber at the dainty writing desk in the corner—stocked with stationery and a goose quill pen next to a bottle of ink, and a silver candelabra with five new white wax candles just waiting to be lit after sunset—she knew the room had been lovingly prepared for Diana. Madeline found herself, at that moment, quite unable to pick herself up, as she usually did, and dust herself off.

She thought about Diana then. How everyone loved her and praised her, while comparing Madeline's shortcomings in the very next breath.

Madeline had never been bothered by it before, not deeply anyway. She'd not permitted herself to be bothered by it, and she was always firm when it came

to her emotions and keeping them in check. She could
sweep away the most painful insults or degradations
with a mental wave of her unfalteringly strong will.

On that account, in childhood and adulthood, too,
she'd crushed any interest in wishing for—or com-
peting for—the kind of attention Diana received.
Madeline had never expected to participate in the
same game, nor had she wanted to; she was much
happier going her own way, spending time alone, outdoors in the garden, while Diana preferred to socialize
and charm anyone and everyone who crossed her
path.

Today, however, for the first time, Madeline felt
the sharp claws of envy boring under her skin. Adam
had not been charmed by her, not in the least. He'd
looked right through her, just as he had all those years
ago when he'd come to the house to court Diana.

Determined not to spend another beastly moment
feeling sorry for herself, Madeline rose, slipped her
tiny stockinged feet into her black buckled shoes and
prepared to venture downstairs.

At the top of the wide staircase, however, she heard
someone call her name. In one of the rooms, lying on
a huge, fluffy, canopied bed, was a pretty and very
pregnant young woman. She couldn't have been more
than eighteen.

"You must be Madeline," she said cheerfully.
"Mrs. Dalton told me you were sleeping. Come in,
come in."

Madeline moved all the way into the room.

"I'm Mary, Jacob's wife. He's off in the fields today, planting the spring crop. You'll meet him at supper.''

"I'll look forward to it," Madeline replied. She glanced discreetly at Mary's full belly with an open book leaning upon it. "How are you feeling?" she asked.

"I'm fine. I've had some pains and the doctor suggested I rest until the baby comes next month. Please sit down.''

Madeline sat in an upholstered chair beside the bed.

Eyes warm and caring, Mary leaned forward and gently touched Madeline's hand. "Mrs. Dalton told me what happened—that you thought you were coming here to marry Mr. Coates. I felt terrible when I heard it. It must have been very distressing for you. Are you all right?''

Surprise, more than anything, shook Madeline. Mary may have been young, but she was astute.

"Of course, I'm fine. It was just a misunderstanding.''

"Misunderstandings can sometimes be more than that.''

Madeline swallowed hard over the lump that suddenly rose in her throat. "Yes, but honestly, Mr. Coates and I were strangers to each other. There were no hurt feelings. I should have guessed something was wrong initially, before I set out for Nova Scotia. I should have known he would want Diana. They were close once, after all.''

Mary nodded and leaned back, but Madeline suspected that the young woman knew what was really going on.

A part of her wanted to confide in Mary, but Madeline bit back the urge. If in time, Adam did marry Diana, Madeline would never want anyone to know how she herself had loved him. She didn't want everyone to pity her as the poor, brokenhearted spinster sister. That would be the worst fate imaginable. Her pride would never be able to endure it.

Madeline politely stood. "I should go downstairs to see if I can help with supper. Can I get you anything?"

"No, thank you. Mrs. Dalton usually brings me supper on a tray."

Feeling a little shaken, Madeline nodded and left the room, promising to return later for a visit and perhaps a game of cards. She walked down the stairs, sliding her fingers along the smooth oak handrail that swept round in a scroll to the newel post at the bottom. She ventured into the stone kitchen at the back of the house to find Mrs. Dalton at the large fireplace, spooning drippings over a crispy-looking hen on a spit. The glorious smells of roasting poultry filled Madeline's senses and her mouth began to water.

Mrs. Dalton wiped her hands on her apron and straightened, then noticed Madeline in the doorway. "Hello, dear. Come in and sit down."

Madeline moved into the room. "After six weeks at sea, Mrs. Dalton, this kitchen smells like paradise. Can I help you with anything?"

"Not today. You've just arrived. Tomorrow you can help."

Just then, footsteps pounded over the wide floorboards in the center hall and stopped in the doorway.

Madeline, somehow recognizing the sound of Adam's boots, turned with a sudden nervous sensation in her belly.

"Miss Oxley, may I speak with you, please?" His tone was serious and steely.

She swallowed. "Of course."

He led her into his private study, a large room with dark green wallpaper and a fireplace flanked by bookcases built into the walls. The rug was soft under her shoes.

Adam stopped in the center of the room, faced her and clasped his hands behind his back. "I realize you've barely had a chance to settle in, but I would like to send Jacob back to the fort this afternoon with the letter, to see that it gets to Halifax with the next traveler."

"The letter?"

Distracted, she gazed at Adam's dark features—the set of his jaw, the straight line of his nose. His black coat was gone now, and he wore a white linen shirt with plentiful gathers off his broad shoulders, and a navy silk embroidered waistcoat that hugged the masculine shape of his torso.

He had filled out since the days she'd known him in Yorkshire. He had been slender then. Now he seemed stronger, more muscular. She suddenly thought of all her romantic daydreams during the crossing, how she had imagined Adam kissing her and touching her on their wedding night. She'd imagined all of it in great detail—the way he would look at her with desire and love in his eyes. She'd imagined him laying her onto his bed and covering her body with his own. The feelings of love she'd experienced at those moments had seemed so true. They *still* seemed true.

"The letter to my solicitor in London," he said. "I wish also to write to Diana, of course. You mentioned you had the address where she is staying."

Torn abruptly from her fantasy, Madeline felt a heaviness settle in her stomach. "Yes, I have it. In one of my trunks. But I haven't unpacked them yet. I don't know where—"

"They're upstairs in Penelope's room. You were resting when they arrived and I did not wish to disturb you."

"I see." Speaking to him now, she had to remind herself that whatever she had fantasized about during the crossing was just that—a fantasy. She and Adam were strangers. There was nothing between them. *Nothing.*

"I'll get it right away," she replied in a congenial tone, then turned to go.

"Madeline—" He took what sounded like an anxious step forward.

She stopped but didn't turn around. She didn't want to see his face.

Nor did she want him to see that her smile was not real. She didn't want him to know that she was disappointed or unhappy or affected in any way. She didn't want him to know anything.

"Thank you," he said simply, and there was a hint of regret in his voice.

Regret? Over what part of the day, exactly? she wondered.

She nodded and walked out of the room, all the while trying to ignore the questions and hopes still dashing about in her brain. Trying to ignore the way her skin had erupted in gooseflesh just from the mere sound of his voice and the way he looked, standing before her, here in the flesh.

Oh, it would not do her any good to continue her fantasies about him. To continue to think of him in a romantic way. She had to stifle these reactions. She had to remind herself ten times a day if necessary that he was likely going to be her sister's husband one day soon.

If she knew what was good for her, she would throttle her hopes and never let them get away from her again.

Chapter Four

Madeline sat at the long, oak table in the dining room, trying very hard not to look at Adam, because every time she did, the urge to stare at him was something close to crippling.

She couldn't explain it. She didn't want to stare. She wanted all these desires to go away. She thought they *would* after what had occurred at the fort, after he'd humiliated her and accused her of deceiving him. She thought that the cold, hard reality of the man Adam had become would jolt her out of her fantasy, and that she would feel nothing for him.

Unfortunately, instead of feeling nothing, she felt everything. One minute she was angry at him. The next minute, after all her ministrations to remain indifferent, she was caught up in the intoxicating dream of him. To be in his presence here tonight made her feel almost short of breath. He sat at the head of the table, his clean, white neckcloth presented in a neat ruffle, his large hands strong and sure. Why couldn't she stop noticing how handsome he was?

She found herself wishing most ridiculously that he

had turned out to be a crotchety old man with bad teeth and no hair.

Forcing her eyes to stay focused on her plate, she cleared her throat, and the sound made everyone jump. All of the family was present, all except for Mary, and Madeline wondered uncomfortably if this silence was normal.

"Why is everyone so quiet?" Penelope asked.

Madeline dabbed at her lips with a damask napkin, curious as to how Adam would answer the question.

His voice was deep and calm. "We're hungry, Penelope. That's all."

"But we're always hungry at supper."

"Perhaps it's because we have a guest, and we're all trying to be on our best behavior."

Penelope lifted her sweet gaze toward Madeline and smiled, then returned quietly to her eating.

A hush fell over the room again. Silverware clinked against china plates, the clock ticked audibly, and Madeline knew that they were all aware of the mix-up, and had now had time to discuss it privately amongst themselves…to whisper and pass judgments about her. Did they believe Madeline had been involved in the manipulation? Did they think she was deceitful or self-serving? Or did they suspect the embarrassing truth and sympathize with her, as Mary had?

She dabbed at her mouth again with the napkin and decided it was long past time to make some polite conversation. "Jacob, Mary told me you were working in the fields today. What are you planting this time of year?"

The young man across the table, dressed in a pale blue waistcoat, set down his fork before he spoke. "I finished planting potatoes in the high field, Miss Oxley. Then I rode over to Mr. Carter's place to help him plant his."

Madeline noticed the lack of resemblance between Adam and his stepson, Jacob. Jacob possessed fair features—golden hair and blue eyes—while Adam and the other children had strikingly dark coloring.

Madeline was curious, all of a sudden, about Jacob's mother and Adam's late wife. Had she been flaxen haired and beautiful like Diana?

Then Madeline thought about her own appearance—her mousy brown hair, dull with frizzy curls, and her freckled complexion. It was the first time in her life she wished she had been blessed with the kind of beauty that Diana possessed. The kind of beauty that turned gentlemen's heads and rendered them speechless when they first laid eyes upon her.

"Do you have a large crop?" she asked Jacob, forcing herself to disregard such foolish, frivolous thoughts, for she had never put much stock in appearances. She'd always credited herself with having more depth of character than that.

Besides, there was no point dreaming about what could never be.

"Large enough to last through the winter."

She smiled at him, but out of the corner of her eye she noticed Adam wipe his mouth with a napkin, then toss it down as if he were finished. "We raise only enough potatoes to meet our needs." She suspected he was being polite for the children's sake, not hers. "We don't market them."

"What *do* you market?" she asked, deciding she would not let him intimidate her with his silences any longer. She would look him in the eye and if she wanted to know something about Nova Scotian farming or the dykes or even if she wanted to hear him admit that he'd been rude to her that day, she was going to say what she pleased. "Corn?"

"No. It's the same with corn as it is with potatoes—only enough to meet our own needs. The marshes here are better suited toward pasture and meadow." He picked up his glass and looked away, as if he were finished not only with his dinner, but with her questions as well.

She couldn't help pressing him. "Animal husbandry, then? And hay?"

"Yes, Miss Oxley. Hay."

Adam turned his attention back to his dinner, and Madeline could see that he had no interest whatsoever in talking to her, nor any interest in even looking at her.

She would have liked to call it indifference, but as she watched him and the way he looked about the room, the way his dark brows drew together in a frown, she realized with some annoyance that it was more than that. The man flat out resented her presence here at his table, for she was the reason Diana was not here, and he was obviously still angry about that. He only felt obligated to see to Madeline's welfare because she was Diana's sister and he didn't want to jeopardize his future with her. Like Madeline herself,

Adam was probably thinking that she could one day be the children's aunt, and for that reason alone, he wanted to keep things affable.

Adam's continued silence for the rest of the meal forced Madeline to think more seriously about what she should do. She couldn't live in a house where she was not wanted. She'd lived like that in her father's house long enough. And worse, she could not stay here and watch Diana arrive and live happily ever after with Adam and his children.

Madeline decided with firm conviction she would look for another situation as soon as she could. She would be long gone by the time Diana arrived to claim her prize.

Inside the barn the next day, Adam lifted a heavy sack of seed grain onto his shoulder and carried it to the wagon. He set it down with a loud *thwack* and mentally kicked himself for being so hard on Madeline during the past twenty-four hours.

What was wrong with him? He used to be better with people, women in particular. He used to enjoy charming them and making them happy, and he had always presumed they were honest and forthright, for his mother, God rest her soul, had been a good, kind woman.

That was before his break with Diana, and before his marriage to Jane.

Unfortunately, Jane had taught him that not all women were what they seemed, and he had to be exceedingly careful. In the beginning, not long after Diana had married Sir Edward, Jane had been a rock of sensible wisdom and understanding, helping Adam through that painful time. Recently widowed and looking after her son, Jacob, she had shared her bed with Adam, and it was there where they both found comfort during difficult times.

When they discovered she was with child, Adam had married her. It was only after the marriage certificate had been signed and they were living as man and wife, that she'd revealed her true nature.

So here he was, presuming the worst about a gullible young woman who had trusted her father and crossed an ocean to become Adam's wife, when he should be going out of his way to apologize for the situation and to ensure her comfort and happiness.

On top of that, she was Diana's sister, and if things worked out the way he hoped, he and Madeline might one day be brother and sister by marriage. He needed to guarantee that Madeline was safe and well-cared-for, and he supposed it wouldn't hurt to cultivate a friendship.

Slapping his hands together to brush away the grain dust, he heard a throat clearing behind him, and turned. There in the doorway stood Madeline, wearing a pretty blue-and-white-striped day dress, with a white lace scarf tucked neatly into her neckline.

Lord, she'd grown into a lovely young woman, he realized suddenly. It was hard to believe he was looking at the same freckle-faced child he remembered.

Adam blinked a few times, then found himself comparing Madeline to Diana. Madeline wasn't lovely in the same way as her older sister. Diana was indisputably beautiful. One knew it the first instant one saw her.

Madeline, however, was more of an enigma. He discovered now—as he noticed the color of her dark brown eyes, so deep and discerning—that she required a longer look, a more careful study. There was an innocence about her because of her youth, but beneath that soft exterior, almost in full contradiction, there seemed to be a firm, immovable strength that revealed itself gradually. And a stubbornness he'd already experienced firsthand. He could see it as clearly now as he could see the pink ribbon on her lace cap. She looked as if she could survive anything.

He wiped his hands on his breeches as he approached her in the doorway. "Is there something you need, Madeline?"

She held her chin high and prepared to speak, as if she were bracing herself for a scolding for interrupting his work. Had he truly been that surly toward her? With a sharp pang of regret, Adam accepted that he had and promised himself he would try to be less gruff.

"I would like to go to the fort," she announced.

"Why? Did you forget something?" Bloody hell, he sounded gruff again.

She seemed to put enormous effort into forming her response, to speak clearly and succinctly and not shrink before his tone. "No, but I would like to speak with the Ripleys. Or I could send a message, if someone is going that way."

He leaned a shoulder against the door frame. "No one's going, at least not that I know of."

"Well, if no one is going, I would like to take a horse myself." She raised her chin again, almost daring him to say no, and he found himself oddly impressed by her tenacity.

Nonetheless, there was no way on God's earth that he would let her ride out into the wilderness alone. "I couldn't let you do that."

"Why not? I could find my way. I'm quite sure I remember the road."

He backed away from her, then lifted another sack of seed onto his shoulder. "'Quite sure' isn't good enough. Some of the paths can be obscure. I'd have to take you myself, but as you can see, I'm busy."

He tossed the seed onto the back of the wagon, and Madeline jumped at the loud *smack*. "Then tell me when."

"How about the day after tomorrow?" He went for another sack.

She said nothing, and he had the distinct impression that his answer wasn't the one she was looking for. He felt her determined gaze upon him, watching him pick up the bag of seed and carry it to the wagon.

"I'd like to go sooner," she said.

He dropped the sack onto the pile, then crossed toward her and leaned against the door frame again. He rubbed a thumb along his stubbled jawline. "What's the hurry?"

"I wish to see about working for the Ripleys."

Distracted briefly by the wind lifting the wispy curls that had escaped Madeline's hairpins and now hung loosely at her delicate shoulders, Adam tried not to let his gaze wander downward, for that would lead his eyes to her neckline.

He felt uncomfortable with his awareness of her neckline all of a sudden—and the fact that he was curious about it, for he should not be noticing anything like that in this young woman whom he had known as a child.

He labored to bring his attention back to where it should be: on the situation at hand and her question about leaving to work for the Ripleys. What should he do?

He had already sent his proposal to Diana, who—if fate was kind this time—would arrive before the fall harvest. What would she say if she knew he had not at least attempted to keep her baby sister safe in his home, and well-cared-for?

"There's no need to leave." He did his best to sound hospitable and not quite so ogrelike. "You're more than welcome to stay here with us as long as you wish."

"Thank you, but no."

"No?"

"No."

God, she was like a brick wall. "Miss Oxley, you're in a strange land. I apologize for the way things were between us yesterday, but that's no reason to be stubborn about—"

"I'm not being *stubborn*. I only wish to make my own way here."

Hell, he'd insulted her. "Let me start again. Your plans have been hampered, and it's partly my fault that you're here."

She blinked a few times. "Partly your fault? Yesterday, this was all *my* fault for not having a mind of my own."

He deserved that, he knew, so he raised his hands in mock surrender. "You have a point, and I'm sorry."

He suddenly felt inarticulate and flustered talking to her—this child who used to follow him and Diana around like a little lost puppy. Lord, how things had changed. He didn't feel as though he was talking to a lost puppy now.

"Why don't you want to stay?" he asked, hoping to steer the conversation into gentler waters. "If you want to earn your way, I could always hire you as a governess myself."

"I don't want a charity position."

"It wouldn't be charity. Penelope and Charlie both need more than what Mrs. Dalton can give them. I've been considering hiring someone for quite a while, in fact..." He was rambling now. Lord Almighty, he'd *really* lost his touch.

Madeline shook her head. "I'm sorry, I can't."

"Care to tell me why not?"

After a long pause, she gave a frustrated sigh as if he was forcing her to reveal more than she wanted to. "Because if Diana accepts your proposal and comes here to marry you, I'd rather be elsewhere."

Adam gazed at her drawn expression and the way she was pursing her full lips. He hadn't expected *Diana* to be the reason Madeline would not want to stay. "Are there problems between you two?"

"No, I just don't want to be dependent upon her."

He rested his hands on his hips. "I can understand that you don't want to be in the position of servant to your sister, but it wouldn't be that way. You would be a member of the family."

Their conversation stopped dead while they stood in the barn doorway, staring at each other. She seemed unable to think of a rebuttal.

For a second or two, he thought he had managed to persuade her, then she pressed her shoulders back and spoke firmly. "Thank you for the kind offer, but I would prefer to be on my own. I'd like to go to the fort tomorrow."

He said yes—only because he knew there was no point in arguing, for she was not going to give in— then watched her turn away from him and walk back to the house, her gait swift and true.

Once again he saw the young Yorkshire lass who had never let anyone tell her what she could and could not do. Back in those days, that willfulness had frustrated him when he'd wanted to be alone with Diana, just as it frustrated him now, when he wanted to keep Madeline here, safe in his home.

Something was different today, however. Adam could feel his blood warming to her, for she was no longer the child she once was. She had become a woman, and he found himself admiring her for, of all things, knowing her own mind and settling for nothing less than what she wanted.

Chapter Five

After dinner, Madeline sat by the fire in the parlor, mending one of Penelope's caps, while the children played cards at the table. She had just threaded her needle, when two shiny black boots and a pair of muscular legs in tawny brown breeches appeared in her line of vision. She glanced up at Adam, who was gazing uneasily down at her.

He gestured at the chair opposite hers. "May I?"

"Of course."

He sat down and crossed one long leg over the other. The fire snapped and crackled, and the children burst into laughter about something.

"I must apologize again," he said quietly, "for the way I treated you yesterday at the fort, and for the way things have turned out."

Madeline poked her needle through the white lace cap on her knees. Oh, she didn't want to have this conversation. She didn't want to experience Adam Coates trying to be *nice* to her. She'd gotten along fine the way things were—first being accused of deceiving him, then enduring his silences and cool reticence. She'd been perfectly happy telling herself that she was lucky to have been spared a marriage to him. She didn't want to go back to feeling otherwise.

"It's not your fault."

"No, but I do feel responsible. If I had never sent the proposal, you would not be here among strangers."

Madeline was careful not to let her cool exterior crack. "You're not a stranger, Mr. Coates. Not entirely. I did know you once. A long time ago."

"Yes," he replied thoughtfully, "it was a long time ago, wasn't it? Who would have guessed the years would pass so quickly?"

She lifted the needle high over her head to pull it through the seam. "They do pass quickly, don't they? It seems like only yesterday that you rode into our yard for the first time." *You wore a long, black cloak.*

The firelight flickered across his face as he held her in his contemplative gaze. Madeline felt her blood rush. She hoped it was not coloring her cheeks.

"Refresh my memory," he said with interest. "Did we speak to each other much?"

She took time to clear her throat. "Not very much, no. I was young."

"Not so young that you didn't enjoy a magic trick, as I recall."

A warmth moved through her. She hadn't thought he remembered anything beyond her bothersome presence—intruding upon his private moments with Diana and refusing to leave when they asked her to.

"You used to make a shilling disappear. Then you would retrieve it from behind the butter crock."

He smiled. "I do the same trick for Penelope now, but instead of the butter crock, I retrieve the shilling from her nose."

Madeline laughed. The beat of her pulse eased a little.

"You were Penelope's age then," he said.

"I was."

"Looking at you now helps me to remember." He stared at her for a long, lingering moment. "You seemed curious about the farm last night at dinner. Or were you just making conversation?"

"Someone had to," she said with a hint of humor, which garnered another smile from him. "But I was genuinely curious as well."

"If you like, on the way to the fort tomorrow, I could show you around the area. It's the least I can do after what happened."

Madeline felt her mood lift slightly. "I would like that very much. Would we see some dykes? I'm curious as to how they work."

He nodded, looking pleased with her enthusiasm. "Do you enjoy riding?"

"More than anything."

"Then I'll take you down onto the marsh in the morning."

She eagerly agreed and the conversation turned to Yorkshire. Madeline told Adam news about some of the people he once knew, and he asked about the earl who had been his landlord, and how the tenant farmers were faring with all the rent increases.

An hour later, it was time to retire. The boys went

upstairs and Adam stayed behind to snuff out the candles.

As Madeline climbed the stairs, feeling invigorated from her first pleasant discourse with Adam, she found herself anxiously anticipating their morning ride. There was a sweet fluttering in her belly, not unlike the way her belly had fluttered aboard ship, when they were nearing the coast.

She stopped on the landing halfway up the stairs, and squeezed the railing tightly in her hand. This nervous, giddy feeling was not a good thing.

Perhaps she should not have accepted Adam's invitation. Perhaps she should have feigned disinterest and requested that he take her straight to the fort.

But that would have been lying, and she had truly wanted to go, so much so that she had momentarily forgotten about her unbending intentions to protect her vulnerable heart. She could only hope there would be no harm in it.

Before breakfast the next morning, Madeline passed by Mary's open door. Mary lay quietly on the bed, her blond curls splayed out upon the pillow, her expression solemn as she gazed at the bright sash window. Her head turned when she heard Madeline's heels across the threshold.

"Madeline. I'm so glad you're here. Please, come in." She tried to sit up.

"Am I disturbing you? You look melancholy."

"Melancholy? I was thinking of Jacob and our baby and hoping all will go well."

Madeline sat down beside the bed and covered

Mary's hand with her own. "I'm sure everything will be fine."

"I wish the doctor thought so. He's ordered me to stay in bed until after the baby comes, and sometimes…good heavens…sometimes I think I'm going to go out of my mind. He allows me to take a turn about the room only twice a day, just to keep my legs in working order, and it's all I can do to keep from bolting out the door to escape and be with Jacob and feel his arms around me. I miss him so much, Madeline, sometimes I think I'm going to disintegrate and crumble into a hundred tiny pieces. And here I am, all alone in this room staring at the same four walls day after day, doing nothing but worrying about having this baby. Oh, I wish he were here with me now."

A wave of commiseration for what Mary must be feeling coursed through Madeline. Childbirth. So much could go wrong. She squeezed Mary's hand again. "I'm sure that when you hold your baby in your arms for the first time, all this will be forgotten."

"You're probably right." Mary's voice brightened a bit, but Madeline knew the girl was still anxious.

"Do you like Nova Scotia?" Mary asked, changing the subject. "Or are you anxious to go home?"

"No, I'm not anxious to go. There's nothing for me there. My father doesn't need me. I'm more of a burden than anything. I want very much to make my own way here."

"What will you do?"

"I'll be a governess."

"For Mr. Coates?"

The question lodged like a musket ball in Madeline's heart. "No, not for Mr. Coates. I know a family from the ship who I think would be pleased to have me work for them. They have four young children and we're going to see them today."

"Why *not* Mr. Coates?"

Madeline stumbled over a few possible replies, none of which would do.

Thankfully, Mary continued talking. "He's going to need some help soon, I think. I used to help out with the children, but after the baby comes, Jacob and I will move into our own home before the end of the summer. Jacob already has our fields planted."

"What about Mrs. Dalton?"

"Agnes loves the children, certainly, but she does so many other things, she doesn't have time to teach them their numbers. And it matters a great deal to Adam to have his children schooled."

Madeline didn't know what to say. She supposed there wasn't really anything *to* say. She had already made up her mind.

"I should hate to think you'll be leaving us so soon," Mary said. "You've only just arrived, and I like that you're here with us."

"Yes, but it was my sister Mr. Coates meant to bring, and if she comes, then I should—"

"Wouldn't you want to live here with your sister? Were you not close?"

There was that question again.

Madeline didn't know how to answer it. How could she explain that the problem was more about Adam than it was about Diana, and her feelings were too complex to even understand them herself?

One minute she found Adam cold and unfeeling. The next minute, he was apologizing and talking about shillings in noses, making her feel giddy and nervous when she knew she shouldn't be feeling anything but a sisterly regard.

Adam belonged to Diana and there was no point in hoping she could ever be with him. Not when she was so certain that Diana would come.

Besides all that, how could Madeline be sure that if she expressed her deepest feelings, the entire household wouldn't know by sunset?

That would be far too humiliating.

"My leaving has nothing to do with Diana. I'm simply a very independent person."

Mary smiled. "I guessed that about you. You were very brave to come all the way from England by yourself, and then, to have your hopes dashed." She shook her head. "In my opinion, Mr. Coates owes you at least a comfortable place to stay as long as you like. None of this was your fault. And don't be in any hurry to find employment, either. Take your time and be sure to find the right position."

"I will," Madeline replied. "But it wasn't Adam's fault, either," she added, wishing afterward that she hadn't leaped so quickly to his defense.

Mary gazed at her knowingly for a long, agonizing moment before she finally nodded and reached for the cards.

Adam and Madeline started off at a trot through the early morning haze, the thumping of the horses' hooves mingling pleasantly with the chirping of sharp-tailed sparrows in the leafy sugar maples. Frost covered the ground and glistened like a blanket of tiny diamonds in the sun.

Madeline looked about at the low fog hanging over the land. "Is it unusual to have frost so late in the spring?"

"Not for Cumberland."

"What about the crops? How do you manage to get everything done when you have to wait so long for the ground to thaw?"

"We plow in the fall. But don't worry, this won't last much longer. In another week, you'll be fluttering your fan everywhere you go."

"I'm not worried," she replied, unable to stop herself from smiling. "And I still haven't seen any of those *mosquitoes* you were so adamant about the other day."

Her teasing tone made him smile, too. "Ah, yes, the mosquitoes. They're as big as groundhogs, you know."

"Groundhogs!" She laughed. "What do you take me for, Adam Coates? I may be a young Yorkshire lass, but I do have a head between my ears."

"So I've learned," he conceded.

They galloped up the ridge. Adam showed her where the barley and wheat would be planted, and pointed out the fields for oats and flax along the plowed uplands.

When they reached the crest, Adam pulled his mount to a halt. Madeline stopped beside him, finally able to look down at the great marsh below, stretching before them for thousands of acres, like a vast green, grassy sea.

"All this was created with dykes?"

He nodded, and she felt him watching her, studying her as she gazed with fascination at the magnificent vista below.

"How much of it is yours?" she asked.

"I own only a fraction of it. The rest goes on for miles inland. The local farmers work together to maintain it and protect it from the tides."

"Does everyone do their rightful share?"

"Unfortunately, no. There are a number of absentee landowners. I'm pushing for the county to appoint an official committee to insure that—at the very least—the marsh as a whole continues to be maintained."

"Yes, of course. You need to preserve this."

"Preserve it, yes, but if we are enterprising, we could build it as well."

He kicked in his heels and led the way along the top of the ridge to a road down the hill. Soon they reached the bottom and followed a narrow path that crossed the lowlands.

"We're below sea level now."

"Really? May I see some dykes?" Madeline could not keep the exhilaration from her voice.

"Of course. I'll take you to the river."

They trotted leisurely across the chilly marsh, the horses' foggy breaths puffing out of their noses. The scent of wet marsh mud somewhere in the distance touched Madeline's nose, and she inhaled its glorious freshness.

Seated high in the saddle, she looked down at the drainage ditches dug into the meadows like deep gashes, carved by a giant, swift knife. She doubted any of this work had been swift, however. All this would have been dug out by hand. Some of it by Adam's hand.

She tried not to imagine that. It wouldn't do her any good to picture him with his sleeves rolled up, his muscles straining against the physical force of driving a dyking spade into the dirt. Just thinking about it now made her body tingle in the strangest places.

They reached a dyke—a long, narrow hill, stretching like a giant snake along the bank of the meandering river. It went on and on as far as the eye could see.

"This was all built by hand?"

"Yes, by the Acadians."

Adam dismounted and helped Madeline down. He took her hand to lead her up the steep side of the grassy dyke. From the top, she peered down into the river.

"The tide is low," Adam said. "When it comes in from the bay and the water level rises—almost to where we're standing—the dyke will keep it from spilling over onto the marshlands."

"Has it ever overflowed?"

"Several times over the years, for different reasons. Neglect mostly."

"What happens to the flooded land?"

"It's put out of production for at least two years. The salt water has to be drained off, then rain and snow has to leach the salt out of the ground. But perhaps I'm telling you too much. I'm sure you're not interested in the science of it.''

''Of course I am. It's fascinating, Adam.'' Too late, she caught herself using his given name, as she had so many times in her daydreams.

His head turned. She refused to look up at him. How could she? She was afraid he would see the awe in her eyes, and know how desperately she had wanted him the day she'd stepped off the boat.

''Sounds like a risky way to farm,'' she continued, trying to keep her tone light, pretending she hadn't even noticed that she'd used his given name.

''Perhaps.'' He finally turned his attention back to the river. She swallowed over her heart, now thumping in her throat.

''But good management dulls the risk,'' he said. ''The dykes are well worth the effort. We don't have to clear forests, there are virtually no stones, and we don't have to fertilize the marsh soil. It's already fertile enough. We can even use the marsh mud to fertilize the uplands.''

''Sounds like a perfect scenario.''

''Nothing is ever perfect, Madeline.''

Madeline. Hearing him use *her* given name sent a flurry of gooseflesh down her back. He spoke with such a deep, resounding voice, yet her name spilled past his lips with fluid grace and buoyancy.

She looked him straight in the eye. ''I'm all too aware of that.''

For a long moment, he gazed at her in the sunshine. She wondered what he was thinking, what he thought of her, what he saw. Was he trying to understand her meaning? Was he wondering what kind of a life had shaped her into the person she was, or was he looking into her eyes and wishing he was looking into Diana's?

He turned his gaze toward the river again. "Perhaps we should go."

"Yes, we should." *We definitely should, before I feel more of what I shouldn't be feeling.*

But she didn't want to leave. She wanted to stay here with him—here alone on the dyke with the sun on her cheeks and the breeze in Adam's hair and the sound of her skirts whipping lavishly in the wind.

Then she thought of her sister and knew that even if Adam wanted to stay here with her, too—which he didn't—it would be wrong.

He tried to lead her down the steep slope, but she let go of his hand and broke into a run.

Adam laughed. "Are you all right? You practically flew down, Madeline!"

She burst into a fit of laughter herself. "I'm fine!"

He walked her to her horse and helped her mount. As she settled into the creaky leather saddle and gathered up the reins, he discreetly took a section of her skirt in his large hand and flipped it over to cover her leg, which she hadn't realized was exposed almost to the knee.

Good God. Her belly went *whoosh* as his hand brushed over her petticoats.

Without even acknowledging that anything had been amiss, Adam mounted his own steed. Madeline felt a tremor of disappointment that he had not flushed or nervously cleared his throat or expressed some other kind of abashment. Then she chided herself.

Why she should think Adam would feel awkward or shaken at seeing her leg was beyond her, for men had never stumbled over themselves with her the way they did with Diana. They looked right through Madeline as if she weren't there. She did not stir passions in men, and that fact was demonstrated to her yet again, as Adam hadn't even *noticed* her leg. He flipped her skirt as if it was the folded-back corner of a faded tablecloth.

She wondered then what it would be like to be Diana, to always feel beautiful and to know she captivated men wherever she went. What power Diana must have felt when they dissolved at her feet.

The horses started walking in the direction of the fort, and a moment of disconsolate silence hovered over Madeline.

At last, Adam spoke. "Care to race?"

Madeline shook her head. "No, I don't really think I'm up to it." Then she kicked in her heels and swindled a head start across the grassy marsh, just to put some distance between them and avoid any more reminders that she was invisible.

Adam galloped after Madeline but did not push to win the race. He intentionally lagged back a bit in order to recover his composure after the shock of his intense response to the unexpected, startling sight of Madeline's long, slender leg.

Desire had sparked inside him, red-hot like a blacksmith's poker left too long in the fire.

He immediately attributed the response to his frustration over Diana's failure to arrive, for over the past few weeks, his eagerness to see her again had mushroomed into a burning, aching need. Madeline was a part of those long-ago days, and her presence here had no doubt brought it all closer to home and stirred what had been dormant in Adam for what seemed like forever.

If he was aware of Madeline's shapely leg or the creamy, soft-looking skin at her neckline, it was only because she was a woman, and he had not seen many "new" women since he'd arrived here in this remote section of the world. He would probably react that way to any feminine feature.

Adam then tried to picture his beloved's face, and wondered if her leg would be anything like her younger sister's, for he was sure he had seen some firm muscle in Madeline's calf. He suspected that Madeline didn't spend a lot of time sitting. She seemed to enjoy the outdoors.

He watched her ride ahead of him. She was indeed an accomplished horsewoman.

He wondered further where he and Diana would be now if she had come as she was supposed to. Would he be riding across the marsh with her? Would she be curious about the dykes, like Madeline was?

He preferred to imagine they would be married already and in bed together, for he had been without her too long. And after the bit of fire he'd just experienced, he decided firmly that he was even more starved for Diana than he knew.

Chapter Six

Adam and Madeline rode up the steep, grassy hill to Fort Cumberland. They dismounted outside the main entrance and led their horses into the courtyard.

A voice rang out. "Miss Oxley!"

Madeline turned and recognized the caller. John Metcalf, a young man who had traveled on the ship with her from Yorkshire, was approaching, ax in hand. He had come alone to Nova Scotia to rent land until he could earn enough to buy his own and send for his brothers. This morning, he looked as if he'd been hard at work, splitting wood and perspiring in the sun.

Madeline smiled and walked to meet him halfway. Adam waited near the barracks.

"Hello, John. It's good to see you. Have you been settling in?"

"Yes, Miss Oxley. Though I haven't found a place to call my own just yet."

She remembered his optimism on board ship, speaking ambitiously about the fertile soil in Cumberland, and how he planned to acquire enough land to someday make something of himself. "I'm sure you'll find what you're looking for soon enough, John. Have you been to see the marshes?"

"Yes, and it's fine land, but I knew it would be." He peered over her shoulder.

Curious to know what had caught his attention, Madeline turned. There was Adam, standing by the barracks, watching their conversation. When he noticed her looking at him, he glanced the other way.

"So you didn't marry him after all?" John asked quietly.

"No."

"Were you very disappointed?"

Madeline cleared her throat. She didn't want to talk about this—not with John Metcalf, not with anyone. "I barely knew him."

"He's older than I thought he'd be." After a pause, John settled his gaze upon her again. "Will you return to Yorkshire?"

"No. I haven't decided what I'll do exactly, but I do hope to remain here. For the time being anyway."

Madeline couldn't help thinking that after spending the morning with Adam, so full of knowledge, wisdom and experience, John's eyes looked particularly youthful.

"So, what *are* you doing at the fort this morning?" he asked.

"I came to see the Ripleys."

"Ah…"

Did she detect a hint of disappointment in his tone? She was probably imagining it. He couldn't possibly be hoping she was here to see him. Men never had hopes about her.

"They're staying in there." John pointed toward the barracks where Adam stood.

"Thank you, John. I must go now. It was nice seeing you again. Good luck finding land." She returned to where Adam was now leaning against the barracks.

"An acquaintance from the ship?" he asked, still watching John.

"Yes. His name is John Metcalf." Why did she feel uncomfortable answering that question? Was it her own foolish sense of loyalty to Adam? Did she feel she should not be talking to single young men?

"Did he bring a family with him?" Adam asked.

"Not yet. He plans to send for his brothers as soon as he finds property to lease."

Adam watched John intently for a few more seconds, then escorted Madeline to the barracks.

They knocked on the Ripleys' door, which almost immediately opened before them. Adam removed his hat and held it under his arm.

"Madeline! How wonderful to see you!" Mrs. Ripley pulled Madeline into her arms, then stepped back. "Is everything all right?"

"Of course. Mr. Coates was very kind to bring me to visit you today."

He bowed at the waist and settled his tricorn hat back on his head. He was so gentlemanly, so courteous and elegant. And how handsome he looked in his hat.

"I shall be in the courtyard, Miss Oxley." Then he left them.

With his departure, Madeline felt the same way she felt when she was in her garden and a cloud moved in front of the sun.

Mrs. Ripley closed the door behind him and sat down on one of the beds with Madeline. "Why did you come? Has it been difficult for you? Have you been crying? Do you want to go home?"

"I'm fine." Madeline laughed at Mrs. Ripley's flair for the dramatic, but at the same time, she couldn't bear the thought of everyone thinking she was heart-broken and pining away. She needed to set them straight, even if she wasn't being completely straight with them or herself.

"Now that I'm here and I've had a chance to get to know Mr. Coates, I see that we wouldn't have been suited to each other anyway. He's a good deal older than I am, and he's not at all the man I remember. Honestly, I have not shed a single tear. I am glad things turned out the way they did. He and Diana are meant to be together, and he has already sent another proposal to her. In fact, it was I who encouraged him to do so."

The older woman touched her hand. "But he's such a handsome man. Surely it's been at least a *trifle* difficult to bear, living under the same roof with him."

"Not at all. He's been a perfect host, more like a father figure. Really, he seems very old to me."

A father figure? Seems very old? She was more skilled at hiding her feelings than she'd thought.

It was time to change the subject. "May I ask, Mrs. Ripley, if you've found suitable land yet?"

"Yes, we found a very promising spot—a farm near Amherst township. A section of the marsh is included and the ground is plowed, and a full crop of potatoes has already been planted."

A rush of hopefulness surged through Madeline. "That's wonderful news. Will you be moving there soon?"

"As soon as the present owner vacates the house in two weeks."

Two weeks! Madeline tried not to sound too delighted about it. "Well...the reason I came is...I wonder if you might have need of a governess. Or even a housekeeper. Or both."

Mrs. Ripley was quiet a moment.

Madeline shifted on the hay-filled tick. "I'm sorry, I didn't mean to sound so anxious. You'll need time to discuss it with Mr. Ripley, of course. Perhaps I could return for an answer tomorrow."

She made a move to stand, but Mrs. Ripley clasped her hand.

"No need to come back, Madeline. We would be delighted to have you. We've been saying that ever since we met you."

A cry of relief spilled from Madeline's lips. "What good news."

"We'll come by early, two weeks from Wednesday, to pick you up." Mrs. Ripley hugged Madeline. "I'm very happy. In a couple of weeks, we'll all be together, and we can finally start to build a new life."

Madeline rested her cheek on Mrs. Ripley's shoulder. "I will be counting the days."

A short time later, Madeline said goodbye to Mrs.

Ripley and found Adam sitting on a bench in the courtyard, conversing with some local tradesmen. He immediately stood, left the men to themselves and crossed to meet her.

"Will you be returning with me?" he asked. The question came abruptly out of nowhere.

"Yes, to stay only temporarily. The Ripleys found land near Amherst township and in two weeks, I'll be able to move into their new home and begin work as their governess."

His gaze swept over her face and settled on her eyes. His voice grew quiet. "I see. Well, that *is* good news."

"They're just waiting for the other family to remove themselves. The papers have already been signed."

"Already signed. More good news." Adam's tone was as cordial as always, but beneath it, she thought she detected a hint of disappointment. Could it be he had enjoyed her company and conversation this morning more than he had expected?

No, surely not. He was simply disappointed because his children would continue to live without a governess of their own.

He offered his arm. "Shall we go?" He escorted her to their horses, tethered near the fort's entrance.

Suddenly an unexpected sadness moved through her.

She chastised herself, for those feelings made no sense. She had accomplished what she'd set out to accomplish this morning. She'd found another situation. She should be overjoyed.

Perhaps a small part of her had still not let go of
the dream.

She tried to ignore it and told herself that soon,
when she was settled into a new life with the Ripleys,
all this would surely pass.

Days later, Madeline ventured outside to feed the
chickens. She closed the kitchen door behind her, but
started at the unexpected sight of Adam pushing the
plow behind a yoke of oxen in Agnes's vegetable
garden. The sleeves on his loose, linen workshirt were
rolled up to his elbows; he wore no waistcoat. He
labored hard to push the plow, his muscles straining
as he strove to keep the furrows straight.

She stood motionless, watching for a moment, re-
alizing how much she loved to watch him work. The
sight of him, with dirt on his clothing and perspiration
dampening his face, made her skin tingle all over with
gooseflesh. She could have stood there and watched
him all day. He was rugged and strong, like the land
itself. He was a part of it. He worked it, handled it,
nurtured it.

Then she began to entertain the most indecent
thoughts. She imagined him alone in his bedchamber
at night, taking off his shirt in the candlelight, preparing for bed. What would his bare chest look like,
and what would it feel like to her touch? What would
it be like to share a bed with him and feel those huge
hands moving over her body? She imagined they
would feel callused and rough, yet warm and gentle
at the same time.

Shaking herself out of those improper thoughts,

Madeline started off toward the chicken coop. She stepped inside. There was a cackling frenzy, then the hens settled as Madeline made her way about, collecting the eggs from the nests of hay while she tried not to think any more indecent thoughts about her future brother-in-law.

A few minutes later, she stepped out to the barnyard, where more hens pecked at the dry ground. She reached into her bucket and sprinkled the feed at their feet.

A tiny voice caught her attention. Madeline turned. Penelope, resting her cheek on her arm and looking quite decidedly bored, watched her from the other side of the fence. "Father said you'll be leaving us soon."

Hearing dejection in the young girl's voice, Madeline labored to sound cheerful. "Yes, Penelope, I've been hired as a governess and housekeeper for a family I met during the crossing."

"Are they a nice family?"

"Yes, they're very nice."

Penelope picked her way around the fence. Her gait was shy and uncertain. "Do they have a little girl? Or just boys?"

Sprinkling more feed onto the ground, Madeline held out the bucket for Penelope to lend a hand, thinking it would do the girl good to feel useful. "They have two boys and two girls. The oldest is ten and the youngest girl is only four."

"Does the youngest one know her numbers yet?" Penelope kept her gaze fixed on the chickens.

"Not yet, but I'll begin teaching her right away."

"I could count when I was two."

A breeze fluttered Madeline's skirts and she stopped what she was doing to gaze down at Penelope, who seemed to be searching for approval. Madeline was more than happy to give it to her, for she knew what it was like to spend a lifetime feeling deprived of it. "That's excellent. You must be very bright."

Penelope shrugged and sprinkled her grain on the ground. "Do you like those children more than you like us? Is that why you don't want to work for Papa?"

"Oh, no, Penelope! It has nothing to do with you and the boys. It's just that my sister will be coming here, and when she arrives, you won't have need of a governess. You'll have a new stepmother."

"But Papa says she won't be here before autumn. Why do you have to leave now?"

Because if I don't leave now, it will be too painful later.

"It's just the way things are. I've already promised the Ripleys."

Penelope was quiet a moment. "I never knew my real mother."

A heaviness settled in Madeline's chest. She stopped what she was doing and touched Penelope's shoulder. "I know, sweetheart, and I'm very sorry. I never knew my mother, either, and I know how it feels."

Madeline shuddered inwardly at the memories of her lonely childhood, of never being held or cuddled the way other children were. Her own father had never offered her any affection—only blame and disdain, for having been the instrument of his wife's death. That fact had led to his favoring Diana all through their lives.

Madeline found herself wondering more about Adam as a father to these children. Was he affectionate? Had he ever blamed Penelope for Mrs. Coates's death, as Madeline's father had blamed her?

"Papa says that Mama had a good heart," Penelope said, "and that she could thread a needle with her eyes closed."

Madeline made sure to keep her tone cheerful. "That's quite a talent. I don't believe I could do that."

"Nor can Mrs. Dalton. Or I. But I keep trying. Papa says it just requires practice."

Madeline held the bucket while Penelope dug into it for more feed. She felt a sudden, strong connection to the girl beside her.

Penelope's tone brightened. "Is your sister anything like you?"

Now, there was a good question, Madeline thought. She had to think very hard to come up with some similarities to offer Penelope. "We both grew up on the moors in Yorkshire. And we both like the color blue."

"Does she look like you?"

"Not at all. She has blond hair and blue eyes and she's very beautiful."

"You're beautiful, too."

"Thank you, Penelope, that's very kind of you to say. You're a sweet girl."

"I'm not trying to be kind, or sweet. It's the truth."

Feeling a pleasant swell of warmth, Madeline turned the bucket upside down and dumped the last of the feed onto the ground. Then she and Penelope went into the barn to fill another bucket for the hogs.

"Will you come and visit us when you're living with the Ripleys?" Penelope asked.

Even though she knew future visits would be difficult, Madeline couldn't bring herself to refuse Penelope's invitation. "Yes, of course I'll come."

A short time later, Madeline and Penelope started back to the house. They had just reached the kitchen door and were discussing a new cookie recipe, when a gut-wrenching scream cut through the still, morning air and pitched Madeline's heart into her throat.

Chapter Seven

"Whoa!" Adam angled the plow to a halt, wiped a sleeve across his damp forehead and turned toward the house. He listened intently, not altogether certain what he'd heard. There. There it was again—another cry from the upstairs window.

Dropping the reins, he bolted for the door. He nearly wrenched it from its hinges as he threw it open and ran through the kitchen toward the stairs. Two at a time he took them, until he reached the top, crossed the hall and skidded to a halt at Mary's open door.

She was sitting up on the bed, panting and screaming Jacob's name while Madeline leaned over her, trying to calm her. "Everything's going to be all right now, Mary. I'm here."

Penelope dashed into Adam's back. "There you are, Papa! I tried to find you!"

Adam turned to her. "Go out to the south field and fetch Jacob. Tell him Mary's time has come, but first go and get Mrs. Dalton."

Panic flitted through Penelope's wide eyes. "She's not here! She's gone to the market!"

Adam glanced at Madeline again, who was trying to convince Mary to lie back against the pillows. "Find George, then. Tell him to saddle a horse and fetch Dr. Hudry."

"I will!" Penelope hurried down the stairs.

Another terrorized scream from Mary shook Adam to the core and summoned hot, agonizing memories. Jane's screams had sounded the same. For the rest of his days, Adam would never forget the desperation in his wife's voice just before Penelope had come into the world—the tears and the sobs and the pleading to God for mercy. He was sure she'd known she was dying and, from his seat in the hall outside the closed door, he could do nothing to save her.

The guilt afterward had been excruciating, for how many times over the years had he wished for things to be different with Jane? How often, when she was ranting and smashing things, had he wondered what life would be like if she were not there?

Adam thrust those thoughts away and said a quick prayer for Mary. His children's happiness meant everything to him, and he did not want Jacob's young wife to be taken from them now, when she and Jacob were so deeply in love and eager for the future.

Madeline pulled the quilt back and tossed it into the corner of the room.

"What can I do?" Adam asked.

Fear showed itself in her eyes, but her voice was calm. "Is there no one here? Just us?"

"Just us for the moment. Penelope has gone to fetch Jacob, and George will go for the doctor."

Adam watched Madeline contemplate the situation,

as if she were playing it through in her mind and anticipating what she would have to do.

A feeling of powerlessness moved through him. All he could do was trust her with his daughter-in-law's life.

"Have you done this before?"

She met his gaze squarely. "Yes. Twice in York-shire, and the midwife explained everything to me along the way. We'll get along fine, Adam. Breathe, Mary. That's it. In and out."

He stood in the doorway, watching Madeline move around Mary, talking to her and telling her what to do, her voice always composed and reassuring.

"Adam, could you get me hot water and towels, please?" She sounded wholly in control, and her confidence eased the tight knot that had formed in his gut. "Then you can leave us alone." With her eyes, she told him not to worry.

He left the room to do as she asked, and thanked the good Lord for sending Madeline to them when He had.

Jacob pounded a fist against the door frame in the hall. "How much longer is this agony going to last?"

Mary screamed again, her cries muffled behind the locked door, but no less disquieting for Adam and Jacob, who waited restlessly outside.

Adam stopped pacing to reassure Jacob again. "This is normal, son, especially for the first child. I remember the night George was born...it seemed to take a week, but it was only six hours."

"Six hours! It's only been three so far!"

Adam strove to maintain a confidence he did not feel, not when Mary was screaming so much louder now.

Where was the damn doctor? George hadn't been able to find him.

"I know it's difficult, but all you can do is wait and pray. Perhaps you'd be better off outside, where you can't hear what's going on."

"No. If she has to endure this, so must I."

Jacob collapsed into the chair in the hall and buried his face in his hands. He shook almost violently with silent, pain-racked sobs.

The sight of him weeping was like a knife in Adam's chest, twisting with excruciating exactness, for his children were his life. His love for them was greater than anything he could ever have expected or comprehended, and to see his son suffer was grueling agony.

Another cry came from inside the room. This time, a baby's cry.

Jacob looked up, his eyes full of tears. "Was that what I thought it was?"

Before Adam had a chance to reply, the door creaked open and Madeline walked out. Her hair was damp with perspiration around her forehead, her face pale. She wiped her hands on a bloody cloth.

Jacob almost leaped out of his chair. He took one look at the blood smeared on Madeline's apron and teetered, as if he were about to faint. Adam grabbed onto Jacob's arm to steady him.

Madeline smiled. "Congratulations, Jacob. You have a daughter."

The air sailed out of Adam's lungs. Surely, the weight of the whole world had just lifted from his shoulders.

Jacob stood. "Is Mary all right?"

"You can ask her yourself." Not even the sun could compete with the purity and brilliance of Madeline's smile as she delivered this welcome news.

Jacob hastened into the room, leaving Adam and Madeline alone in the hall. They both stood in silence, staring at each other, recovering from the anxiety they had both been harnessing for the past three hours.

Adam gestured toward the chair. "Why don't you sit down? You look to be in need of a rest."

"Thank you."

An immense upwelling of fondness and gratitude moved through Adam. Madeline had been a great champion today. She had kept Mary safe and brought a beautiful new life into the world. She had made Jacob a happy, lucky man, and that made Adam a happy, lucky man, too.

"No, I must thank *you*. What would we have done if you had not been with us today?"

She made light of his compliment. "Everything went smoothly. Mary's built for childbearing. You'll have a whole house full of grandchildren before you know it."

Adam gazed at the young woman sitting across the hall from him, her hair tousled and toppling from its bun, her cheeks now flushing from the stress of the morning. How was it she could be a mere four years older than his stepson, Jacob, yet seem a whole lifetime older in maturity and experience?

"Blimey," he stammered, trying to sound full of humor, when he was not at all accustomed to trying so hard to sound anything at all. "The years have caught up with me. I'm an aging grandfather."

Her eyes shone with self-assurance again. "That is not how I see you, Adam. I see what lies ahead, not what has already gone by."

He could not resist probing further. "And what do *you* think lies ahead?"

She thought carefully before she spoke. "New beginnings, great happiness and love."

"Do you mean Diana?" he asked quickly. Too quickly.

An uneasy sensation prickled through him. *What kind of question was that? Of course she meant Diana.*

After a long pause, she simply smiled and stood. "I should go and see if Mary needs anything."

Adam cleared his throat. He felt unexpectedly flustered and unsure what to say next. "Of course, you must go." There was that gruff voice again. "I'll go and spread the good news."

He made a move to leave, but Madeline caught his arm. "Please, Adam, come first and see your granddaughter."

A warm, familial pride moved through him. Madeline was right of course. He should be among the first to see the babe. This was all so new to him. Thank God sensible Madeline was here to guide him through this.

He followed her into the room, where Jacob was standing in front of the large window, holding his

firstborn child in his arms. Dazzling sunshine lit up
Jacob's fair features—so much like his mother's—
and reflected off the tears of joy on his cheeks.

Adam felt his own eyes cloud with tears. It was an
extraordinary moment he would never forget.

Jacob turned to show off the babe in his arms.
Adam moved softly toward them. Only the infant's
tiny face was visible from beneath the white swad-
dling blanket—her beautiful, tiny red face. She made
quiet little fussing sounds and pursed her puffy lips.
Adam touched his knuckle to her fat little cheek and
felt love move through him in a powerful, potent rush.

"Look, Father, isn't she beautiful?"

"She's a treasure, Jacob." His voice shook.

Mary watched from the bed, smiling. Madeline
moved toward her and wiped a cool, damp cloth over
her forehead and face.

"Congratulations, Mary," Adam said, bending to
kiss his daughter-in-law on the cheek. "You did
well."

A single tear spilled from her eyes. "I couldn't
have done anything without Madeline. She was so
encouraging and knew exactly what to do. I would
have been terrified if she had not been here to tell me
that everything was going to be all right."

Adam glanced over his shoulder at Madeline, who
had moved to the other side of the room. She lowered
her eyes at Mary's compliment, turned her back to
him and wrung the cloth out in the basin.

Adam's heart trembled with gratefulness. He could
not let the moment pass without letting Madeline
know how much he appreciated what she had done

for them today. He crossed the room and took her by the arm, gently urging her to face him. "I'll never forget this, Madeline. Thank you." Then he laid a warm, light kiss on her cheek.

As he caught the scent of her hair in his nostrils, felt the warm, silky softness of her cheek beneath his lips, his body responded with a subtle buzzing sensation. He had the most intense urge to hold her a little closer and embrace her more fully. To run his hands over her back and let his lips linger longer upon her skin, and to kiss her again in other places: her hair and her forehead, down her cheeks to her neck.

Surprised and bewildered, Adam pulled back. He searched around inside himself for explanations. He had dismissed the spark he'd felt when he'd helped her onto her horse that day on the marsh. He had attributed it to his frustration over Diana. Could he dismiss this, too? Could he blame this on the intensity of the moment?

Thankfully, Madeline didn't seem to sense any change in him, maybe because she'd kept her eyes lowered. She turned from him to face the washbasin again, and Adam sucked in a deep breath as he backed away from her and struggled to retrieve his sobriety.

Throughout the next week, Adam did manage to deny what he'd felt when he'd kissed Madeline in Mary's bedchamber. Over and over, time and time again, he told himself that it was gratitude and nothing more, for he had come to depend upon Madeline a great deal since she'd delivered the baby.

She had been caring for the infant, reading to the children in the evenings, helping Agnes in the kitchen and with the chores. She was also giving Penelope impromptu music lessons. Then, after the children were in bed at night, Madeline sat with Adam in the parlor, listening to his concerns about the marshlands and encouraging him to continue his campaign to preserve them.

Like a newly sown field after a long, cold winter, Adam felt awakened and more confident about the task of safeguarding and expanding the land that belonged to him and would one day belong to his children and grandchildren. Yes, he and Madeline had become good friends. But nothing more than that, he assured himself.

Then one morning, Adam descended the stairs just as the back door opened and Madeline walked into the kitchen carrying a basket of eggs. She began to hum as she pulled off her shawl and hung it on a peg by the door. She wore a dress Adam had not seen before, with red printed flower sprays over a white background, and a muslin neckerchief covering her bosom.

Or perhaps he had seen the dress before but had simply not noticed it.

Well, he noticed it now. He noticed a lot of things now—like the feminine curve of her neck and shoulders, and the delightful wine-colored blush of her soft, moist lips. For once he let himself gaze deliberately at her bosom. It was hard to believe those ample, womanly breasts had not even existed all those years ago. Now they were full and round beneath that neckerchief, and he found himself wishing she would take the blasted thing off so he could see the deep crease between them.

He watched Madeline for another few seconds as she whisked the eggs, and he grew increasingly uneasy with his thoughts and the way his eyes were locked on her, as if he would stare at her all day if it were possible.

Just then, Agnes walked out of the dining room with an empty platter in her hands, and he felt as if he'd been caught stealing cookies from the jar.

In reality, this was much worse than that.

He cleared his throat. "Good morning, Agnes." Then he walked with exaggerated aplomb into his kitchen.

Madeline turned, her voice cheerful and melodic as she greeted him. "Good morning, Adam. Breakfast will be ready soon."

He picked up a warm biscuit from a pan cooling on the table and bit into it. The moist flavor of the biscuit melted exquisitely on his tongue. "These are spectacular, Madeline. Did you bake them?"

He sensed Agnes hovering around like a busy bee behind him, listening. His awareness of her presence, and a feeling of self-consciousness, was a great deal sharper than usual.

Madeline's eyes lit up at the compliment. "Yes. I added some sweet, dried savory to the dough."

"Savory, you say…" He took another bite. "Magnificent."

Near the door, Agnes pulled on her shawl. "I'm

going to the barn to do a few chores before breakfast.'' With that, she was gone.

Adam remained in the kitchen, watching Madeline
pour batter into an iron pot on the fire. She was so
quiet. So calm all the time.

Suddenly he yearned to know more about her and
her life before she came into his, and he couldn't
resist the curiosity. He sat down at the trestle table.
''Did you cook for your family at home?''

''My father had a housekeeper, but I was always
in the kitchen helping her, if I wasn't in the garden
digging in the dirt. Of course, neither of those things
my father approved of, but he gave up trying to stop
me after a while. To be honest, I doubt he ever expected me to do what Diana did.''

Her voice trailed off, and Adam was intrigued.
''Which was?''

Madeline looked at him and giggled. ''I don't
know, Adam. She spent so much time away from
home. She was constantly with our aunt in London,
and when she came home she always looked beautiful. She was skillful with an embroidery needle, too,
so I suspect she spent a lot of time doing what most
well-brought-up young ladies do.''

He laughed. ''Are you saying you were not brought
up well?''

''I'm saying I was not as socially ambitious as most
young women my age.'' She threw him an apologetic
look. ''I beg your pardon, Adam, I did not mean to
insinuate anything about Diana.''

''I didn't think you had.''

She stirred whatever she was cooking in that huge

pot. "Diana and I were eleven years apart, and we had very different childhoods."

Why did he have the feeling she was still apologizing for what she'd said about her sister?

Adam watched Madeline a little longer. The desire to know more about her and the person she was beneath the surface she showed to the world would not leave him, so he simply gave in to it. "How so? Diana spent time in London with her mother and aunt. What about you?"

Madeline moved away from the fireplace to the worktable. She reached for bread dough that she must have set to rise before she'd gone out for the eggs. "Mother died when I was born, so I never took any trips to London. Father went, of course, and continued to take Diana with him, but I was just a babe, so he left me at home with the housekeepers. Habits form, I suppose, and as I grew older, he continued to leave me behind."

"Did that bother you?"

"No, I hardly noticed. It was the way things always were, and I never questioned them. To be honest, I grew to look forward to their trips, so that I could have more freedom at home to do what I wanted."

"Were you lonely?"

"No. At least I didn't think I was. I found much to interest me on the moors and in the garden, and later, in books. I know that when you came calling on Diana, I might have seemed lonely, the way I followed you about—" she glanced at him sheepishly "—but I think I was more curious than anything. About what you and she talked about and did together. I had never seen a romance before." She flipped the heavy dough over and smiled at him, an appealing smile that made the hairs on his arm prickle. "Is it too late to apologize?"

"If anyone deserves an apology, Madeline, it is you, for we were young and selfish. You were just a child, and we should have included you."

That apology, he decided, was long overdue.

He absently twisted his wedding ring around on his finger. Madeline stopped kneading. "I've noticed you have not taken that off."

"My wedding ring?" He turned his large hands over and looked at them. How candidly they revealed his age. "No, I couldn't bring myself to."

"You must still miss her a great deal."

Adam laid his hands flat on the table. "It's not so much that...." He had never spoken of Jane to anyone, at least not about their imperfect marriage. He wondered why he was compelled to do so now, with Madeline—a young woman who had never been married herself and probably assumed that every romance had a happy ending. "I believe it is guilt that keeps me from taking it off."

Madeline sat down across from him and gently clasped his hand. "Guilt? Adam, surely you can't blame yourself for her death."

"What husband wouldn't when his wife dies on the birthing bed?" She squeezed his hand. "But more than that, I regret the misery in our marriage. Jane was an emotional woman. She cried over a chipped plate, or flew into a rage when the fire would not light on the first try. In the beginning, I was sympathetic and spent a great deal of time trying to appease her, when I was not walking on eggshells, for fear of setting her off. Later, as the years passed, I felt nothing when she wept, for she was not rational. My sympathy dried up, and she knew it. Things only got worse after that.''

"I had no idea, Adam. What about the children? Did they suffer also?''

''Penelope, of course, knows nothing, and the boys, thank God, were too young to recognize what their mother was going through. Mrs. Dalton was very good at distracting them or taking them out of the room when Jane was having one of her 'spells' as I used to call them.''

He began to twist the ring again, remembering the earlier days. ''It's odd, when I married her, she'd seemed so sensible. Looking back on it now, I see that the things she said to me were just words. Even if she knew what was sensible and what was not, she could not control her emotions. We married too quickly. She had known about Diana, and I don't think she ever believed for one minute that I was over her. I think that's what made Jane unbalanced.''

Madeline continued to hold his hand, accepting what he had confessed without pushing him for more. He felt a weight lift in his chest.

"I cannot believe I burdened you with all of that,'' he said, hoping to lift the somber mood that had descended upon the kitchen. ''The melodramatic regrets of an old man's life.''

''You are not old, Adam, yet you keep saying it.''

It was true, he had been feeling his age more than usual lately. Since Madeline had arrived.

How could he tell her that *she* in all her youthful splendor, by bringing forward the past, had forced him to look inside himself at the man he once was, and the man he had become?

Gazing across the table at her cheerful, tender countenance, into eyes that actually saw the *old* Adam, he wanted to be that man again. Could he?

For the first time in many years, he felt the scattered remnants of his old self bucking within.

Then he reminded himself that Diana was coming, and *she* was the reason for all this, even though Madeline had been the one to help awaken him and make him see that he could change.

He began to tell himself that Madeline's arrival here—and his surprisingly strong responses to her—were happening for a reason. God had intended it. After all, if Diana had come first, and seen the empty shell of the young lover she remembered, she might not have stayed to see things come around right.

That realization disturbed Adam more than he could say. Did he have no confidence in Diana? Did he not trust her to be different this time?

Suddenly the kitchen door swung open, and both Adam and Madeline jumped. Agnes stepped inside, her gaze falling to Madeline's hand upon Adam's.

Madeline pulled her chair back and stood, returning to her bread dough which sat like a dry lump of clay on the worktable. She began to knead it again, asking Agnes about the weather.

Agnes hinted at nothing untoward—she never

would—and rambled on about the hogs being in an awful tizzy over the water trough.

Adam stood up to leave, but Agnes stopped him. She wrung her hands together with an uncharacteristic nervousness. "Mr. Coates, before you go, I wonder if I may have a word with you."

"Certainly. What is it, Agnes?" Good God, was she going to chastise him for sitting alone in the kitchen, holding hands with his future sister-in-law?

"I beg your pardon, sir, but may we speak in private?"

Hell, she *was* going to chastise him.

They walked together into his study and Agnes paused by the door, still wringing her hands together. "I have something difficult to tell you, and I hope you will not be...I hope you will not be..."

Adam fumbled for his handkerchief and offered it to her. She took it and blew her nose. "I promised myself I wouldn't cry. You've seen enough of that in your life, sir."

"Nonsense, Agnes," he replied softly. "What is upsetting you?"

She collected herself. "I am afraid I must leave you and the children."

Chapter Eight

His housekeeper's words came at him as if through a tunnel filled with echoes. "Leave us? Why, Agnes? You've been with us forever."

"I have indeed, Mr. Coates, and my years with you have been good ones, the best of my life. I love the children like they were my own, I do. But I have a chance to live in my own house now. I'm to be married."

Adam had to sit down. "Married? To whom?"

"To a man from Maccan, sir. We've been meeting every Wednesday at the market in Amherst."

He took a moment to digest this news. "I noticed you've been late returning. I thought you were simply taking more time for yourself."

"Well, I have been, sir."

"Yes, of course you have been. He's a good fellow, is he? Dependable? Trustworthy? I won't have you marrying any dangerous or unscrupulous character."

"He's a good man, Mr. Coates. A widower like you. He owns his own farm."

Adam leaned back in his chair as the news settled upon him. "The children won't be happy to see you go."

"Nor will I be happy to leave them, but I will visit often. I promise you that."

Adam stood. "I suppose congratulations are in order, then. I'm happy for you, Agnes. You deserve every joy life brings you."

He pulled her into his arms and held her. She buried her face in his chest and wept.

"When will you be leaving?" he asked, his own voice trembling.

"The end of the week."

"The end of the week? So soon?"

"Yes, sir. I thought it a good time, since Madeline is here and taking such good care of things."

"But she's not staying. She's leaving in a few days."

Agnes blew her nose. "Yes, but I doubt you'd have any trouble convincing her to stay, if you explained the situation."

"I've already offered her a position, and she's dead set against it. And she's headstrong, Agnes. Surely you've seen that."

"I have, but she's only headstrong in the face of what she doesn't want. And she *wants* to stay here."

"How do you know that?"

"I just know. Any fool can see it."

"Any fool but me. Honestly, I've tried to convince her."

"I reckon you'll have to try harder, sir."

* * *

That evening, after the supper dishes had been washed and put away, Madeline ventured into Adam's study to look at his books. It would do her good, she thought, to immerse herself in an intriguing story for the next few days, to help pass the time.

Candelabra in hand, she made her way down the dark center hall, the heels of her shoes tapping lightly over the wood floor. The door to Adam's den was open, but inside, the room was black, the curtains drawn and keeping out the moonlight.

She carried her candles in to the tall bookcase on the far side of the fireplace and held the light up to the spines of all the books, delighted by the simple pleasure of smelling them.

There were so many. Surely every one of Shakespeare's plays. She had not yet read King Lear. Perhaps she would begin with that one.

As she knelt down and let her fingers graze over others closer to the floor, she found new temptations—Homer, Hobbs, Norton, Milton, as well as a number of other authors whose names she did not recognize.

She pulled out something by Samuel Richardson—a thick novel called *Clarissa, or The History of a Young Lady*. Madeline set her candles on the floor and opened the book. Just then, she heard footsteps come into the room. She stood quickly, stepping sideways in a panicky effort not to singe her skirts on the candles.

Carrying his own candelabra, Adam slowly approached and bent to pick up hers. He set it in a safer place upon a desk.

"Did you think I was a ghost?" he asked.

She smiled. "I wasn't sure. You surprised me."

"I do apologize. I thought I heard you come in here. Have you found anything that interests you?"

Heart still racing, Madeline cleared her throat to speak. "I was just about to look at this one."

He came to stand next to her and held his candles over the book she held. "*Clarissa*. Are you sure? I believe it's the longest novel in the English language."

Madeline laughed.

Her reaction seemed to amuse him. With a smile, he said, "It's no joke, my dear," and furtively slid the book out of her hands. His were large and strong, yet graceful as he ran his fingers over the lettering. "Do you know anything about it?"

"No, nothing."

"The characterization is magnificently sustained, but it's very tragic. I wouldn't recommend it to everyone. It all depends upon your tastes."

"I'm open to anything if it's well written. I've read my share of tragedies." *I've lived my share, too.*

"Well, don't let me influence what you choose. Taste in literature is very personal."

He handed *Clarissa* back to her. Their hands touched briefly, but he shied away, as if her fingers were hot to the touch. Madeline thought of their conversation in the kitchen that morning and colored fiercely. Did he regret confiding in her, and had he been uncomfortable with the way she had held his hand? Perhaps this was his way of telling her that he knew she was attracted to him, and he intended to discourage her.

She was glad she would be leaving soon.

Madeline put *Clarissa* back where she found it. "Can you recommend something else? Perhaps something shorter?"

Adam held his candles up to the titles on a higher shelf. Madeline stared at the strong line of his jaw in the flickering candlelight and wished she could reach out and run her fingers along the shadow of stubble.

He looked over the spines for a few seconds. He seemed intimately familiar with where everything was. "Have you read any Shakespeare?" Then he smiled down at her. "Of course you have."

She returned his smile. "Yes, but not everything."

"What about *Measure for Measure?*"

"Yes, I've read that one."

"What did you think?"

"I thought the ending was hurried."

He continued to look over the titles on the spines, tilting his head to the side to read them, running his fingers over the embossed lettering. "I thought so, too."

Madeline stood back, watching, enjoying these precious moments of conversation with him, talking about books. She realized now that she had come to understand him on a deeper level these past weeks— staying up late to talk about the marshlands and what he wanted to accomplish to ensure their survival.

She now felt a certain compatibility with him, for she, too, valued good land, and knew how important it was to nurture and maintain it. All her life, she'd toiled in her own garden at home, proud of her accomplishments, always delighted to see the green shoots sprouting out of the dirt. The feel of the soil under her fingernails—even though Diana had badgered her for being so irresponsible about her hands—had always provided her a secret pleasure.

"What about *Twelfth Night?*" Adam asked, bringing her thoughts back to the present.

"I've read it."

"Did you like it?"

"Very much. It was hilariously complicated."

He smiled at her and nodded in agreement. Then his attention went back to the books.

"What about *The Merchant of Venice?*"

"I've read it."

"The Merry Wives of Windsor?"

"Read that, too."

He smiled down at her and said good-naturedly, "Perhaps it should be *you* doing the recommending, instead of me."

She laughed. "Are there any books here, Adam, that you *haven't* read yet?"

"Only a few. I read most of them in Yorkshire, when Jane was alive. I needed a distraction, I suppose."

Madeline found herself gazing into Adam's eyes in the candlelight, wanting to fill in all the years he had been absent from her life. In a moment of abandon, she chose to ignore her resolve to keep her emotional distance and began asking questions she had no business asking.

"Tell me more, Adam. Tell me about the day you decided to leave Yorkshire."

He set his candelabra on a table. "Surely you don't want me to bore you with that."

"I do. Tell me why you left your home when you had spent your entire life there."

Somewhat reluctantly, he began. "Well, knowing I was going to spend the rest of it working someone else's land, and earn nothing to pass to my children weighed heavily for me. I was tired of seeing my hard work go to support my landlord's mistress's apartments and baubles. Then one afternoon, his agent came by to discuss the harvest, and Agnes, wanting to be a good hostess, served him tea in Jane's best china—china we had received as a wedding gift from my family. Mr. Westing took one look at his teacup and the silver teapot, and said that if we could afford china like that, we could afford to have our rent raised."

Madeline felt her temper flare. "Poor Agnes. I hope she didn't blame herself."

He gave Madeline a look that told her otherwise. "It was only a few weeks later that the lieutenant-governor of Nova Scotia came to recruit families to emigrate, and I was more than ready to hear him out. We came here on the very first ship and made a fresh start."

"And now, you're a landowner."

"Sometimes I pinch myself."

Madeline thought of what it must have been like, for Adam to sell everything, uproot his family and venture across an ocean into unfamiliar lands, when his children were so young. Penelope would have been only five years old. And Adam—without a wife to support his decision, or keep him company during the lonely years settling into a strange place—must have often questioned himself and worried for his children's futures.

Madeline smiled warmly. "You've done well for your family, Adam. You should be proud."

He nodded and let his gaze linger upon her eyes for a second or two, then he raised his left hand to look at it. "You know, I think I should take this off now."

"Your wedding ring?"

"Yes. After our conversation about Jane, I've been feeling less burdened by what had been keeping it on my finger." He pulled it off and put it in one of his desk drawers. "I have you to thank for that, Madeline. How can I ever repay you for your kindness?"

Even in the candlelight, Madeline could see his face go pale. He spoke awkwardly. "And I suppose it would have been bad form to still be wearing it when Diana came. Thank you," he said again.

Madeline simply nodded to hide her own face going pale or flushing with pink. She wasn't sure what it was doing, only that her cheeks were burning. For she had a dozen ideas about how Adam could repay her for her so-called kindness.

Adam regained the composure in his voice. "So, I've told you why I left Yorkshire. What about you? Why were you so eager to leave your home and marry a man you barely knew?"

She stared at him blankly.

"Good heavens, Madeline, that came out not at all the way I meant it to."

"It's all right, Adam, you're right. I acted hastily, knowing nothing about where I was going or who I was going to. I was just so happy to be leaving, I suppose I stuck my head in the sand."

Maybe she fudged the truth a little, leaving out the part about wanting to marry *him* because he was the man of her dreams, but she couldn't very well tell him everything.

"Why would you be so happy to leave? Was your father that much of a tyrant?"

Odd, that Madeline had come to Nova Scotia to escape and hide from the scandal that had ruined her, yet now found herself wanting nothing more than to revisit it again and confess everything.

She supposed she wanted to feel closer to Adam, even though she knew it was wrong and foolish.

Lord help her when Diana arrived.

"My father was part of the reason I left Yorkshire, but not all of it. Mostly I wanted a fresh start, for I discovered the hard way that a woman's reputation is as fragile as glass and, once broken, not so easy to put back together."

Adam gazed at her with interest. "What happened, Madeline? You weren't..."

She quickly shook her head. "No, it never came to that, but it's not what happens to a woman that matters as much as what *appears* to happen. When I was eighteen and visiting Stanley Hall to tutor Lord Jeffrey's children, the local vicar followed me out into the garden and attempted to compromise me, for which I gave him a black eye.''

Adam's face lit up at that. ''Good for you, Madeline.''

''Well, I thought so, too, but my father, alas, did not. He paid the vicar a large sum to marry me, but I refused. The story got out, don't ask me how, and the vicar blamed *me* for seducing him. My reputation was ruined, and the vicar lost his position and insisted on keeping the money for compensation. Father never forgave me for not marrying the man. Before that, I always felt he tolerated me. I may never have believed that he *loved* me—not like he loved Diana— but afterward, I knew he out-and-out despised me.''

''He despised *you!* His youngest daughter! For defending herself against a lecher! I can only pray that if Penelope ever encounters a man like that detestable vicar, she will have your spunk and spirit, and give him *two* black eyes.''

Madeline tried to smile, but the familiar shame and embarrassment that her father had pressed into her for years came upon her, despite her deep belief that none of it was her fault. She lowered her gaze to the floor.

To her surprise, Adam's strong arms enveloped her and pulled her close into the warmth of his chest, where the shock of being held by him—the profound sense of release—took her breath away. She could feel the heat from his body, smell the outdoors on his clothes. She could even hear his heart within, beating against her ear. A quiver surged through her.

Then, the intensity of it all unleashed a flood of tears.

"Madeline," Adam whispered, stroking her hair and rubbing her back. She tingled as he spoke her name. "It wasn't your fault. Whatever torment or grief you endured these past years has not followed you here. You're in *my* care now, and I would defend your honor to the death if I had to. I only wish I had known you then. I would have been your champion."

A rush of new feelings coursed through her: an unfamiliar, steadying sensation that came with the knowledge that someone was on her side. Someone believed her and sympathized with her. For the first time ever in her life, she felt valued and appreciated, as if she were part of something. Part of a family.

God! What kind of fool was she to think she could go on denying that she loved this man? Since she had arrived here and had her dreams crushed, she had convinced herself that he was not real. That whatever she believed him to be was born of her imagination and her illusions of him.

Now that she knew him, now that she had seen who he truly was inside, she knew all of it was true, and more. He was the most beautiful, incredible man she had ever known.

Suddenly, she trembled with grief. It was like someone had died, for she had to remind herself that he would never be hers.

At last she managed to grapple with her feelings and drew away from him. "I'm so sorry, Adam, I don't know what came over me."

"You have been wronged, Madeline, and no one has been there for you. You deserve a good cry."

She tried to laugh, even though she felt as if her insides were being ripped out. "I suppose I do."

She accepted the handkerchief he offered. Madeline wiped her eyes and blew her nose.

Adam reached to brush a few loose strands of hair away from her face. His touch was gentle and loving and filled her with agonizing longing. "You deserve a better life, Madeline. You have suffered a great injustice."

Lowering her gaze again, she nodded. "That's why I wanted to stay here in Nova Scotia, even after I found out you had wanted Diana, and not me."

"I do want you, Madeline," he said softly.

She trembled again. What did he mean by that?

All her rational instincts warned her not to misinterpret his words, not to allow herself any false hopes that he might want her in a romantic way.

At the same time, just thinking about it lifted her hopes and shone a tiny beacon of light into her heart.

Treading cautiously, she managed to get a few shaky words out. "I beg your pardon?"

"I mean, I want you to stay with us. I *need* you to stay."

Carefully, meticulously, she pressed him for his true meaning, for she had learned her lesson once and learned it well, and she would never again presume anything about Adam. He would have to hit her over the head with a marriage proposal first. "I don't understand."

He looked deeply into her eyes. "Mrs. Dalton is getting married. She's leaving us in a few days, and

I am desperate. I need you to stay, at least for a while until I can find another housekeeper.''

An angry tightness squeezed around her chest. ''You want me to be your housekeeper?''

''Well, that was your plan, wasn't it? To support yourself here? You can be sure this is not a charity position, Madeline. I truly need you.''

''But I've already promised the Ripleys.''

''Whatever they're paying you, I'll double it.'' When she made no reply, he added, ''I'll triple it, then.''

With a forceful swallow, she pushed down the anger she had no business feeling, for Adam was doing nothing wrong by asking her to stay, and her rational mind knew that. She had buried and hidden any feelings for him, and to him, she was his future sister-in-law, nothing more. She was, as she had always been, invisible.

''You can't leave us now, Madeline, not when you've become such a friend to the children. They adore you. *I* adore you. We could all be so happy together if you will just consider staying.''

She tried to see into the future, tried to imagine how this could possibly turn out well for her.

She pictured Diana arriving and becoming Adam's wife. Madeline would be forced to watch them retreat to their bedchamber together every night, and wish it was *she* in Adam's bed and in his arms.

She would have to listen to them talking and laughing and going off alone like they used to do all those years ago. She could not imagine a worse fate.

Adam cradled her chin in his big hand, and in the

dim flickering candlelight, she saw the pleading in his eyes. Oh, if it were a different kind of pleading—one filled with passion and desire—she would never be capable of resisting what was forbidden to her.

"Please, Madeline, don't leave. I couldn't possibly get along without you, not now. We have become such good…such good friends."

She felt his thumb stroke her cheek, and she ached to touch him. The delicious, inviting musk of his body overwhelmed her senses.

They stood by the bookcase, staring at each other. Madeline could smell his shaving soap and the dripping candlewax and the books on the shelves beside them. She could even hear her own heart throbbing in her ears.

Adam was still caressing her cheek. She felt so intimate with him! If he thought her a child, he was wrong. She was a woman, a woman who wanted to belong to him, body and soul. Was there a chance he could ever see her that way? What if Diana *weren't* coming? Would he open his eyes to Madeline then?

That thought jolted her.

What if Diana didn't come? Wasn't it possible? Wasn't there a slim chance that by the time she received Adam's proposal, she might have already remarried? Her mourning period had ended months ago, and Madeline had not spoken to her since then. Adam's proposal would take at least six weeks to get to her. Wasn't there a chance? And wasn't there a chance that Adam could fall in love with Madeline in the meantime?

Lord, what was she thinking? She was not a devious person. She loved her sister, and if Diana *was* going to come, Madeline could not steal the true love of her life out from under her.

But Adam was the love of Madeline's own life as well. Why should she sacrifice her happiness for Diana, who had always gotten the best of everything and had *chosen* to throw Adam over for a better catch years ago, while Madeline had suffered and been punished for something she could not control. For being born feet first. That had not been her fault, and the fact that she had never known her mother was as painful and damaging to her as it had been for everyone else.

Still, the fact remained that Adam loved Diana, not Madeline, and Madeline wasn't sure she would ever be able to change that, even if she tried. Diana had been the love of *his* life, after all.

"Well? Will you stay?" Adam asked, still stroking her cheek, and she realized it was a seduction of sorts—maybe not a sexual one, and maybe not a conscious one, either, but an effective one all the same, for it found its mark.

She could not fathom leaving him.

"Yes, Adam, I'll stay."

Chapter Nine

The sky was blue and the sun warm over the south field as Adam, Jacob and George planted the season's first crop of barley. The boys were spread out across the field, working diligently with their bags of seed slung over their shoulders, straw tricorn hats shading their downturned faces from the sun.

Adam stopped for a moment to kneel down and pick up a handful of dirt. He felt its coolness in his palm, studied its dark, rich color between his fingers.

Glancing upward at a hawk soaring freely overhead, Adam thought about his conversation with Madeline in his study a few nights ago, when he'd remembered what it was like in Yorkshire, farming the land that was not his.

Back in those days, he'd never stopped what he was doing just to touch the earth for pleasure's sake. He'd touched it, of course, to see how wet or dry it was, or how sandy it was, but he'd never felt like this when he did. He'd never felt the physical rush that made him smile. It was as if this land was a part of himself, and to see it flourish was as satisfying as seeing Penelope squeal with delight when she accomplished something she'd set out to do. Or seeing Jacob smile at Mary with love and pride in his eyes.

Adam was glad Madeline had decided to stay. She understood him and the things he cared about; she made him see all the things he should be thankful for, instead of the things he had lost. He wondered fleetingly who did that for her. Who did she have to talk to?

Just then, Adam noticed a rider ascending the ridge, along the road from the marshland below. Adam let the dirt slip between his fingers, brushed off his palms and started toward the stranger.

The young man stopped on the road and dismounted. "Hello there!"

As Adam stepped over the plowed furrows, he recognized the caller. It was the young man from Fort Cumberland, the fellow who had spoken to Madeline.

Adam reached the edge of the field and greeted him. "Good day to you. John Metcalf, isn't it?"

John's eyes lit up for some reason as they shook hands. "Yes. Did Madeline mention me?"

Ah, the reason for the visit was clear now. Adam felt the muscles in his back stiffen slightly. "She told me your name after she spoke to you."

"I see." He glanced around, over Adam's shoulder, at Jacob and George in the field. "Your sons?"

"They are. What can I do for you, Mr. Metcalf?"

John removed his hat. "Well, I'm here for two reasons. I was hoping you might be able to point me in the direction of some land to lease. Someone told me you had some acreage leased to a fellow on Fort Lawrence Ridge.''

"That I do. Two spots there, actually. As well as another place near Sackville township.'' Adam didn't know why he was telling John about the other places. None of them were vacant.

John's shoulders rose and fell with what looked like a nervous sigh. "Are you looking to lease anything at the moment?"

"No, I've got excellent tenants. Hardworking men with families.''

"They're not looking to buy and move off anytime soon?"

"If they were ready to buy, or wanted to, I'd sell them the land they're living on.''

He nodded in understanding. "Do you know of any other farmers who are looking to lease some land? I haven't had much luck finding anything.''

Adam removed his hat and wiped his forehead with a sleeve. "Can't think of anyone offhand. Have you tried the Petticodiac?''

"The Petticodiac! That's miles away!"

Adam paused. "You seem to have your heart set on Cumberland.''

"I'd like to stay near the folks I got to know on the ship, sir, and as far as I know, they're all looking to settle around here.''

Adam watched John perspire in the hot sun. "Ah. Well, you could try River Hebert. Or Maccan.''

John stared blankly at Adam. From the look on the young man's face, Adam guessed those places were a little too far as well.

"I reckon I'll just have to keep looking," John said, putting his hat back on. He glanced at Jacob and George again. "You need any help? Till I find a place of my own, I'm temporarily for hire."

Adam cleared his throat. "Not presently, John. I'll keep you in mind, though, at haying time. I usually hire a few hands then."

An awkward silence rolled around them.

"What was the second thing you came to speak to me about?" Adam asked.

John's face flushed red. He swept his hat off again. "Well, sir, I came to ask your permission to..."

He paused and swallowed. Things were quiet. That hawk was circling overhead again.

Adam pressed him. "Yes?"

"To call on Madeline," John finally said.

For a moment, Adam didn't know what to say. He had suspected this was coming, and wasn't entirely comfortable with the fact that he'd hoped John would choke on his words before spitting them out.

Quickly Adam told himself that he would feel the same way if Penelope was older and a young man came to court *her*. Adam would naturally want to refuse him, too. He wouldn't, of course, unless he had a very good reason to.

Was there a good reason to refuse John?

God, why couldn't he think of one? He *wanted* to think of one!

Adam hesitated for another moment and the awkward silence from a few minutes ago mushroomed into something almost intolerable.

"Was Madeline expecting you today?" Adam asked.

If the answer was yes, he would feel irritated, even though he knew there was no reason to feel irritated. It would be irrational, ridiculous, and he was not a ridiculous man.

"No, sir. I wanted to ask your permission first. I presume you're acting as her…as her…not her father, but her—"

Father!

"Guardian?" Adam finished for him.

"Yes! Guardian. Thank you, sir."

Adam shifted his weight from one foot to the other. He didn't like the way he felt. He didn't like this ill-tempered mood, when only moments ago in the field, he'd felt on top of the world.

"When do you wish to call on her?" he asked John, only because he had to.

John's face went pale, and Adam realized that his tone had intimidated the young man. He should have regretted it, but he didn't. Wasn't it the guardian's purpose to intimidate young suitors?

"I would like to call on her today, sir, if I have your permission." His voice cracked on the last word.

Adam took a long, deep breath and replaced his hat on his head. "All right. For one hour."

The color returned to John's face as he backed away. "Thank you, sir."

Adam made no reply. He simply watched John's lively, youthful energy as he practically leaped onto his horse.

"Good day, sir!" John galloped off, down the road toward the house.

Adam stared numbly at the cloud of dust rising behind the ardent, thundering hooves. He suddenly felt an ache in his back from bending to plant the barley. Why was he feeling it now, of all times?

He *knew* why, and it worried him more than he cared to acknowledge.

No, it *more* than worried him. It damn well scared the hell out of him.

Feeling the muscles in his jaw clench, Adam turned and walked back across the field. Damn that John Metcalf for making Adam wish he was a younger man, and that it was *he* who was riding up to the house to call on Madeline today.

There was no point denying it. He was jealous!

As soon as he admitted it, however, the other night in the den came hurling back at him. He had been working so hard not to think of it, but now, he couldn't push the recollection away: his hands on Madeline's body, the sweet smell of her soft skin and sinuous locks of hair, the enticing moistness of her lips—it all stirred him into a whirlwind of impassioned awareness.

Adam halted in the field and stood there, dumbstruck.

He shouldn't have held Madeline in his arms, shouldn't have touched her. Now his mind had something solid to work with—an innocent moment to repeat in his memory, over and over.

Lord help him, if he was alone with her now, feeling this new, unbidden hunger, he wasn't sure he'd be able to resist her as he had the other night when she was gazing up at him with tears on her cheeks and adoration in her eyes. He might very well take advantage of the attraction he'd thought he'd sensed in her, too, for these feelings of his had suddenly become impossible to explain or deny.

How long had it been since he'd held a woman in his arms? he wondered ruefully. Not since Jane had died, and to be honest, he had stopped holding her long before that, when doors were routinely slammed in his face after nightfall.

Now he felt like a bear waking from a long, cold winter in the den. He was ravenous.

He all at once realized with a disturbing torrent of dread, that his world was about to become intensely complicated.

Madeline was sitting in the kitchen plucking a hen for dinner, when a knock sounded at the front door. She rose to answer it, but Agnes, who had not left them yet, answered it first.

It was John Metcalf. He was standing on the front step, nervously hugging his black tricorn hat to his chest. He said something to Agnes, and she invited him in. His apprehensive gaze fell upon Madeline, and she knew that she was the reason he had come.

Agnes turned toward Madeline. "You have a visitor."

"Good morning, Miss Oxley," John said.

Madeline reached around to untie her apron in the back. "I'll be right with you, John."

She went into the kitchen, glanced at the half-plucked hen that would have to wait, then laid her apron over the back of a chair and washed her hands in the rinse bucket. Smoothing some of the loose sprigs in her upswept hair, she returned to the front hall.

"What brings you here, John?"

"I came to see you, Miss Oxley. Mr. Coates said it was all right. Just for an hour."

Her heart stumbled clumsily over John's answer. "You spoke to him?"

"Yes. I met him on the road just now. He and his sons were planting in the field."

"And you asked if you could..."

"Call on you, yes."

Call on me? No one ever calls on me.

Madeline swallowed with difficulty and had to struggle to find her voice.

She wished that her thoughts didn't fly directly to Adam in these circumstances. She wished she wouldn't wonder how he would feel about John courting her. She supposed at the very least, he would worry that he was going to lose another housekeeper.

But maybe, just maybe, John coming to call on her would make her become *visible* to Adam. Maybe Adam would see her as a woman for once, and notice that another man had found her attractive, even though she had a hard time believing it herself. "I see. Would you like to come in?"

John gave her an appreciative smile and followed her into the front parlor.

Agnes headed for the kitchen. "I'll make some tea."

Madeline sat down on the chintz sofa while John sat on the other side of the room in a green upholstered chair. For a few minutes, neither of them spoke, while John's eyes wandered around the room, looking at the framed paintings on the walls, the brass face on the tall-case clock that ticked away in the silence. He gazed at the piano in the corner, then wiggled in his chair as he reached down to touch the rich, velvet upholstery on the seat.

"Mr. Coates has a fine house," he said.

"It's very comfortable."

"It's *more* than comfortable. It's a palace compared to most places around here. Maybe we should start calling him 'Lord of the Marsh.'"

Not caring for John's cynical tone, Madeline rubbed a thumb over her fingers. This was going to be a very long hour.

Adam stood under the warm morning sun, his boots firmly planted in the dirt, and removed his hat to wipe his forehead with a sleeve. The wind was nonexistent today. Everything was so damn still. Everything except the insects, which were humming and buzzing a steady cacophony.

Damn his thoughts, for buzzing a cacophony, too.

He hoped Madeline was all right at the house. Maybe he should go and check on things.

No, surely that wasn't necessary. He was just making excuses to interrupt, to thwart John Metcalf when Adam had no business thwarting anything to do with Madeline.

Whatever improper feelings he had for her, he had

to bury, for Adam had already proposed to her sister. More than proposed. He had sent the necessary documents for a proxy marriage to take place, and it was out of his hands now. The proposal was on its way across the deep blue Atlantic, and Adam could not make the ship turn around. Nor should he want to. Diana was supposed to be the true romance of his life, the one he'd always wanted and the one he continued to want at this moment.

The number of times he'd had to convince himself of that lately was beginning to irk him.

He settled his hat back on his head and tried to return to planting, but despite his desire not to think about Madeline anymore, it dawned on him that perhaps Agnes was not in the house with her and John.

Adam hadn't thought about stipulating that to John or returning to make sure that Agnes was there. What if she was in the barn when John had arrived, and Madeline was alone in the house to greet him? They'd have no chaperon.

Bloody hell, he was no good at this. He'd never played this role before. He hadn't expected to be in this position until Penelope had matured a number of years. A *good* number of years.

When he'd sent for Diana, he'd expected a bride, not a ward.

Hell, he was making excuses again. Madeline was not his ward. She was a woman, and sometime over the past few weeks, he'd become all too aware of that fact.

He gazed across the field at Jacob and George working diligently. For a long time, he watched them, then he flinched at the direction of his thoughts again as he asked himself: If the proposal to Diana was not pending, would he go up to the house now and interrupt John's visit, then begin to court Madeline himself?

His head began to throb. Good God, how was he going to handle this? He reached into his bag for more seed and sprinkled it onto the field.

He knew one thing. He was not—absolutely not!—going to return to the house and make a fool of himself. He was going to stay right here. And *dammit,* if he knew what was good for him, he was going to wrestle this reckless, taboo infatuation into submission.

Not two minutes later, feeling thoroughly ashamed of his ineffectual will, he dropped a final handful of seed onto the ground and stomped up to the house.

Chapter Ten

Madeline, listening politely to John tell her about his family in Yorkshire, had just raised her teacup to her lips when the front door of the house swung open.

Adam stepped in and paused in the doorway. Their gazes met and locked. He looked a little flustered for a moment, almost angry at himself, then the room went silent.

Madeline set down her cup. Adam glanced briefly at John and nodded, then his boots thumped down the hall toward the kitchen.

She wondered if something was wrong. Should she go to him to ask if he was all right and, if there was a problem, try and help somehow?

Her heart began beating a breakneck rhythm against her ribs. She took a deep, calming breath to allay it, telling herself that Adam's moods and problems were not hers to sort out, at least not when she had a gentleman caller.

Agnes, who sat beside Madeline on the sofa, said nothing. She didn't seem startled or surprised. She just drank her tea.

The conversation then resumed.

A few minutes later, Penelope came down the stairs and joined them in the parlor. The sight of the child's huge brown eyes and the sound of her little girl's voice brought a smile to Madeline's face. Penelope told them about the baby's strong grip, how she had grasped Penelope's thumb in her hand and not let go even when Penelope had tried to gently shake her off.

Madeline suddenly wondered what Adam was doing in the kitchen all this time. Had he noticed the half-plucked chicken? Was it in his way if he wanted to sit down at the table? Or was he simply listening to their conversation?

"So there's a good chance my brothers will come, too, if things work out for me here," John said. Madeline realized she had missed something of the conversation just now.

"Shall we take Mr. Metcalf for a walk?" Penelope suggested. "We could show him the swing."

"You just want someone to push you," Agnes said good-naturedly.

"I'll push you," John offered.

Penelope stood and Madeline set down her cup to go with them.

"I'll tend to this," Agnes offered, tidying up. "You three go out and enjoy the good weather."

Madeline followed Penelope to the door, but sensed Adam's presence, watching them. She glanced briefly back at the kitchen, and sure enough, he was standing there, silently sipping coffee, staring at her. His gaze was dark and intense.

Her skin prickled with awareness and a longing to

stay behind and ask him if something was wrong, for she sensed he was not himself, but instead, she forced herself to ignore the impulse. There was no sense nurturing the intimacy of their so-called friendship, and feeding forbidden feelings that were already dangerously out of control.

She followed the others outside, where a spotted sandpiper was perched on the stone bench near the birch grove. Penelope began to tiptoe toward it with her hand outstretched, as if to make friends.

Grateful for the distraction, Madeline watched her, then felt John's gaze upon her face.

"That bird," he said, "will make a mess on your bench. She doesn't feed them, does she? That'll only bring more of them around."

Madeline kept her gaze fixed on Penelope, whose shoulders slumped in disappointment when the tiny bird flew away.

"I believe she enjoys the music they make," Madeline told him.

He shrugged at that and followed Madeline, who led the way up the hill, on a footpath through the trees. Along the way, Penelope skipped ahead, stopping in a dusty clearing to pick fragrant, bright yellow chamomile along the edge of the wood.

John talked about how much trouble he was having finding a place to live, and Madeline listened graciously to every word. He told her about all the people he had met at the fort the past week, and the farmers he had met on his quest for good land. He spoke of the farms and the livestock and the crops, told her about his plans and ambitions.

He was a handsome young man, she decided, noticing the way his tawny hair curled around his face in the front. In the back it was tied in a neat queue. Madeline supposed that if there were more young, unmarried women in Cumberland, they would probably be fighting over him.

Madeline ducked under the branches of some birch saplings, then pointed at a towering old oak. ''There's the swing.''

Penelope ran and hopped on. John hurried to catch up, and she laughed when he spun the swing around, then let go. Penelope twirled in dizzying circles, her skirts flapping in the breeze.

Madeline leaned against the thick tree trunk, its bark covered in lichen and small patches of green moss, and felt the cool air caress her cheeks. She watched John pushing Penelope on the swing and wondered about him.

Was this visit the beginning of a courtship, or was he just being neighborly? Unfortunately, she didn't have much experience with this sort of thing. No young man had ever come to call on her in Yorkshire. Not even once.

John didn't know about her past, of course. So here he was.

Would it matter, she wondered? If he knew, would he still come? She had heard that single women were scarce commodities here in Cumberland, so perhaps the men would be less choosy and more willing to settle for less. Beggars couldn't be choosers, after all.

Oh, what a horrible, horrible insult. To both herself and John. She chided herself for it. John was a handsome young man, a very good catch. He was not a "beggar," and she was not a batch of useless, second-rate goods, even if she was invisible to most men.

She wondered further, if John decided to come calling again after today, and again after that, would she ever tell him what had happened? How would he react? Would he be as understanding and supportive as Adam had been?

You're in my care now, and I would defend your honor to the death if I had to. I only wish I had known you then…I would have been your champion.

A jovial screech from Penelope pulled Madeline from her thoughts, and she stepped away from the towering oak.

"Perhaps we should go back," John suggested. "Our hour's up. I wouldn't want to displease Mr. Coates on my first day."

My first day. So he did plan to come again.

Madeline waited for Penelope to hop off the swing and lead the way down the hill, then tried to figure out exactly how she felt about a return visit from John Metcalf.

Agnes was married in a private ceremony in Adam's home, followed by a wedding breakfast of blueberry pancakes with maple syrup, poached salmon, maple-pecan scones and fresh apple spice cake for dessert.

Shortly after noon, she drove off with her new husband and left Madeline behind, in full charge of the household. Madeline immediately settled into her role, cooking all the meals for the family, helping

Mary care for the baby and spending time with the children.

One afternoon the following week, Madeline completed her midday chores early and decided to reward herself with a short walk along the road that overlooked the great marsh. Clouds were thick and heavy overhead and the ground was still damp from a morning rain. In the distance, a thick fog encased the forested ridge on the other side of the marsh, and Madeline could smell the salty tang of the sea.

She'd had no time to herself lately, she realized as she watched the toes of her boots peek out from under her skirts with each long stride.

Not that she was complaining. Quite the contrary. The truth was, she enjoyed it. She and Penelope and Charlie had been studying multiplication, and yesterday they decided to hold a spelling bee Tuesday evening after supper as a special entertainment for Adam, who had been away the past few days and would be returning this afternoon.

Adam had traveled to Halifax to meet Nova Scotia's new lieutenant-governor, the Viscount Blackthorne, and speak with him about establishing a committee to maintain the marshlands. Lord Blackthorne had just arrived from England a month ago, and eager to be an auspicious representative for King George, was familiarizing himself with the colony and addressing land issues.

Adam worried that some of the absentee farmers in Cumberland were neglecting their sections of the marsh, and that their negligence could affect all of the farmers if anything unpredictable occurred.

Adam believed that Lord Blackthorne might be receptive to his concerns, for it was a well-known fact that the aging aristocrat had relations in Yorkshire, and for that reason, seemed genuinely interested in Cumberland and its success. He'd been quoted as saying that "Yorkshire farmers were the best around."

Madeline walked down the steep ridge to the lowlands, where Adam had taken her riding a few weeks ago.

It seemed like ages had passed since that day, she thought, for they knew each other so much better now.

Hoofbeats came thundering behind her. She turned. Adam sat astride his big horse, his black coat flapping in the wind, looking for all the world like a prince riding toward her. His white shirt was clean and his neckcloth tied in a perfect knot at his collar. There was no dirt or dust on his riding boots today. Even the brass buttons on his coat were polished and shiny.

Her belly swarmed with a fluttering sensation that she tried to beat down.

"Good afternoon, Madeline." He pulled his horse to a halt beside her.

"Hello, and welcome back."

"Was everything all right while I was gone?"

"We were fine. How was your trip?"

"Very good, thank you."

Adam knew he had been avoiding Madeline lately, and had hoped his time in Halifax might have cooled his unwise attraction to her. A part of him had also hoped that his feelings had been induced by John Metcalf's visit and a basal manly competitiveness that had nothing to do with Madeline specifically; perhaps it was merely a hankering to be young again.

But as Adam gazed down into Madeline's clear, wide eyes and regarded her gentle, innocent beauty, he felt his body quicken and knew that with or without John Metcalf, this was more than a fleeting infatuation. He had been dreaming if he'd thought a few days in Halifax would eradicate it.

His horse restlessly stomped his hooves. "May I join you? I have much to tell you about my journey."

"Yes, please, Adam. I've been wondering about your progress. Were your ideas well received?"

He dismounted and walked beside her, and told her of his meetings at Government House. Adam had been a guest at two formal dinners, where at one, he sat next to a future English duke.

"Oh, Adam, when you left Yorkshire, did you ever imagine such a thing?"

"No, I did not. I must say, however, that I was pleasantly surprised by the young man's genuine interest in Nova Scotia and his eagerness to converse with local citizens, regardless of rank or wealth. Life is different here, Madeline. A man without rank can rise to become whatever his ambitions will allow."

Adam felt a surge of pride for the decision he had made and the risks he had taken bringing his family to an unfamiliar land.

"And what about the marsh?" Madeline asked. "Did you discuss it with Lord Blackthorne? Was he sympathetic to your concerns?"

"He was, indeed. He intends to come soon to see the Tantramar, and I invited him to be our guest."

Madeline stopped on the road. "Adam! A *viscount* will be staying with us? My word! What will I feed him?"

Adam laughed. "You'll have plenty of time to think about it. He won't be here for at least a week."

"A week! Oh, you're teasing me now!"

"How can I resist, when you squeal with such sweet charm."

It was a joke—they both knew it—but Adam could see the blood rushing to Madeline's cheeks and knew that the compliment had unnerved her. The fact that she was not accustomed to compliments yanked at his heart, and he wished he could spend the next decade of his life showering her with them.

He attempted to fill the awkward moment with conversation. "I do know that he enjoys our local fiddle-heads, as well as corn fritters and brandy snaps, and anything made with blueberries."

"Well, that gives me something to work with. How long will he stay?"

"Only a few days, long enough to see the marsh and meet some of the local farmers. Then he'll continue on to the Petticodiac and the Saint John River Valley."

They spoke more about the events during Adam's visit to Halifax, and he enjoyed this time alone with Madeline, for he knew he could never conquer how much pleasure he derived from their conversations, nor was there any point in conquering that particular aspect of their relationship. They were supposed to be friends, after all.

Then he had to broach another subject, one that was

a little less pleasurable for him. "By the way, I met John Metcalf this morning, on my way by the fort. He was riding to Jollicure. He's still looking for land."

"Oh?" By the tone of her response, Adam guessed that Madeline didn't know anything about Metcalf's current comings and goings, and Adam couldn't help feeling a little glad.

"You didn't see John while I was gone?" he asked.

"No, not at all. I've been very busy. Did you stop to speak with him?"

"Yes." Deliberately, Adam did not elaborate.

"And what did John say?"

It was decidedly rotten of him, making her beg for information like this, but Adam wanted to see just how curious Madeline was about John Metcalf.

Apparently, she was curious enough to press him for the details, and he felt a twinge of disappointment even though he had not wanted to care.

"He asked about you, naturally, and wanted to know if he could visit again tomorrow afternoon and spend another hour with you."

Madeline stared straight ahead. "What did you tell him?"

"I told him he would have to ask you himself, for I didn't know what your wishes were, nor did I even know where you were in order to ask you."

"But you found me."

"Yes, I found you. Mary told me you had gone for a walk, and I took the chance that you would go this way, along the same route we explored together a few weeks ago.''

They walked in silence for a few minutes. The horse, still plodding along behind them, snorted in the damp air.

"In the future," Adam said, knowing that *he* was the one now pressing for information, "if John asks me if he may visit you, what would you like me to tell him?"

Madeline stopped. Adam stopped, too, awaiting her answer.

"Are you asking me how I feel about John? If I *want* him to come calling?"

He stared directly into her eyes. "Yes, that's what I'm asking you."

Adam felt a surge of impatience.

"Yes, I would very much like John to call on me again."

Adam squared his shoulders. "Very well, then."

They continued walking.

Adam tried to subdue the displeasure that was clinging to him, following him like a shadow. God, this was all so bloody confounding. His head was reminding him that he was engaged to Madeline's sister, while his heart and body were refusing to believe it. There was a full-blown battle raging inside of him.

Just then, Madeline slapped her neck. "Ouch! What was that?"

Adam moved toward her to clap his hands beside her ear. "A mosquito. Looks like they've found us."

He inspected his palms, then wiped away the tiny corpse.

Another little fly came flitting, floating around Madeline. She took a few steps backward, but the insect followed.

Adam waved his hand in front of her face. "They must like the way you smell."

"What do you mean, the way I smell?"

"The flower water you use."

He was embarrassed for having revealed that he'd noticed.

"Shove off, you nagging beasts!" She began to wave her hands about, then took off in a run along the path.

Adam couldn't resist laughing. "See? I told you! We should go home! It's all this damp weather. It will be better up on the ridge."

Not wasting another moment, Madeline ran back to Adam, who turned his horse around.

They walked quickly up the hill, where a welcome breeze began to blow. "You're right, there aren't as many up here."

"Not at the moment, but I wouldn't stand still for too long."

"You mean we can't stop to catch our breath?"

He shook his head, his brows creasing in a teasing way. "Not a wise thing to do on a wet day on the marsh."

By the time they reached the top of the ridge, they were both breathing hard with exertion.

Madeline's voice was light and airy as she spoke. "That was a good walk. I feel exhilarated now."

"Exhilarated? I could hardly keep up. I think I need to rest my weary bones."

"Well, don't do it here, the mosquitoes will have you for dinner."

"You're quite right, and I wouldn't want that. Then I would miss the spelling bee you have planned for tomorrow evening. Wonderful idea, Madeline."

They reached the gate, and Adam opened it for her. She brushed by him but stopped. "Ouch!" She slapped her neck and inspected her hand. "Another one! He bit me! Cheeky creature. I'm bleeding. Look."

Adam inspected the squashed mosquito in her hand, surrounded by a few drops of blood. "He certainly had a bellyful. Let me see."

He moved a few wispy hairs aside and pulled back her lacy collar to examine the back of her neck. Sure enough, there was a red spot already swelling.

Madeline lifted her upswept hair so Adam could see the whole area. All at once, the world around him seemed to disappear, and all he could see and feel was Madeline's presence before him, her feminine scent, her soft, smiling nearness.

Her skin was smooth, like peach cream. What he wouldn't have given to touch his lips to the warmth of her neck, then turn her toward him and kiss her mouth, to feel her sigh and whimper with amorous pleasure against him. How he wanted to slowly slide his hands under her collar and ease them down the inside front of her gown, to feel the silky, fleshy texture of her breasts...

He jumped when Madeline spoke. "Well?"

Adam cleared his throat and stepped back. He broke into a sweat under his wool coat. "You'll be itchy, but you'll live."

He thought of what day it was, tried to anchor himself in reality. His proposal to Diana might very well be in her hands at this moment. She might be scrolling her name to become his wife.

God, if Madeline ever recognized the lust he felt for her, she would think him a low, faithless scoundrel who could not be trusted.

What the hell was he going to do?

Whatever happened, however he decided to handle this situation, he had to keep his integrity and his honor intact. But how? What was the *right* thing to do?

Before he had a chance to realize what he was asking or why he was asking it, he took hold of Madeline's arm to keep her from going into the house. "Madeline, will you tell me something?"

"Of course."

"Is Diana still the same? Has she changed at all?"

Madeline's eyes met his disparagingly. "She's still very beautiful."

"No, I mean, has she changed in other ways? Is she still the same person? Does she still like to ride?"

"She and Sir Edward used to go fox hunting quite often."

"They were close, then? Do you think...do you think she's over him, and *ready* for another marriage?"

A breeze blew a wayward lock of hair into Madeline's face. She closed her eyes, then gently pushed the hair away. "I can't say with absolute certainty, Adam, for we did not speak intimately with each other, but I do know that you were always the love of her life. She said that to me once, years after she married Sir Edward. She said you would always be the man she dreamed of."

A month ago, that news would have put him in the clouds. Today, it filled him with dread and confusion. "Do you think, when she receives my proposal, that she will come?"

There was something intense in Madeline's expression, in the color of her eyes and the set of her jaw, as if the certainty of Diana's arrival was the most elusive thing in the world to her, too.

"If she is free, yes, I think she will come."

Then Madeline pulled her arm out of his grasp and quickly went ahead of him through the gate.

Chapter Eleven

Adam walked into the house, went straight to his private study and closed the door behind him. Good God, did he truly not *want* Diana to come? He'd been so sure that she was the only one he had ever—or could ever—love.

He walked to his desk, opened the bottom drawer and pulled the cedar box out. He found the tiny key in one of the pigeonholes and unlocked the box, then rifled around inside it, his big hands searching for the miniature he still possessed after all these years.

There. He found it.

For a long time, he stared.

Adam hunted in his mind for the memories of Diana, the *real* woman, trying to remember how he had felt when he was with her, trying to bring back those feelings. His young heart had been hopelessly besotted. He'd felt intoxicated from the sound of her voice, weak at the sight of her face.

He stared at that face now, waiting for the longing to come. Trying to *make* it come.

He saw only a picture. He felt nothing. No surge

of longing. No heat, no vigor. His blood was racing, yes, but that was from holding Madeline's arm, trying to keep her there with him outside the gate, beseeching her for answers.

Answers to what? To how she felt about him? How she felt about Diana?

He reached for the letters in the box—letters Diana had written to him after she'd married Sir Edward. They'd continued for almost a year. She'd written intimate things to Adam, reminisced about their times together, and he'd known she was unhappy.

Of course he never wrote back. He could not encourage her, and he was married himself by that time. She had made her choice and he did not wish to prolong the misery. Neither hers nor his.

After a while, the letters stopped coming and he had presumed she'd forgotten him and grown into her role as another man's wife.

Thank goodness Jane had not known about the letters. At least he didn't think she had. If she had gone through his things and found them, it would certainly have explained some of her anger and insecurities.

Lord, so many hearts had suffered. Adam squeezed his forehead with his hand, racking his brain for an answer, a plan, a proper course of action.

In the end it was his heart that guided him. He knew what he had to do.

"I love you, more than anything in the world. You're planted so deeply in my heart, sometimes I think you must have been born there. Not even a poet could express what I feel for you, my darling."

Madeline heard the words spill tenderly from Mary's lips, just as she stepped into Mary's open doorway. Chessboard in hand, Madeline froze. She saw Jacob leaning over the bed, kissing his young wife.

Just then, everything on the board—the kings and queens and knights and pawns—started to slide and Madeline had to fumble in a panic to keep from dropping the entire game onto the floor with a resounding crash.

"Madeline!" Mary called out, surprised but not the least bit sheepish over what Madeline had just seen and heard. She rose from the bed, straightened her skirts and went to greet her. "Come in. Oh, bless your dear heart, the baby just fell asleep and I'm in need of some distraction."

Madeline handed the chessboard over to Mary. "Well, I should leave you two...."

"No, no! Please come in. Jacob was just trying to leave and I wouldn't let him."

He stood. "Yes, Father's waiting for me. We're preparing to drive a herd of beef cattle to Halifax."

"To Halifax?" Madeline asked. "But he just returned."

"Father won't be going, just George and I and a few fellows from Jollicure. We'll start out early tomorrow and be back in a week."

He kissed Mary on the forehead and whispered something secret in her ear that made her giggle and gaze at him flirtatiously.

"See you at supper, Madeline." He smiled at her as he left the room.

Madeline moved all the way in and sat in the chair by the window.

Mary began to set the chess pieces in place on a table. "Say you'll start a game with me, Madeline."

"I shouldn't. With all the preparations for Lord Blackthorne's arrival…"

"Just fifteen minutes, then I'll come and help you." Mary's blue eyes flashed at Madeline. "Besides, you can't leave now. You still look flushed."

Madeline felt her cheeks turn an even deeper shade of pink. "Flushed?"

"Yes, from walking in on Jacob and me. I apologize. We didn't know anyone was upstairs."

"I should have knocked."

"No, the door was open. We should have been more discreet, but sometimes, I just can't help myself. I can't help telling Jacob how much I love him."

With a twinge of sadness that seeped into her bones and ached like an old wound on a damp day, Madeline stared absently at the chess pieces. Ever since her conversation with Adam out on the road, she'd felt flustered and disconcerted in the most bothersome way, and she hated that she did not know what was going on and how he felt about her.

When she'd tried to leave and he had taken her arm and pulled her toward him, she could have sworn she'd seen passion in his eyes, that he'd wanted to kiss her. But that couldn't have been true. It must have been wishful thinking on her part. No man had ever felt passionate about her.

Nevertheless, her heart had leaped into her throat and it had taken every ounce of self-control she possessed to keep from kissing him first. How she had wanted to.

Then he asked about Diana, and Madeline had been knocked backward and off her feet, back into her secluded, solitary place.

Now, to walk in on two young lovers who seemed to know so much more than she did about love and life, she suddenly longed for some new understanding. She wanted to feel she was knowledgeable and capable, that she could handle and understand her emotions when it came to Adam.

"You spill out your hearts to each other," she said to Mary. "You hold nothing back. I've never seen anything like that before."

Mary's voice brimmed with sincerity and an odd hint of commiseration. "What other way is there to love someone? There's no need to keep it inside. Jacob likes it when I tell him I adore him, and I like it when he tells me. Love is as much about what you say and do and what you show, as it is about what you feel inside, because the one you love can't read your mind. Besides, it feels wonderful to tell him. I can't stop myself. I know it sounds trite, an exaggeration, but my heart swells every time I say it." She moved her first pawn.

While Madeline considered her own first move in the game, she found herself wondering what it must be like to feel so free to give and receive love.

She supposed she'd never had any example of it before. She'd never had a mother and a father who would express things like that to each other, nor did anyone express such things to her. She could not imagine telling someone she loved them. Was it something a person got used to? Like jumping into the cold ocean? Shocking at first, then it almost began to feel warm?

How did Mary become so secure in her belief that Jacob would not break her heart in return? Madeline could see for herself that Jacob shared Mary's feelings, but when did Mary come to know that? Who took the chance and declared their love first?

Maybe they just knew how the other person felt.

Would Madeline ever *just know?*

She knew John Metcalf was interested in her, but he was not passionate, the way Jacob and Mary were. At least she didn't think so. Maybe that came later.

With Adam, on the other hand, she knew how he felt, because he continued to make his feelings about Diana known. As Mary said, love was about what you said and did and showed, not just about what you felt, and Adam had already told Madeline that after all these years, he still loved Diana, and he'd asked questions about her today.

Madeline found herself wondering what Adam would do if he knew how Madeline herself felt. If she came right out and told him.

Then, while she waited for Mary to make a move in the game, Madeline began to fantasize. She imagined that if she did tell Adam that she adored and wanted him, he would take her into his arms and tell her he felt the same way, and together they would somehow find a way to resolve the situation with Diana. Adam could retract the proposal, and if the proxy marriage had already been finalized, well…marriages could be annulled, couldn't they? Yes, Diana would be angry, but she would recover from it, the way everyone recovered from pain in their lives. No one was safe from it.

Madeline rested her cheek on her hand and tried to imagine Diana receiving the news that Adam was jilting her. *For her younger sister.*

Diana would be shocked out of her petticoats to be sure, Madeline thought mischievously. Diana would probably break something. A piece of china. A mirror. Madeline could almost hear her sister screaming like an old witch for someone to come and clean up the shattered glass at her feet.....

Lord, what a child Madeline was. Still.

She had to give up these foolish dreams, for she was coming dangerously close to making a fool of herself and spoiling any chances of continuing a relationship with this family, whom she was growing to love, after Diana came.

It was her turn in the chess game, but as she gazed down at the board, she could see no logical way to move her pieces.

"Mosquito," Penelope said with very precise diction. "*M-o-s-q-u-i-t-o.* Mosquito."

Everyone clapped. She sat down beside Charlie on the chintz sofa.

Charlie rose to stand in front of the fireplace like a soldier, his arms planted firmly at his sides.

Madeline picked up the next card and read the word printed upon it. "'Tempestuous.'"

Momentary panic dashed across Charlie's face.

"Tempestuous. *T-e-m-p-e-s-t-u-o-u-s.* Tempestuous."
He quickly sat down.

"This is getting tense," Jacob said.

Madeline glanced at Adam, who sat in one of the
wing chairs with his legs crossed, his temple resting
on an index finger. He was watching her. Feeling a
whoosh of butterflies in her belly, she quickly picked
up another card.

"George, it's your turn."

George rose and took his place in front of the fire.
"I'm ready."

Madeline read the word. "'Apprehension.'"

George spelled it correctly, and the bee continued
for another hour until Penelope finally took the prize,
after George and Charlie both misspelled *dilemma*
and she proudly got it right.

After much applause and congratulations and the
presentation of the award—a cream cake in the shape
of a trophy—the children made off to bed, and Mary
went into the kitchen to feed the baby and tidy up
before going upstairs to join Jacob.

Madeline was left in the parlor to collect and put
away the spelling cards she'd made, while Adam
moved the furniture back into place.

"Are you ready for Lord Blackthorne's arrival?"
Adam asked. "A ship is arriving from Halifax tomorrow, and he should be on it."

"Almost. Mary has been a wonderful help to me."

All too aware that she was alone with Adam in the
candlelit room, she stood up to leave him—a little too
quickly.

He gently squeezed her arm. "Won't you stay and have a cup of tea with me?"

She tried to keep her voice steady and polite. "I really shouldn't. Tomorrow will be a busy day."

His expression was impossible to read. "Of course. I understand, but will you come to the fort with me tomorrow to meet the ship? I would be proud to have you at my side, Madeline."

Proud to have you at my side. Oh, with words like that, how could he even think she would refuse?

His beautiful eyes and his deep silky voice reduced her to a puddle of melting resolve on the floor. The idea of being alone with him even for an hour was a temptation too powerful to resist. "I would be delighted."

With a charming, flirtatious smile, he released her arm. "Sleep well then, and I'll see you in the morning."

She nodded and said good-night, picked up a lit candle and turned from the room. Madeline reached the top of the stairs and made her way down the back hall to her bedchamber. She set the candle down on her bedside table and noticed the book, *Clarissa,* lying unopened on the bed.

She had not read a word of it. She'd been too busy with her household duties. She'd been spending all her free time with the children and the baby, feeling as if she had to make up for a lifetime of missing companionship—like a starving street urchin who has just been presented with a feast.

Madeline decided to return the novel to Adam's den, at least until after Lord Blackthorne's visit. She took the candle with her out into the dark hall and down the stairs, and tiptoed into the study. She set her candle on his desk, went to the bookcase and slid the book into the empty space on the shelf, then returned to the desk for her candle.

She had her finger through the grip when she noticed a miniature lying there beside it. A miniature of Diana.

Madeline's heart broke a little at the sight of it, for she had been hoping again…but she somehow managed to keep her head out of the stars. This was the reality. She knew it. It was not a shock or a surprise.

She let her fingers roam over all the letters spread out on the desk, letters from Diana, written years ago. Madeline picked up one of the letters, held it next to the candle and read a few words.

> *My darling Adam, how deeply I regret the way we parted and how I made you suffer. You were my one true love, and I betrayed that love. If I could see you one more time, I would not trust myself not to run away with you and correct all my mistakes, for I may be another man's wife, but my heart will always belong to you. I will go on dreaming that one day, we will be together again—forever—as we were meant to be….*

Madeline closed her eyes briefly, searching for the strength to put down the letter and read no more of it, for it felt like a vise around her heart, crushing it. Madeline picked up her candle and walked out of the room.

* * *

Early the next morning, Adam waited anxiously for Madeline, who was upstairs, dressing to go to the fort to greet the lieutenant-governor. It was not Lord Blackthorne's arrival that was making Adam anxious, however. It was something much more profound than that, for Adam had a letter in his pocket.

He remembered sitting in his study the day before, deliberating over what to do about the situation with Diana. He hadn't thought he could go one more day without somehow telling Madeline how he felt about her, and at that moment, he had known he could not marry her sister.

Yet, he'd already sent the proposal. It was on a ship bound for London. What if Diana had already received it and wanted to come right away? On the contrary, she might send a letter turning him down and he would be free, but could he wait six weeks or more to find out? Could he go on for that long, keeping his desires for Madeline in check? He sincerely doubted it.

So with a new sense of purpose, Adam had sat down at the desk, reached for a clean parchment, picked up his quill pen, dipped it deeply into the ink and begun his letter to Diana: the retraction of his proposal. And if necessary, the request for an annulment.

It had been a difficult thing to do, but he knew it was the right thing. For everyone.

Now Adam paced up and down the hall, still waiting for Madeline to come downstairs. He patted the letter in his pocket. He couldn't wait to hand it over to the ship's master.

Of course, Adam couldn't actually propose to Madeline until he'd received a reply from his solicitor, affirming that Adam was free, but he could at least explain to Madeline what he had done, and assure her that Diana would not be coming to Cumberland.

He was eager and impatient to take the first step toward a life with Madeline if, God willing, she would ever have him. He supposed that after today, he would have plenty of time and opportunity to *make* it happen, for he had every intention of fighting for her. By God, he was going to give John Metcalf a good run for his money.

Just then, Penelope came running down the stairs. "Father, may I take Thunder out for a ride on the marsh this morning?"

Adam cleared his throat and cupped his daughter's soft chin. "Have you had breakfast?"

"Yes. I had two eggs and a slice of corn bread."

"Then yes, you may take Thunder out, but stay on the path."

"I will! Thank you, Father!" She bolted past him and out the front door.

He heard a rustle of silk behind him and turned.

There stood Madeline, wearing a fine peach-colored floral gown, her hair pulled into an elegant bun and decorated with pearl combs, beneath a ber-gère straw hat trimmed with flowers. Her short, tight sleeves were trimmed with a triple layer of lace flounces just above her elbows, and at her neck, she wore a white crossed handkerchief to cover the deep, square décolletage.

Adam could barely speak. How could he ever have imagined she was plain?

"You look exquisite, Madeline. I…"

There were no words to describe how she affected him. All he could do was bow deeply to her, as if she were a duchess and he, her humble servant.

She laughed. "Oh, Adam, you flatter me."

"The lieutenant-governor will fall over himself when he sees you."

"I certainly hope not!" she replied, her smile beaming.

Adam offered his arm. "Shall we go then, my lady?"

"As you wish, sir." She looped her arm through his and they went outside to the waiting carriage.

As he helped her into the seat, he remembered the first time he'd set eyes on her at the fort. She had come here as his intended bride. She had been willing to marry him that day. If only he had known what he knew now. He should have called for the reverend right there. If only he had known how his feelings would change.

He climbed in beside her and flicked the lines. They turned up the road and drove into the woods.

Along the way, they talked about the marshes and discussed which sections to show Lord Blackthorne. They discussed the entertainments they had planned for him, and what songs Penelope should sing first, for she had rehearsed a number of them.

By the time they reached the fort, the wind had

picked up. The British flag was snapping noisily atop the mast, and Madeline had to hold on to her hat to keep it from flying off her head. They saw the schooner still a distance away in the basin and decided to wait inside the courtyard until it reached its berth.

There was an entourage at the bottom of the hill, lined up at the wharf—buggies and carriages that must have traveled overland to meet the viscount here.

Adam and Madeline marveled at the pomp and ceremony of it all, and Adam felt a surge of pride to be Lord Blackthorne's host in Cumberland. Then he thought of the letter in his pocket, and a sense of excitement joined the pride, for he would eventually—*soon,* he hoped—be free to pursue Madeline.

Finally, when the schooner drew near, Adam and Madeline drove down the cart road to meet the lieutenant-governor. They parked the buggy behind the others and walked to the gangplank, now lowering onto the dock.

The deck of the schooner was crowded with officials and footmen, and Adam could see the bright colors of ladies' gowns. Good Lord, had Lord Blackthorne brought the entire population of Halifax with him? Adam hoped he would have room for all of them in his home. And food, and enough entertainment. He hoped they weren't expecting a ball or anything of that nature. Cumberland was a farming community.

Lord Blackthorne emerged from the crowd and was the first to disembark. "Good day, everyone!" he shouted.

He was a portly man with gold-rimmed spectacles and a powdered wig with horizontal rolls. He wore a cream satin coat, trimmed with sham buttonholes and embroidered in blue lace. His breeches were also made of satin, with silk-clocked stockings and a shiny buckled shoe on one foot, but not the other, for it was a wooden stump.

It was a well-known fact that the viscount had lost his leg in the war with the French, twenty years earlier.

He walked down the gangplank, his wooden leg tapping lightly, and Adam prepared to introduce Madeline. Adam froze, however, when he looked beyond the lieutenant-governor's shoulder and met the eyes of the woman coming down behind him.

Dressed in silks and satins and fluttering her fan ridiculously in the driving wind, she smiled broadly at Adam.

He struggled to keep his balance, for the woman approaching, flashing her blue eyes at him, was Diana.

Chapter Twelve

Dumbfounded and bewildered, Adam struggled to maintain his composure.

Lord Blackthorne appeared before him, looking all around at the vast green landscape. "Mr. Coates! What a magnificent countryside you have here."

Adam forced himself to greet the viscount and make some audible response.

Lord Blackthorne gestured behind him. "As you can see, I brought another flower to add to it, and what an exceedingly great pleasure it is to do so."

Adam remembered a conversation he'd had with the viscount one evening at Government House when they were enjoying a glass of brandy together.

"Are you married, Mr. Coates?"

Adam had swirled the amber liquid around in his glass. "No, my lord. I am widowed, but I've recently proposed to a woman I once knew in Yorkshire years ago—Lady Thurston. She, too, is widowed. Her younger sister is here now, and we're awaiting my lady's arrival."

"What's the woman's sister doing here?"

So Adam had been forced to explain the mix-up....

Lord Blackthorne slapped Adam on the back, shocking him back to the present. "I've come on the same schooner as Lady Thurston! What an extraordinary coincidence, what?"

Diana moved to stand beside Lord Blackthorne, who seemed to enjoy the opportunity to bring two long-lost lovers back together again. "Adam Coates, may I present your betrothed, Lady Thurston."

Adam's heart throbbed in his ears as he forced himself to meet her sparkling gaze. *Diana...*

She looked as young and slim and perfect as the first day he had met her, sixteen years ago. Almost nothing had changed, save a line or two around her eyes. Her smile was the same, her full lips were the same, her tiny, dainty nose...it was all the same.

Diana—his Diana—here in the flesh. The shock of it. It was incomprehensible.

She smiled and tilted her head in that old, familiar way. He was shaken by how well he knew her mannerisms, as if they were etched in his heart and mind and soul.

"Adam," she said, "how wonderful it is to see you again. It seems like a lifetime." Her voice was the same, too—rich and velvety like a song.

He felt everyone's eyes upon them, as if they all knew the situation and were waiting to see what would happen next. Of course, no one knew the *real* situation, that he had a letter to break off their engagement searing a damn hole in his pocket.

He turned to look at Madeline, somewhere behind him. God, his chest was aching.

Madeline stood tall and unruffled, her hands clasped together in front of her. As he turned, Diana turned, too, then Madeline moved forward to greet her sister.

The whole scene was excruciating to Adam, like something out of a bad play. They hugged each other, and it was all Adam could do to keep himself from demanding an explanation. What was Diana doing here? She couldn't possibly have received his proposal and arrived so quickly. It wasn't feasible.

Madeline smiled warmly at her sister. "What are you doing here so soon? We didn't expect you."

"It was your letter, Madeline. Thank goodness, you sent it!"

"My letter?" Madeline replied, sounding confused. "It was Adam who wrote to you after I arrived, but you couldn't have received that yet, and have traveled all this way."

"No, no! *Your* letter! Don't you remember? You wrote to tell me you were leaving Yorkshire to marry Adam, that father had arranged it."

Madeline's brow furrowed as she contemplated her sister's explanation. Adam watched the scene with a sick feeling in his gut.

"Naturally I went to see Father about it," Diana said, "for I knew something was wrong. I knew he must have done something absolutely beastly, for Adam would never have wanted to marry *you*. He would have wanted *me*."

A hush fell over the small crowd. Madeline held on to her hat against the driving wind and her skirts whipped around her legs.

Adam felt Madeline's humiliation as if it were his own. He stepped forward. "It was a misunderstanding, that's all."

He turned to look at Madeline's profile in the sun, to try and see what she was thinking. Her eyes were downcast.

God, he wanted to hold her. He wanted to lead her away from here and take her into his arms and tell her that he wanted *her*, not Diana, and that Diana's unexpected appearance—though a shock to be sure—only served to confirm that fact to him.

He decided firmly that he would do everything in his power to make it right.

Lord Blackthorne interrupted the awkward silence with his deep, booming voice. "Well, it's all worked itself out now. Lady Thurston and I had a fine opportunity to get acquainted on the ship, and I say, you can imagine my surprise when she explained who she was and why she was en route to Fort Cumberland. Small world, is it not? For it was I who had the pleasure to assure her that her sister had not married Mr. Coates, and that if Lady Thurston had remained in London, she would have received a more recent proposal herself. Naturally, she was overjoyed to hear it."

Diana elaborated, directing her words at Adam. "Yes, well, I was a bit concerned that you might have already married Madeline, out of guilt or a sense of responsibility for her, after what had occurred. As I'm sure you must know, that would have been devastating for me." She looked around, her cheeks flushing.

Adam didn't know what to say. She was gazing at him, waiting for something....

Madeline shook her head. "I would never have allowed such a marriage to take place, Diana."

It was her pride talking, Adam knew it, and it only made him respect her more.

Diana hugged Madeline again. "Oh, you are the dearest sister in the world. There are none more loyal than you. Thank you, Madeline. My *heart* thanks you. You cannot imagine how little I slept during the crossing, worrying that I would be too late." She faced Adam again and her gaze was intense. "For I have dreamed of this day."

Lord Blackthorne interrupted again. "Well, we shall have a grand time over the next few days! I have much to learn about the Tantramar, and I'll enjoy watching two lovers reunited, getting to know each other again. I could not have planned my visit for a better time."

To Adam, however, the timing of everything could not have been worse.

During the trip home, Lord Blackthorne rode up front in the buggy with Adam, so that he might see some of the marsh and ask questions, which left Madeline to ride in Diana's coach with her sister and her maid, Hilary.

Madeline realized that part of the entourage she and Adam had seen at the fort was as much for Diana and her maid and two grooms, as it was for the lieutenant-governor and his retinue. She supposed her sister was still an English lady—a wealthy one at that—and had certain expectations about how she should live her life.

Madeline wondered with some concern how Diana would adjust to the simple country life in Cumberland, where tilling and harvesting were more important to most people than keeping up with the latest Paris fashions.

The convoy of carriages descended into the woods along the narrow cart road, and the sound of sharp branches scraping against the roof of the coach unnerved Diana. "Heavens, I had no idea the land was so uncultivated here."

"It's not uncultivated," Madeline explained, "maybe just a little thick here in the bush, but Adam's farm is fully cleared, with fields of grain already planted, and hay almost ready to be harvested down on the marsh."

Diana smiled. "Father told me that Adam had made something of himself, that he's grown quite wealthy. He said Adam owns more land here than anyone in the area. Is that true?"

"He has indeed come a long way since the days we knew him in Yorkshire."

Her sister smiled and leaned back. "I always knew he would rise to something wonderful. And oh, he has grown even more handsome, don't you think, Madeline? I thought I was going to fall off the boat when I saw him, dressed so finely in that embroidered waistcoat, his eyes so strikingly intense. The sight of him brought it all back—all the memories of my youth when I was so desperately in love with him."

And when you jilted him to marry a baronet.

Madeline's thoughts were full of acid and she knew it. She chided herself, of course, but at the same time accepted that she couldn't help feeling resentful. Here was Diana, coming to take Adam for herself and make him hers. All she had to do was flutter her long, seductive eyelashes, and it would be done.

"You've been quiet, Madeline. Were you that surprised to see me? I always suffer when you're quiet. Why must you do that to me, when I have come all this way and I want very much to talk."

Why is everything always about you? "I'm sorry, Diana. I don't mean to be quiet, it's just that I've been working hard the past few days, preparing for Lord Blackthorne's arrival. Of course I'm thrilled to see you."

"Ah." She gazed studiously at Madeline. "May I ask, what is your role at Adam's house? You're not…keeping house, or anything like that, are you?"

With that tone, she might as well have said, "You're not *eating dead worms,* are you?"

Madeline arranged her skirts on the shiny blue leather seat. "As a matter of fact, I am. I'm also governess to the children, and I'm tending to the vegetable garden with my very own hands."

Diana gazed out the window at the passing spruce branches, still scraping against the sides of the coach. She threw Madeline that look—that *you-just-like-to-shock-me-because-you're-hateful* look.

Perhaps there was a bit of truth to it today. Madeline wanted to shock Diana. Let her know that Adam was not an aristocrat and he didn't expect his future sister-in-law to be one, either.

"I forgot," Diana added, "that you always liked getting your hands dirty in the gardens. I never understood that."

Madeline felt guilty suddenly, for purposefully trying to exasperate her sister, who had just traveled across an ocean to be with Adam, whom she loved. No matter how angry or resentful Madeline felt, she could not forget that. Diana loved Adam, too.

She reached for her sister's hand and held it. "We were always different, Diana. We still are, but that doesn't mean we can't try to be close now that you're here. We're a long way from home."

Diana's beautiful smile reached her eyes and made them sparkle like jewels. No wonder everyone who met her fell in love with her.

"Yes, we must get to know each other all over again. After all, you're the only true family I have here. At least until I become Adam's wife."

That last comment struck Madeline like a slap, but she made a firm decision not to feel sorry for herself any longer. Fate had played its hand today and had sent Diana early. It was clear that Diana truly loved Adam, and he most certainly loved her, so it was time for Madeline to accept that and try to be a dutiful sister.

Adam spent the early part of the afternoon seeing to everyone's needs and ensuring that his guests and all their servants had places to sleep. Agnes had arrived to help out, and Mary was doing her part, too, while Penelope watched the baby. By the time everyone was settled, it was time for supper.

They dined on fresh beef with gravy, fiddleheads and Yorkshire pudding, with chocolate squares and gingerbread cake for dessert. Adam sat at one end of the long table, while Lord Blackthorne sat at the other, his pleasant laughter filling the room with mirth. The food was delicious, the children were polite and entertaining, conversation was engaging, yet Adam was reeling in discontent.

He watched Diana eat her dessert, gracefully, delicately, while she shone with witty remarks and curious questions for the lieutenant-governor about his property in England and his new position here in Nova Scotia.

Her beauty was remarkable. She possessed shiny golden hair and blue eyes, a flawless complexion, and she wore a flattering gown of the latest fashion, trimmed in precious gold lace. She was the perfect hostess, even though it was not yet her party to host. She was any ambitious man's dream of a wife.

Yet, her physical magnificence left Adam feeling listless and unresponsive. It was Madeline's simple beauty that attracted his attention now.

He sipped his wine and watched her. She listened politely to Diana's stories, smiled demurely at Lord Blackthorne but, for the most part, was quiet. There was a sweet shyness about her, a shyness that he adored, for it was gentle and kind. He loved that she valued the things he valued: family, home, the land. She didn't care about lustrous jewels or society gossip. She was more interested in watching Penelope chase a squirrel, or helping Charlie with his numbers, or seeing the first tomato plant sprouting out of the soil.

Beneath all that, she was strong and capable, and as Adam watched her now, dipping her gingerbread cake into the cream on her plate, he knew that Diana's arrival had changed nothing. Whether Madeline was aware of it or not, she had stolen his heart.

Did Madeline even have the slightest idea how he felt about her? he wondered. Did she suspect anything when she looked into his eyes?

Lord Blackthorne directed a question at Diana. "Tell me, Lady Thurston, what do you think of Cumberland now that you're here?"

She raised her wineglass. "I believe I have never seen a more fascinating landscape, my lord. The sheer size of the marsh is astounding. Yet I have not seen any tenant farms, Adam. Where are you hiding them?"

The viscount laughed at her intended jest, but Adam wasn't sure Diana understood that her joke had just revealed her ignorance of the colony. He tried to correct her as kindly as possible.

"Mostly I farm the land myself, and though I do rent some land to other families, the returns are incidental. I only wish to keep those farms productive until the children are ready to move onto them—if it is their desire. I don't wish to profit from them. The families I rent to are merely in transition until they can buy land of their own."

Diana cleared her throat. "You farm this yourself? You must at least hire hands."

"At harvest time, of course, but my sons and I can

manage most of the work ourselves throughout the year.'' He winked at Charlie, who smiled proudly in response.

By the blank look on Diana's face, he sensed she was imagining him actually pushing a plow. She seemed to have a hard time swallowing.

Lord Blackthorne changed the subject, and Adam decided he would have to resolve this situation as soon as possible. He could not go on misleading Diana, nor could he continue keeping his true feelings for Madeline to himself. He would have to do the right thing, as swiftly and gently as he could, and do his best to spare any further heartache.

He had an uneasy feeling, however, that no matter how carefully he handled this situation, it was going to be bloody.

With Lord Blackthorne's presence in the house, it was necessary for Diana and Madeline to share Madeline's bedchamber, the one that should have been Diana's to begin with. As Madeline slipped into the cool sheets beside her sister, she felt as if *she* were the guest.

''Is it true,'' Diana whispered to Madeline in the darkness, ''that after you arrived, Adam sent instructions for a proxy marriage? Lord Blackthorne told me so on the ship, but of course I never received the proposal so I wouldn't know for sure.''

Madeline hugged the coverlet to her chest. ''Yes, it's true.''

''Adam must have been terribly anxious to have me. It still seems like a dream. Oh, how disappointed he must have been when it was *you* who arrived that day, and not me. Was he very angry? I'll wager he wanted to brain Father.''

''Yes, he was angry.'' Madeline knew her sister wanted to hear all the details, but damned if she was going to give them to her. She simply couldn't, not without revealing how heartbroken she had been and continued to be.

''Oh, Madeline, I can still barely believe I am here in Adam's house. You cannot imagine how, over the years, I have dreamed of seeing him again.''

Madeline rolled onto her side to face her sister. ''Was it difficult for you, being married to Sir Edward when you could not forget Adam?''

Diana nodded, and Madeline was suddenly curious about more of her sister's deeper feelings.

Madeline thought of Mary and Jacob and how they'd always told each other every thought and feeling, and consequently, Madeline decided that even though she was having a hard time with the situation now, she should try to think of the future and nurture a closer relationship with Diana. She was flesh and blood, after all, and wasn't it time Madeline reached out to forge a true bond with someone?

''Did you love Sir Edward at all?'' she asked.

Diana blinked up at the ceiling. ''He was my husband and I respected him, but it wasn't easy being his wife. I was young and naive when I married him and I had no idea how the world worked. I thought I was marrying into a fairy tale—becoming *Lady* Thurston—but to them, I would always be a tenant farmer's daughter. Edward only married me to badger his mother. He already had his heirs from his first *proper* wife. I was just a pretty reward."

"But he seemed so in love with you."

"It was lust, Madeline, not love. Part of the curse of being beautiful, I suppose." She rolled over to face Madeline, and stroked her curly hair. "You're lucky. When a man falls in love with you, he will love you for what you are on the inside, not what you look like on the outside."

Despite what Madeline felt was a backhanded compliment, she smiled consolingly at Diana in the dim, flickering candlelight. "Adam truly loves you, Diana. You can be certain of it. If it had been lust, he would not have carried a torch for you all these years—a torch that still burns as brightly as the day it first sparked into flame."

Diana sighed. "That's what I try and tell myself. It's what kept me going when the reality of my marriage sank in. I had to believe that somewhere out there, Adam loved me. Even when he married Jane, I clung to that hope."

Madeline confided in her sister. "I read one of your letters to him. He kept them, Diana. All of them."

"He did?" Diana's voice beamed with surprise and happiness. "He never answered them. I feared he had crumpled each one."

"No, he still has them and he treasures them."

Diana rolled onto her back. "I am so happy, Madeline, to be reunited with him at last. It's inconceivably romantic, as if we were meant to be together. That it's our destiny and God is making it happen. Will you stand with me on my wedding day?"

Madeline swallowed over the painful lump in her throat. "I will be honored." Then she yawned and rolled over onto her side, facing the wall. She tried to keep her voice from trembling as she closed her eyes and said wearily, "Good night, Diana."

Chapter Thirteen

For the next two days, Adam escorted Lord Blackthorne all over the marshlands, explaining the workings of the dykes and the *aboiteaux*. When the lieutenant-governor realized that entire hay crops would be lost and the land would become inoperable if the dykes were not maintained, he became more open to the idea of establishing stronger requirements for the farmers, as well as attaining some funding for yearly maintenance.

Feeling pleased with the results of the visit, Adam and the rest of his family said goodbye to Lord Blackthorne and his servants, and waved to the convoy of carriages as it rolled with a flourish out of the yard.

Adam took a breath. Instantly everything seemed quiet. He turned to see Diana and Madeline standing arm in arm, smiling and waving one last goodbye.

"Congratulations, Adam," Madeline said. "You've done it."

He would have liked to hug her then, to twirl her around and celebrate, but Diana was smiling at him and he could not.

"Congratulations for what?" Diana asked, and Adam realized he had not explained his concerns about the marsh to her, nor had she asked why he and the lieutenant-governor had gone riding every day. Had she thought it was merely a social visit?

When he didn't answer right away, Madeline answered for him. "Adam has just secured Lord Blackthorne's support to fund the maintenance of the dykes and protect the marsh."

"Protect it from what?"

"From flooding."

"Flooding? Heavens." The information barely had a chance to reach her ears, when she turned toward Agnes. "Mrs. Dalton, what time is lunch being served?"

"One o'clock, my lady."

Without another word about the marsh, Diana turned to go into the house. "Well, I best go and dress, then. It will be our first meal alone as a family, and I want it to be special. Will you summon my maid please, Mrs. Dalton?"

Adam watched her, feeling dumbfounded, trying to remember what he had expected when he'd sent his proposal to her originally. He'd thought he'd known Diana, but he hadn't. He only knew a fantasy of her, what he *wanted* her to be.

A moment later, everyone was gone, and Adam was left alone in the yard. A longing flared through him, and he could not keep it buried any longer. The time had come. He would break off his engagement to Diana today.

* * *

After lunch, Madeline heard the tapping of hoof-beats up the driveway, and knew Adam had returned from his inspection of the fields. She sat up straighter on the bench, forcing herself to ignore him—she would not turn around to look—and fight the clattering, painful awareness inside her heart.

She smiled warmly at John Metcalf, who had come this windy afternoon to tell her about the farm he had just leased. "What are your plans, John? Will you raise beef?"

"I reckon so. I still have some work to do on the barn, though, before I can purchase any stock. There's a hole in the roof the size of a wagon wheel."

"Oh my!" Still trying to ignore the urge to turn and look at Adam, Madeline laughed with John, who began to fidget nervously on the bench. He cleared his throat a few times before speaking.

"The other reason I came, Miss Oxley, is to ask you to accompany me to the summer dance at the Aikens' place. I hear they clear out their barn for a real romp."

Madeline felt her face color. No one had ever asked her to a dance before. She took a moment to consider his invitation, then she pictured Adam escorting Diana and dancing all night long with her.

A quick decision immediately followed, but she was uncomfortable with it. "Yes, John, I would be happy to go with you. When is it?"

"Next Saturday night. I can come by to pick you up at seven." He nearly spilled his tea as he took another sip.

Just then, Madeline heard Adam's footsteps over

the hard ground and sensed his approach. He stopped behind them. This time, she allowed herself to turn on the bench and smile casually. "Good morning, Adam."

"Good morning, Madeline. Metcalf, how are you?"

"I'm fine, sir. I came to tell Madeline that I found land to lease. It's nearby—not more than a stone's throw, down in the lowlands just past the Chapman place."

Adam unbuttoned his coat. "Congratulations. You must be pleased about that."

"I am, sir." John gazed at Madeline and smiled. "I'm *very* pleased."

Madeline felt her whole body tense at John's blatant show of affection for her. It was the first time anyone had ever looked at her like that. It was just like the way Jacob looked at Mary.

Her insides tugged unpleasantly in response.

Perhaps that tugging sensation would become pleasant later on.

Or perhaps not.

What would she do if it did? Or didn't?

She glanced up at Adam, who was still staring icily at John, who was staring starry-eyed at her. Good Lord, she couldn't believe she was having this philosophical debate with herself in front of Adam.

The wind caught the ribbon in Adam's queue and lifted it. She stared blankly at it for a moment, feeling dazed at the sight of his strong jaw and dark eyes, his broad shoulders beneath his coat, and the way he held himself—tall, confident, mature. He was so much more of a man than John was.

But he was not the one who was courting her.

At that instant, she knew with conviction that she *must* make an effort not only to appreciate John Metcalf for all his good qualities, but to encourage him, too. She had to forget about Adam and move on with her life. She couldn't go on pining for her sister's future husband.

She pasted on a smile for John and forced a polite reply past her lips. "I'm pleased, too."

"Well, good," Adam said, his voice deep and booming. "Everyone's pleased. If you'll excuse me now, I have some business to attend to." He started toward the door, but hesitated and turned back. "Madeline, perhaps we could talk this evening. About something rather...important."

With that final word, he left, taking long strides toward the house. Madeline watched after him, wondering what he wanted to talk about.

"Is there something wrong, Madeline?"

She jumped at the sound of John's voice, pulling her back to the here and now.

"You look melancholy," he said.

Madeline pulled her teacup to her lips. "Melancholy?" She struggled for an excuse to give him, to give herself. "I suppose it is this ominous weather." She glanced up at the dark, brooding clouds, blustering across the sky. "I daresay, it looks like we're going to get rain."

No amount of rain, however, could compare to the tempest inside her heart.

* * *

Adam stormed into the house, his frustration reaching a new peak. He detested the idea of John Metcalf courting Madeline, yet he had no one to blame but himself, for he had been stalling these past few days. He was not looking forward to confronting Diana, breaking her heart and sending her home, but if he didn't do it now, he would risk losing Madeline forever.

Adam pulled off his coat and carried it to his den. He walked in and closed the door behind him, but froze there on the spot. Sitting at his desk, reading his correspondence, was Diana.

Startled, she turned in her chair, or rather, *his* chair. "Adam, I thought you were out riding."

He worked hard to keep his voice steady and controlled. "I was."

They gazed at each other for a moment, then she set down the letter in her hand and stood. "I was just…I was just reading these…" She gestured toward the pile of letters on his desk. *Her* letters. "I had forgotten all the things I wrote to you. I'm so glad you kept them."

He took an anxious step forward. "Diana—"

"I remember now, how miserable I was that first year of my marriage and how desperately I'd wanted you back. You were everything to me, Adam, and I was foolish to let you go. This brings it all back, makes it seem like it happened only yesterday."

"It wasn't yesterday, Diana, it was a long time ago."

"Yes, thank goodness, otherwise I would still be buried in loneliness back there."

God, this was wretched.

He gazed at the window and saw Madeline outside still talking to Metcalf. The young man was standing by the bench, and she was gazing up at him, her hand on top of her straw hat to keep it from flying off on a gale.

Adam's insides careened at the sight of her talking to John—or any man who tried to court her, for that matter.

There was no way in hell Adam could take another minute of this. He turned back to Diana, who was now walking toward him, her smile warm and inviting.

Adam breathed deeply. "Diana, we must talk."

Chapter Fourteen

Adam carried his coat across the room and draped it over the back of the wing chair in front of the fireplace. He stood behind it, summoning the right words while Diana moved toward him, tilting her head the way she always did when she was unsure of something.

He gestured toward the other wing chair. "Diana, please sit down." He took a seat across from her.

There were times he wished he was not a compassionate man, that he could act according to necessity and not be affected by it. He had been compassionate for his irrational wife when she'd collapsed in tears or flown into a rage, and he was compassionate now for Diana, knowing he was about to break her heart.

It had always been his weakness—another person's suffering—and he knew it. He also knew he had to work hard to stand strong and do what must be done, no matter how painful it was.

She perched on the edge of the chair, her back stiff and straight, her hands clasped together tightly on her lap, and he detected her wariness.

Perhaps she had sensed the lack of feeling in him since she'd arrived, compared to the days long ago when he'd loved and worshiped her in Yorkshire. Since she'd stepped off the ship here in Cumberland, she'd confessed her happiness to him numerous times, and not once had he responded in kind.

"What is it, Adam?"

God, this was difficult. "I'm afraid we need to talk about the situation here...."

The situation here? Hell, he could do better than that.

"What do you mean?" She reached across to take his hand in hers. "You look so serious. You're scaring me."

He squeezed her hand in return and paused a moment before speaking, then disciplined himself into a steely resolve. "This is difficult to say, Diana, but surely you must recognize that we are not the same people we once were, that there has been a lifetime of experiences between us, and a great deal has changed."

She smiled charmingly. "Well, of course things have changed, and I'm glad. You are a landowner now, Adam. A wealthy one. You have accomplished tremendous things, when before, we were both young and knew nothing of the world."

"It's more than that, my dear. I may have wealth, but I am not an aristocrat and I will never be one. In my heart, I am still just a simple farmer. You, on the other hand, are every inch a proper lady and, in your heart, I think you always were."

She laughed. "I don't understand, Adam."

He shook his head. "I'm not saying this well at all. It…it has nothing to do with rank or class or wealth. It has more to do with—" he touched a fist to his chest "—with our hearts."

"But my heart has always belonged to you. Even while I was married." There was a pleading note to her voice all of a sudden. It tied his gut into a knot.

"Has it really? Or has it belonged to a dream of me?"

"I still don't understand what you are trying to say."

Adam leaned back in his chair, searching for the grit to see this through. "We don't know each other, Diana, and I'm not certain we ever did. Something gave you reason not to marry me years ago, and whatever that reason was, it still exists. We are different people. Your feelings for me have merely been a way of escaping whatever was missing in your own marriage, just as my feelings for you were an escape when times were difficult. We both wanted to return to the past when we were innocent and happy and knew nothing of the kind of pain or loneliness life can bring, but we can't go back to that innocence. All we can do is learn from the past and move forward."

Her jaw clenched visibly and her tone deepened. "What is your point, Adam?"

He suspected she already knew, but he had to say it anyway. "My point is—I don't think we should marry."

Her chin rose as she gathered her dignity around her. "I beg your pardon?"

He forced himself to say it again, as if it weren't

hard enough the first time. "I believe it would be a mistake for us to marry."

The pleading tone returned to her voice. "But...maybe it's...maybe we just need time alone together. We need to start again. How can we enjoy each other in a house full of children? Maybe we should think about sending the younger ones away to school. Then we could go back to what it was like when we—"

Adam felt sick. "I do not wish to send my children away."

She confronted his resolute answer with a look of anger. "This makes no sense. Surely you are not put off me because I have *risen* in life. If anything, you should be honored and grateful that I have come all this way to marry you. I am *Lady* Thurston!"

Pausing to allow her time to let the shock settle in, Adam leaned forward again, resting his elbows on his knees and lacing his fingers together.

"You are a beautiful, charming woman, Diana, and I have had difficulty myself letting go of the dream of you. But that's all it was—a dream. In reality, we are not compatible. You are in love with the man you want me to be, not the man that I am. I couldn't possibly hire other people to do my work for me. I *like* my work. I want to plow my own fields and stick my hands in the dirt at harvest time, and I doubt you would enjoy welcoming me home after I've just slaughtered a hog."

A delicate finger came up to rest under her nose. "Good gracious, Adam, there's no need to be cruel, saying such things to me."

Adam wondered with a sigh which part she considered more cruel: his breaking off their engagement, or his mentioning the hog slaughter.

"You see, Diana, we are not right for each other. You would be much happier with a different kind of man."

She continued to hold her head high. "You sounded like Madeline just now, talking about sticking your hands in the dirt. What is it about dirt that people always like to torture me with it?"

Baffled by her comment—baffled by everything about her—he patted her hand. "I am deeply sorry for bringing you all this way for nothing."

"You are sorry? Sorry!" She snatched her hand out of his grasp and stood. "I spent six weeks on a stench-filled boat with a bunch of laborers! Now, you have the nerve to tell me that *I* am the one who is living in a fantasy! *You* were the one to send the proposal! *You* were the one who started all of this! You've barely spoken two words to me since I've arrived, yet you presume to think you know enough about me to conclude that we are not right for each other. Is it because I am older? Am I not as beautiful as you remembered? Is it my hair? Have you noticed the gray?"

Adam stood. "No, Diana, you are as beautiful as ever."

"Then what, may I ask, has changed since you wrote to Father to ask for my hand in marriage?" Her voice was harsh and demanding.

Not entirely sure how much he should say, or how

truthful he should be, he replied simply, "*I* have changed."

The features of her face hardened; her voice faded to a hush. "How? And why?"

Adam moved to stand in the center of the room. "It grieves me to say this, Diana, but I have changed because I've met someone who…someone who sees the world the way I do. I have learned to appreciate what is here before me in the present, to let go of the past and all the pain that went with it. I have met someone who is, I believe, my true mate."

That last comment shook her physically. "There's someone else?"

"Yes."

"Who? Who has cheated me out of my place in your heart, and stolen you away when I have waited so long?"

"I can not tell you who."

"Why? Are you afraid I will go to her and tell her what a faithless, fickle man you are? That you could propose to a woman one week, and forget her the next?"

"It wasn't as simple as that. I was not cavalier about this."

"Then what was it? How could you sweep me from your heart so expeditiously, after wanting me all your life? Madeline assured me it was so—that you still cared for me."

The mention of Madeline in this conversation unnerved him but, for the moment, he concealed it. "I do still care for you, Diana. I always will, but we are not meant to be husband and wife."

"But the letters…you kept them."

He struggled to keep his composure. "I never meant for you to see those."

"But they were here on your desk, for all the world to see!"

Adam tried to keep his anger in check. "They were locked in a box."

Diana realized her gaffe but brushed it off and pointed a long finger. "The key was sitting out, right there."

He gazed at it on the desk. "A key on a desk is not an open invitation to go through a man's personal belongings!"

"They were *my* letters!"

Good God, why were they arguing about this? Adam pinched the bridge of his nose to try and thwart the headache that was beginning to throb. "You may have them back if you wish."

She glared hotly at him. "Indeed. You're through with them, are you?"

He said nothing. He merely met her gaze, hoping she would see how truly sorry he was.

She marched angrily over to the desk and picked up the box of letters. "I believe I will take them, thank you. And *you*, Adam Coates, can burn in hell."

With that, she walked out of his study. Adam followed her down the hall and into the kitchen, where she threw the box of letters onto the fire. Sparks snapped and crackled and flew into the air, and Diana slapped her hands together as if to brush off the grimy memories.

Alone in the kitchen, they stood face-to-face, staring at each other. Adam didn't know what to say. If she had wanted to slap him, he would have let her, for she deserved some kind of satisfaction for what he'd put her through.

If he could have changed the way things had occurred to have avoided this altogether, he certainly would have. If only he could have seen into the future. He would have sent for Madeline's hand in marriage in the first place.

Life, however, was never as easy as that. He had to face the difficult truth that he had caused Diana great pain and inconvenience, and had also displaced her from her home.

"The least you can do is tell me who she is and where you met her," Diana said.

Adam stiffened. He could not tell Diana that it was her sister he loved, when Madeline herself didn't even know. "I would rather not."

"I deserve to know the truth, Adam. I *want* to know."

He would not waver. He shook his head at her.

"Have you already proposed to her?"

"No."

"Does she know about me?"

"Yes." God, he wanted this to be over.

For a long time she stood there, glaring at him, and when he offered her no further information, she pushed past him toward the stairs. "I'm leaving on the next ship. And I'm taking Madeline with me."

Before he had a chance to realize what he was doing, he was reaching for Diana's arm as she passed. With a quick, tight grip, he stopped her. "Madeline stays here." Diana's startled expression shook his resolve. "At least until I have a chance to talk to her myself."

Diana yanked her arm out of his grasp. Her chest rose and fell with deep, furious breaths. Then her face changed; her voice was like an echo. "It's Madeline, isn't it?"

He met her challenging glare but said nothing, for what could he say when his world was crumbling all around him?

"You've fallen in love with my sister! How could you! How could *she!* She assured me you still cared for me. She pretended to be my loyal sister, when she was betraying me all along!"

"No, she is innocent in this."

"Innocent! An innocent girl does not steal her older sister's..." Diana's outburst halted on her lips. She appeared to be putting all the pieces together on her own, without his help. "She doesn't know...."

He swallowed uncomfortably. "No, and you can't tell her. I need to tell her myself."

"I'll tell her whatever I want! And don't think for one minute that I will sing your praises."

She gathered her skirts and walked quickly to the stairs. Adam went after her. "If you have a kind bone in your body, Diana, you will leave this to me. I love Madeline and I'm going to ask her to be my wife. Don't take this chance for happiness away from her."

Diana continued to scurry up the stairs. "I won't let her marry you. Not after what you've done to me."

"It is not your decision to make. She is a grown woman."

Diana stopped on the landing. "She is my obstinate little sister! She has always been jealous of me, and she probably seduced you just to get back at me for being prettier and smarter and for always getting what I want! No one has *ever* chosen her over me!"

Feeling weak and stunned by Diana's brutal, egotistic honesty, he stood on the staircase looking up at her, squeezing the railing in his fist. It seemed almost impossible that he could have loved her once.

She whirled around with a swish of silks and petticoats and floated the rest of the way up the stairs. A few seconds later, her bedroom door slammed shut.

Adam quickly summoned his thoughts into action. He had to find Madeline before Diana spoke to her. He had to tell Madeline he loved her and explain what had happened with Diana.

He went out to the front porch, but she and Metcalf weren't there.

Returning inside, he took two steps at a time up the stairs and went from room to room, searching, but the house was quiet and still, all except for Diana's maid, Hilary, who was stitching a hem in the hall by the window. "Have you seen Miss Oxley?" he asked her.

She shook her head.

Penelope had gone to Mary and Jacob's house to help them prepare to move in, and the boys were out in the fields. Where was Madeline? He listened at Diana's door but heard nothing and knew Madeline was not in there with her. If she had been, there would be screaming and tears.

He ran down the stairs and out the front door. A violent gale was still blowing, and the sky was churning with dark thunderclouds. He ran to the barn, checked the chicken coop and the vegetable garden, but couldn't find Madeline anywhere.

John Metcalf had been with her last. Had she left with him? Gone riding across the marsh?

One more short search of the yard and the house yielded no results, so he quickly saddled his horse. No matter what it took, he was going to find Madeline. And God willing, he was going to make her his own.

Chapter Fifteen

Adam galloped along the ridge top, stopping to overlook the marsh below, while a brawny, brisk wind blasted him in the face. A storm was brewing, there was no doubt about that, and he had to find Madeline. He needed to explain his feelings to her before Diana had a chance to spoil everything. And she would. He *knew* she would. Madeline was deeply loyal to her sister. If she heard Diana's story first, Madeline would never believe Adam's love was pure. She would never betray her heartbroken sister.

He kicked himself then, remembering the day he had brought Madeline with him to meet Lord Blackthorne's ship. With high hopes and grand intentions, he had carried the letter to Diana in his pocket, yet he had not disclosed a word of his plan to Madeline. He'd foolishly believed he had all the time in the world to woo her. He had stalled, waiting for the right time, and now he might have missed his opportunity altogether. The window had slammed shut on his fingers.

When he didn't see Madeline or John down on the

marsh, he wondered if John had taken her to see his new homestead. Deciding it was a likely place to find her, he turned his mount and kicked in his heels, feeling the first cold drops of rain pelt his cheeks.

A short time later, he was thoroughly drenched and trotting into John's yard. John's horse was tethered inside the open barn, his saddle gone from his back. A light burned in the kitchen window.

Feeling a surge of protectiveness over Madeline, Adam dismounted and strode to the door. How would he handle this, if Madeline was inside? The impropriety of it was one thing; John would have to be dealt with. But what about Adam's more important objective—to pour out his heart to Madeline? He certainly couldn't do it here, and what if he was too late? What if Madeline had fallen in love with John?

Steeling himself against any of those possibilities, Adam knocked on the door. It opened before him, and John stood there in stockinged feet, his waistcoat off, his shirt open at the neck.

Adam felt his gut twist with dread. *Please, Madeline, be anywhere but here.*

Clenching his jaw, he tried to keep his voice low and controlled. ''Hello, John. I'm looking for Madeline.''

John held a half-eaten chunk of rye bread in his hand. He stopped chewing. ''I left her at your house over an hour ago.''

An odd mixture of relief and frustration welled up inside Adam. He heaved with a shaky breath. ''Did she mention anything about going anywhere? For a walk perhaps?''

John shook his head. "No. Why, is she missing?"

Adam recognized the concern in John's voice, saw the flash of panic in his eyes, and knew John's feelings for Madeline—like Adam's own—were genuine. Although there were times he would have liked to put John on a leaky boat back to Yorkshire, he couldn't fault the young man for his affections. He was young and unattached, hoping to begin a new life, and Madeline was indeed a treasure.

Adam descended the steps. "Don't worry, I'll find her."

Not five seconds later, John was shrugging into his coat. "I'll come with you."

"There's no need."

To his credit, the young man persisted. "You need help, Mr. Coates. This storm's getting worse, and if Madeline's not at home, she might be stranded somewhere."

Adam mounted his horse. "All right. I'll meet you back at my house. We'll see if she's returned there. If not, we'll search the hay barns on the marsh. She might have taken shelter in one of them."

With a grateful nod to John, Adam steered his horse directly into the wind and galloped across the rain-soaked field.

Feeling the chill of the first few raindrops strike her skin, Madeline picked up her skirts and hurried into the yard. She entered the house just as the storm unleashed its fury and the skies opened up with a violent downpour.

Thankful to have outrun it, she removed her shawl

and shook away the wetness. The house was quiet and she felt guilty for having been gone so long, but she had needed some time to herself.

After John had ridden away, she had turned to see Adam through the window, sitting across from Diana in his study, reaching for her hand. It had shaken Madeline, for although she had consciously accepted their love, it was another thing entirely to see them alone together, exchanging intimacies. Gazing at each other. Touching.

A tremendous swell of tears had filled her eyes and she'd had to leave the yard. She'd walked up the hill to the towering old oak, sat on the swing by herself and wept until she couldn't weep any longer. She'd needed to weep, for she had bucked her tears for too long.

She realized that although she'd tried to resist and deny it, her desire for Adam had taken over her entire soul and she could not conquer it. The only way to save her heart was to leave. She would have to make her own future somewhere other than under Adam's roof. Whether or not John Metcalf would be a part of that future, she did not know. That remained to be seen.

So here she stood, feeling a little stronger from the tears now out of her system, and determined once again to move on with her life. This time, she would succeed.

She went to light a candle, for the storm had made the house seem almost as dark as night.

Madeline jumped, however, when Penelope came bounding down the stairs. "It's you!"

Charlie came down behind her. "Where is everyone?"

"What do you mean?" Madeline said.

"There's no one here except for Hilary," Charlie replied in a tense, clipped voice. "We returned from Jacob's house, and saw Lady Thurston riding out of the yard toward the marsh on Penelope's horse. She didn't stop when we called after her, and when we came inside, Hilary didn't know where Lady Thurston had gone. And now it's raining."

Hilary came hurrying down the stairs, too. "Begging your pardon, Miss Oxley. We're dreadfully worried."

"Where's your father?" Madeline asked Charlie and Penelope.

The children shook their heads. "We don't know."

Madeline walked to the window and looked out at the rain streaming down in a forceful, almost horizontal torrent. Huge Scotch pines and maple trees in the yard were swaying in the gusting winds, their branches flapping about. Raindrops noisily battered the glass panes. She thought of her sister, getting caught in this. It wasn't dark yet, but it would be soon. Would she find shelter? Or would she become disoriented and get lost?

"Diana doesn't know her way around," Madeline said. "She's never been down on the marsh. Why would she ride off like that?"

"We don't know," Penelope replied.

"And you've looked everywhere for your father?"

"Yes. He's not here. His horse is gone."

Madeline tried to consider all the possibilities. "Perhaps Diana was following him somewhere."

Hilary put her arm around Penelope. "No, miss. Mr. Coates left over an hour ago. He was looking for *you*."

Madeline pressed her palm to her forehead. "For me? Why? I had just gone for a walk."

They all shrugged.

"This is all my fault," Madeline said. "I should have told someone where I was going." She directed her gaze at Charlie. "Is your horse in the barn?"

"Yes."

"Will you come and help me saddle him?"

"You shouldn't go out in this weather," he said. "Father wouldn't want you to."

"Everyone else is out in it. I might as well be, too. Besides, I think your father might have gone to look for me along the road where I usually go walking. If I can find him, I can tell him that Diana is out in this, too. Don't worry, I know my way around, and there's still time before dark."

"All right." Charlie went to fetch his coat. "But I'm coming with you."

Madeline started upstairs to get her hooded cloak. "I was hoping you'd say that."

Splashing through puddles and squinting into the driving rain, Adam rode his horse into the yard. He quickly dismounted, tethered his mount and went inside. The candles in the hall were lit, and as soon as the door closed behind him, Penelope and Hilary appeared out of the back kitchen.

Penelope ran at him and leaped into his arms. "Father!"

He knelt down to hug her. "I'm fine, darling. It's just a little rain. Has Madeline returned?"

"Yes, Mr. Coates," Hilary replied, "but there's been—"

"Thank goodness," he said, overwhelmed by the relief he felt, hearing that she was safe. "Where is she? I must see her right away."

He rose to his feet and continued to hold Penelope's tiny hand. She did not seem ready to let it go just yet.

"Miss Oxley's not here, sir. She returned not long ago, and discovered that you and Lady Thurston had both gone looking for her, so she went with Charlie to find you."

There was a long, tremulous silence as Adam's brow furrowed with disbelief. "She's gone back out? Diana's out there, too?"

"Yes, sir."

"But this storm is getting worse every minute."

"We know, sir. Miss Oxley assured us she knew her way around, and Charlie went with her. Her ladyship, however, was alone."

He went to the door to look out. "This is disastrous. How long ago did they leave?"

"Miss Oxley and Charlie left about ten minutes ago," Hilary replied, "but my lady has been gone almost an hour."

He gathered his coat collar tighter around his neck and opened the door. A gust of wind blew into the front hall. "You two stay here. I'm going to the marsh to look for them. John Metcalf is on his way. When he gets here, tell him what has happened and send him out to look, too.''

''Be careful, Father!'' Penelope called to him from the shelter of the doorway.

He waved at her, then mounted his horse and galloped through the wind and rain toward the top of the ridge. He paused there briefly to gaze below, but saw nothing through the raging storm. His horse nickered, and Adam had to urge the reluctant steed down the road to the lowlands.

On the marsh, Adam called out to Madeline and Diana, but no reply came. The wind howled like a great beast as it gusted over the grasses. The rain stung his face like steel pellets. He continued along the road toward the river, until he decided to cross over a dale to check one of the hay barns.

Within minutes, he noticed his mount was struggling to manage his footing across the wet grass. The closer they came to the river, the deeper the puddles became until they were sloshing through soggy ground and sinking into the mud. It was clear to Adam that the water was not draining fast enough into the ditches. He gazed uneasily up at the darkening sky, the clouds showing no sign of retreat. He called out Madeline's name again, then Diana's, and searched the vast landscape with squinting, burning eyes.

Though his first concern was to find each of them unharmed, he could not deny the hope that he would find Madeline before Diana did.

He continued toward the river and soon realized

that his horse was up to his knees in water, struggling now with each step.

A slow panic began to move over Adam. He stopped on the marsh and peered through the storm toward the river. Perhaps the dykes were damaged.

"Madeline! Diana!"

He spotted a hay barn in the distance and wondered if they might have gone there to seek shelter. Madeline was smart. She would take Diana there if she'd found her.

"Let's go, boy, just a little farther."

Suddenly his horse slumped beneath him and Adam tumbled off, splashing into ice-cold salt water. The shock of it set his heart racing. The next thing he knew, he was struggling to keep his head above water and touch bottom in what appeared to be a flooded ditch.

His horse snorted and whinnied. A few frenzied seconds of panic passed, then they both managed to stagger out of the trench. Still up to his knees in muddy water, Adam pulled himself onto his horse. He shivered with a chill, then called out, "Madeline!"

He heard a cry from somewhere in the distance. "Madeline!" he called out again.

At last he spotted her, galloping across the swampy ground with John Metcalf and Charlie, and he thanked God for keeping them safe. He started off toward them.

"Adam! Help!" Madeline shouted. "It's Diana! She's been hurt! Terribly hurt!"

The words struck him like a mallet. He rode to meet them on dryer ground. "Where is she?"

Dear God, whatever had happened to Diana tonight, it was his doing and he would never be able to forget it.

"She's in one of the hay barns!" Madeline turned to point toward the center of the marsh. "I couldn't get her out! The wind took the roof off and it collapsed on her! She's not conscious!"

He heard the terror in Madeline's voice, felt it in his own chest. All he could do was urge his horse onward. "Let's go. We've got to get her out of there before this whole marsh floods."

John rode up beside Adam. "It's flooding? Good God, you're drenched."

"I went for a swim. We all will, if we don't reach high ground soon."

By the time they crossed the marsh to where Diana was trapped, the entire ground had flooded knee-deep. John and Adam leaped off their horses.

"Where is she?" Adam asked.

Madeline slid off her horse and splashed into the water, the surface littered with limp blades of grass and weeds. She gasped at the shock of the chill. "She's this way!"

Gathering her heavy, wet skirts in her fists, she waded toward the barn door and went into what remained of the damaged structure.

She pointed. "There!"

Adam saw the vivid color of Diana's blue skirt peeking out from beneath some debris and draping over the side of the loft. He felt a sickening wash of dread. The rest of her was hidden beneath the fallen roof. At least she was not in danger of drowning, he told himself, as he climbed the ladder.

John followed close behind. Carefully they tossed boards and planks aside until they could reach her. Adam touched her arm. "Diana!"

She didn't move. He found the pulse at her wrist. "She's alive!"

He and John pulled broken pieces of wood off her, most of them small shingles and splintered planks. When he uncovered her face, he saw that it was scratched and cut.

One larger beam had pinned her leg and was not so easy to move. "John, can you reach the end of it?"

John moved a few more planks out of the way and crawled to Diana's feet. "Yes, sir, Mr. Coates."

"When I say *go,* we'll lift at the same time. Ready?" They each gripped a section of the beam. "Go!"

Groaning at the impossible effort, they pulled the beam off her leg and tossed it aside. Adam scrambled to see where Diana was injured. He lifted her skirts. Her leg was twisted and her stocking was soaked in blood. "This doesn't look good. We have to get her home. Help me, John, that's it, take her arms. Madeline! Bring my horse!"

They handed Diana down like a heavy, limp doll. A few minutes later, Adam was high on his horse, cradling Diana in his arms. The others mounted and they started off across the sodden marsh toward the ridge.

"John, will you fetch the doctor? Do you know where he lives?"

"Yes, sir." Without hesitation, John pushed ahead, struggling over the flooded ground to the uplands, finally reaching the road and disappearing over the hill.

Charlie rode behind Adam and Madeline, all of them keeping their heads down, protecting their faces from the driving wind and rain. It was dusk now, growing darker by the minute.

"Will she be all right?" Madeline asked.

Adam shifted Diana in his arms. "I don't know. All we can do is pray."

They walked their horses along a fence, reaching the edge of the marsh. The road to the uplands was at last within reach.

Suddenly a low, thunderous roar stopped all of them in their tracks. Charlie, behind them, called out, "Father, what's that noise?"

They could see little through the gray, turbulent dusk, but the noise continued, like the terrifying rumble of the sea. Adam turned in the saddle. "Hurry, Charlie, we've got to reach the road!"

His son was farther back, his horse laboring through the shallow waters that had gradually covered the entire marsh around them. "Dante can't go any faster!"

"Try!" They all continued toward the road. Adam was the first to reach dry, higher ground, with Madeline close behind him. "Madeline, take my horse with Diana and go home. I have to help Charlie."

"But I can't leave you here!"

"You have to. Your sister's life depends upon it."

Madeline reluctantly changed places with him.

Charlie called out, ''Father!''

Both Adam and Madeline turned toward the marsh. From their height just above, they saw a wave sweeping toward them at great speed from the river, taking with it whatever stood in its path: hay, fence rails, cattle and sheep. The dykes had all but disappeared beneath the great tidal surge.

Panic welled up in Adam as he watched his youngest son turn to look over his shoulder. Adam ran down the hill. ''Charlie! Ride!''

He heard Madeline calling out to him but couldn't stop. He ran splashing into the water just as the wave swept up behind Charlie and lifted both him and his horse off their feet.

Chapter Sixteen

Adam continued to sprint toward Charlie, finally being swept off his own feet by the waves. Ice-cold water covered his head. He pushed himself to the surface and swam toward his son, who was flailing in the frigid, rough waters, calling for help.

Reaching Charlie at last and gathering his coat collar in a tight fist, Adam hauled him through the water in the direction of the ridge. "Swim, Charlie!"

Frigid waves crashed over their heads; Adam gasped frantically for air. His heavy coat, tangling around him, made it almost impossible to move and stay afloat in the dark waters, let alone swim to shore. The sound of the water surging all around them was deafening and the water was filling his ears and nostrils. He could taste the salt in his mouth, feel the grit of the marsh mud between his teeth.

Adam heard Charlie make a low cry of defeat behind him. He shouted again, "Swim!" and struggled harder against the weight of his clothes. His fingers, in a tight fist around Charlie's coat, ached from the cold, but he would not let go. He would never let go.

Then, by some great gift of fate, another surge swept them both toward the edge of the marsh and Adam grabbed onto a fence pole, the top barely visible in the gray waters. They made their way along the fence and climbed upward to dry ground, where they collapsed in heaps of exhaustion.

Adam turned to look at Charlie. "Are you hurt?"

Charlie shook his head.

From somewhere outside his muddled consciousness, Adam heard the faint sound of Madeline's voice. "Adam! Adam!"

He sat up. The wind gusted past him, pressing his cold, wet clothing hard against his skin. He managed to wave at her.

"I must take Diana home!" she shouted.

He could barely make out what she'd said beneath the roar of the flood. She rode the horse up the hill toward the house.

Adam gathered Charlie into his arms. "Thank God, you're all right."

Charlie sobbed. "What about Dante?"

Adam gazed out over the waters, looking for the horse. Farther out, he could see the heads of his cattle, drifting toward the sea. He saw an entire barn floating away and breaking up. "I can't see him."

Charlie stood. His teeth chattered, and his voice trembled from his shivering. "What's going to happen to him?"

Adam managed to stand, also. "I don't know, Charlie. We'll just have to wait and hope he makes it to dry ground. But for now, we've got to get you home."

* * *

Madeline rode into the yard, her muscles aching from the strain of keeping Diana's limp body on the horse. Just as she approached the door, John Metcalf came galloping in behind.

He dismounted and rushed to Madeline's side. "The doctor's on his way!"

Madeline handed Diana down to John, who carried her to the house.

Hilary and Penelope must have been watching at the window, for they were already there waiting, holding the front door open for him. Madeline quickly led the horses into the barn and tethered them there, then she ran through the pounding rain to the house. She was never so glad to walk into a warm home and see candles burning, smell a fire in the hearth.

She unhooked her cloak and handed it soaking wet to Hilary. "Bring hot water and towels to Diana's room right away. She's badly hurt." Madeline picked up her wet skirts and bounded up the stairs.

She hurried to Diana's room. John was laying her sister on the bed, while Penelope lit candles. When the room brightened, Penelope froze at the foot of the bed, staring dumbfounded at Diana's blood-soaked stocking. Her brown eyes were as big as saucers.

Madeline rested a hand on Penelope's shoulder. "Sweetheart, go and watch for your father. He and Charlie are on their way, and they'll need warm blankets and hot tea as soon as they arrive."

Penelope pulled her horrified gaze away from Diana and nodded. Seeming grateful for a task to focus upon, she turned and left the room.

Madeline moved to the bedside and laid a hand on

Diana's forehead. "She's chilled. Let's get her under the covers." John helped Madeline pull the quilt around Diana. "When is the doctor going to arrive?"

"He had to saddle his horse. He should be here any minute."

Madeline tried to catch her breath. Everything had happened so fast.

"Why hasn't Diana opened her eyes or moved at all? I'm so worried, John. Is this normal?"

"My uncle fell from his horse once, and didn't move for two days."

"Two days? Really? Then what happened?"

"He simply woke up one afternoon and said, 'Who let the fire go out?' He had a few bumps and bruises, but he recovered."

Madeline gazed warmly at John. "Thank you for helping us. We were lucky to meet up with you."

"It wasn't luck. Mr. Coates came to my homestead. It was *you* he was looking for. He was worried, and I offered to help him find you."

She remembered that she had gone for a walk without telling anyone, and all this was surely her fault. Would she ever be able to forgive herself? What if Diana did not recover? Good Lord, she couldn't bear to think of it.

Hilary appeared with the towels, and Madeline pushed her fears aside and proceeded to gently remove Diana's stocking and begin to wash the blood off her leg.

There was some commotion downstairs, the sound of boots thumping over the floor and a lot of questions being asked at once. "John, go and see if that's the doctor."

John left Madeline alone with Diana to cleanse her wounds.

Perhaps it was better that Diana was unconscious, Madeline thought miserably, for if she were awake, the pain would be excruciating. It was obvious to Madeline that bones were broken. How many and where, she couldn't tell, but no normal leg ever looked as misshapen and swollen as Diana's leg looked now.

More footsteps came thumping up the stairs, and the doctor—a distinguished, gray-haired man with gold spectacles—entered the room carrying a brown leather bag. He set it down on the floor and approached the bedside, immediately checking the pulse at Diana's neck, then feeling her head for a fever. His intelligent eyes assessed Diana's full form and settled on her leg. "That looks serious."

Madeline could tell by his voice that he was a Yorkshireman. She moved out of his way to allow him room to examine her sister.

A swell of fear squeezed Madeline's heart. "How is she?"

"It's too soon to tell." He squeezed Diana's calf and all around her knee. "She hasn't regained consciousness at all?"

"No."

He continued to apply pressure in different spots. "The leg is definitely broken. In at least three places." He shook his head ruefully. "Four places."

Madeline tried to keep her voice steady, even

though inside, her stomach was rolling with queasiness. "She's not going to lose her leg, is she?"

The doctor glanced up at her only briefly. "I'll do my best, Miss Oxley."

He moved around the bed and pulled Diana's lower eyelids down with his thumb, then checked around her scalp for a head injury. "Things look fine here. Perhaps she fainted because of the pain." He went to his bag and pulled out a couple of splints. "I'm going to try and set the leg now, while she's still out. Will you stay? I could use your help."

Madeline stepped forward. "Doctor, you couldn't make me leave if you tried."

He nodded approvingly at her and began to roll up his loose linen sleeves. "I'm afraid this is going to take a while."

As soon as Charlie was wrapped in a blanket and nursing a cup of hot broth in the kitchen, Adam hurried upstairs to check on Diana and Madeline. The door to Diana's bedchamber was closed, John was sitting on a chair in the dimly lit hall, and there was an eerie howling from the wind outside. Rain was beating the windowpanes and something was knocking somewhere—a barn door perhaps, swinging open and banging against a wall.

Adam paused at the top of the stairs, imagining what was going on behind Diana's closed door. He glanced at John. "What's happening?"

"The doctor is setting her leg. She still hasn't woken up."

"I suppose that's a good thing at the moment."

They waited silently in the hall. Adam recalled his last conversation with Diana, how he'd broken off their engagement and admitted he was in love with her sister. If he had known how angry she would be, or how determined she would be to find Madeline, he wouldn't have left her alone.

A moment later, the door opened slowly and Madeline appeared. Adam took an anxious step forward. John leaped from his chair.

Madeline still wore her wet clothes. Her hair had fallen out of its knot on her head and hung wet and limp upon her shoulders. Her face was pale and ashen. She staggered to the side.

Adam lunged forward to grab onto her at the same time John did. They each held one of her arms.

"Sit down, Madeline," Adam said. They helped her into the chair. "What's happened? How is she?"

Madeline slid a hand over her hair, pushing it away from her face. "She's still unconscious, but we managed to set the broken bones in her leg."

Relief washed through Adam.

Madeline continued. "But the doctor's not sure if…if she's going to be able to keep her leg. We'll have to wait and see. Even if she does keep it, she might not be able to walk again. At the very least, she'll need a cane. That's the most we can hope for, and we'll be lucky if she manages that."

The idea of Diana having to learn to walk again, or being confined to a pushchair for the rest of her life was like a knife stabbing Adam in the gut. He was responsible for this—for bringing Diana here to this strange land, for breaking her heart and crippling her at the same time.

"I just wish she would wake up." Madeline sobbed with despair.

Adam knelt before her and squeezed her shoulder. "She will. We must all pray, and have faith."

Madeline covered her face with hands that were shaking violently. "This is all my fault."

"It's *not*."

"Yes, I went for a walk without telling anyone and I stayed away too long. With the storm coming, Diana must have been worried about me and gone searching. It was wrong for me to go off like that, not thinking about anyone but myself."

Adam pulled her hands away from her face. "It was *not* your fault, Madeline. I assure you."

"But you were looking for me, too!"

Adam gazed into her beautiful pain-filled eyes and knew he had to convince her that she was the most innocent in all this. He glanced up at John, who was watching uneasily.

"John, will you excuse us? I need to speak to Madeline privately."

God, Adam did not want to tell her now, not like this. But he could not let her go on thinking this was her fault. He had to take control of this situation and, no matter what the consequences, confess the truth.

Chapter Seventeen

John left Madeline and Adam alone in the upstairs hall outside Diana's room. Madeline watched Adam rise to his feet and felt a prickling of uneasiness, for he looked as if he were going to deliver shocking, terrible news. Though what could possibly be worse than what had already occurred that day, she could not imagine.

Adam held out his hand. "Come with me."

Despite her uncertainty, she accepted his hand and followed him to the reading corner at the end of the hall. Floor-to-ceiling bookcases surrounded them, and Adam lit the candles. He sat down in an upholstered chair opposite Madeline, just as he had sat opposite Diana earlier in the day.

"I must tell you something, Madeline."

"What is it?" Madeline stood. "Good Lord, Charlie's not hurt, is he?"

Adam gazed up at her, his face solemn. "Charlie's fine. Please, sit down."

She did as he asked and waited shakily for him to speak.

"God, this is difficult. I don't know how to say this. I don't *want* to say this now of all times, but I must. Madeline, what happened to Diana is not your fault. It is mine."

She stared blankly at him as a numbness poured through her limbs. "How so?"

A muscle trembled at his jaw and he hesitated before answering. "It is my fault because this afternoon, while you were outside with John, I told Diana that I could not marry her."

His words struck Madeline like a bucket of cold water in the face. "But...why?"

Adam met her gaze directly. A vein stood out at his temple. Madeline sat across from him in shock, not certain why he was telling her all of this now.

"I couldn't marry her because I don't love her, Madeline."

She stammered in bewilderment, "But you said you did."

"That was before I knew you."

"But all along, you wanted her to come. The picture...the letters..."

Adam squeezed her hands. "I know this is the worst time imaginable to have this conversation, but as soon as Diana wakes up, you're going to hear the truth anyway, and I would rather you hear it from me. She went riding alone because of what happened between *us*. I told her that I could not marry her, because...because I was in love with you."

For a long time Madeline sat in her chair, immobile, listening only to the sound of her blood pounding in her ears. She stared blankly at Adam.

"You can't be."

He bowed his head.

"You can't possibly love me. I'm nothing."

"You're not nothing. You're everything."

"No, you're confused, Adam, because of what happened today."

"When Diana wakes up," he said, "she is going to tell you exactly what happened today, and make me out to be a rake and a philanderer. She will loathe and despise me more than ever now, because of the accident, and I cannot blame her for that.

"But you must know that I was searching for you so that I could have the chance to explain my feelings in my own way, and to tell you that I am not a dishonorable man. No matter what she tells you, and no matter what you choose to believe, please know that I have grown to care for you deeply and ardently, Madeline, even though I did my best to fight it." His blue eyes bored into hers. "Believe me, I felt that a break with Diana was the right thing to do. I had no idea any of this would happen. If I had known, I would have handled things differently, I assure you."

Adam paused for a moment. He closed his eyes and held them shut before opening them to continue.

"The truth is, when I brought you with me to meet Lord Blackthorne's ship, I had a letter in my pocket which I intended to send to London, a letter which instructed my solicitor there to halt the proxy marriage or annul it if necessary. I had hoped to prevent Diana from coming, to retract my proposal and make things right so that I would be free to love *you*."

Madeline's insides shuddered with an odd mixture

of disbelief and despair. She had long dreamed of hearing these words from Adam's lips, even while she was forcing herself to accept that it would never happen.

Now that it was real she found that she could barely believe it. How could he want dull, stubborn, mousy Madeline over beautiful, bewitching Diana?

"I don't understand. When did your feelings change, and why didn't you tell me?"

"They changed very gradually over time, and I didn't tell you because I was trying to fight it. I didn't want to fall in love with you. I was engaged to your sister, and by the time I was ready to take steps toward winning your heart, it was too late. Diana stepped off the boat."

Madeline covered her face with her hands. "I can't believe this is happening."

He reached for her hand. "Forgive me, Madeline. I didn't mean to cause you or Diana pain."

"But you have, and I don't know what to do. I don't know what you want from me."

"I only wanted you to know the truth."

"And what am I supposed to do with it? I can't be happy about it. I can't accept your love and fall willingly into your arms. Diana is wounded and broken, she may never walk again, and now to learn that she is heartbroken, too?"

A part of Madeline wanted to scream at Adam for waiting until this moment to tell her this. For telling her at all! For what could she do now, but suffer with guilt for the tragedy that had befallen Diana, and a lifetime of regrets for what might have been, if things had been different?

She cleared her throat. "I don't know what to say, Adam."

"Say anything. Scream at me if you like, for I was so wrong about what I thought would make me happy. You must think me a foolish man."

Foolish? No more foolish than I.

Madeline knew she was as much to blame for this accident as Adam, for whether he realized it or not, she had helped cause whatever confusion he was experiencing now. She had acted like a wife to him in all ways but one. She had supported him, encouraged intimacy in their conversations. She'd taken care of his family and cooked for them, and she had been as charming as she knew how to be.

On top of that, Madeline had entertained terrible thoughts, wishing Diana would jilt Adam again so that she herself could pick up the pieces. Or she'd wished that Adam would jilt Diana so that for once in her life, Madeline—the ugly duckling sister—could be the chosen one.

The rain battered against the window, the panes rattled in the wind. Adam and Madeline sat in stony silence.

"I'm so sorry, Madeline," he said. "Will you ever be able to forgive me?"

Madeline felt tears coming, tried to subdue them, but it was no use. She could not be with Adam now, despite what he was saying. She could never be so cruel, so disloyal to her sister when her future was so uncertain. Madeline breathed shakily and forced herself to speak.

"This has been a terrible day, Adam. I doubt you even know what you're saying."

Head bowed low, he shook his head. "I know exactly what I'm saying."

"I'm sorry," she said, her voice quivering, "but I have to go and be with Diana."

Madeline pulled her hand from his and rose from her chair.

"Wait, don't go yet. I need to know. If this hadn't happened, would you have cared for me? Would you ever have been able to love me as a man?"

She stared blankly at him. Her heart was reeling with chaos! She was aching inside. Aching! She loved Adam more than anything in the world and he had no idea. None.

A barn had collapsed on her sister, while the entire world was collapsing around Madeline. How could she possibly manage so much tragedy?

Her voice quavered as she spoke. "How can you not know the answer to that question?"

His face went pale.

She forced herself to search for the courage to continue. "Did you never once suspect that I loved you the first moment I stepped off the ship, and that I have been struggling all this time to crush that love? To defeat my feelings and stop wanting what I believed was forbidden to me?"

Her response was like a blow to Adam's chest. The wind sailed out of his lungs. "You cared for me? But you never revealed it."

"How could I? I was imprisoned by the same things you were. You were engaged to my sister, and I believed that you loved her."

He took a cautious step toward her and touched her soft cheek with the back of a finger. "Madeline...." Her eyes were wide and bloodshot as she gazed up at him. Adam's heart swelled with a relentless, overwhelming love for her. "Don't tell me this can never be."

She blinked, as if in some kind of stupor.

He couldn't stop himself. She was so beautiful, uncertain and disheveled as she was. He lowered his mouth to hers.

A tiny little moan escaped her as he brushed his lips over hers, reveling in the gentle tentativeness of the kiss. Her lips parted and he let his tongue mingle with hers as he cupped her whole face in his big hands. How long he had waited to do just this.

He pulled back from the kiss and whispered as he rested his forehead against hers. "Please tell me we can work through this."

She stepped away from him, her lashes sweeping downward. She sucked in a breath. Was she going to cry?

God, he wanted to hold her. He reached for her, but she took another step back, almost as if she feared him.

"I don't know what your intentions are with Diana," she said. "That is between the two of you, but you must know that nothing can happen between us now. I cannot betray my sister and run off with you, not after what has happened to her. How could I do

that? She still loves you, Adam.'' Madeline put a
hand on her stomach, as if she felt ill. "If she wishes
to return to Yorkshire, I will have to go with her.''

Hands trembling visibly, she backed away from
Adam and returned to Diana's bedchamber.

Adam stared after her for a long time, then leaned
back against the wall and sank numbly with despair
to the floor.

Madeline wasn't sure if it was the morning light
beaming in through the lace curtains or something
else that had awakened her, but as soon as she opened
her eyes, she found herself lying next to Diana, her
head on the same pillow, listening to her sister moan.

Instantly wide-awake, Madeline sat up. "Diana,
I'm here. You're going to be all right. Can you
speak?''

She continued to coax her sister to consciousness,
and when those big blue eyes fluttered open to stare
at the bed's canopy above them, Madeline shouted
with glee and hugged Diana. "Thank you, God, thank
you!''

"Where am I?" Diana asked groggily, both confusion and irritation evident in her voice. "I don't feel
very well.''

Madeline reached for the basin on the bedside table, and Diana retched into it. She continued to moan
with confusion and discomfort.

"My leg…dear God in heaven, it's excruciating.
And my head…what has happened?" She tried to sit
up, but pain forced her back down. Suddenly she

screamed, a shrill, piercing shriek full of agony and fury. ''What happened to me!''

Panic speeding through her, Madeline stroked her sister's forehead. ''You were hurt. There was a storm. The barn collapsed on you, but we got you out. You're safe now.''

''Safe!'' She slapped Madeline's hands away. ''You call this safe? My leg! Get off the bed! Every time you move it hurts!''

Madeline quickly slid off, as gently as possible. ''I'll send for the doctor again.''

''Again? He's already been here? Why am I in so much pain if he's already been here? What kind of doctor is he? Some kind of quack? Ow!''

''He was very good. Your leg was broken in four places, and he set all the bones last night while you were unconscious.''

Diana writhed on the bed, moaning and groaning, so Madeline seized the opportunity to dash out of the room to fetch help. She met Hilary in the hall. Still in her nightdress and running from her room, she pulled a shawl around her shoulders. ''Miss Oxley, is her ladyship awake?''

''Yes, you must ask Mr. Coates to fetch the doctor again. Lady Thurston is in dreadful pain and I don't know how to help her.''

Looking flustered, Hilary nodded. Madeline quickly returned to Diana's room.

''Why aren't you doing anything?'' Diana shouted hysterically. She began to sob and cry and Madeline ran to the bedside to hold her hand.

Just then, Adam practically skidded into the doorway, his white shirt untucked and open at the collar. He froze there with a look of concern.

Diana turned her head on the pillow. When she saw him, she cried out. "Adam! I've been hurt! My leg is broken!"

Madeline saw the guilt and misery in his eyes. "I know. I'm going to get the doctor. He'll be able to help you."

Adam hastened from the doorway, his footsteps pounding briskly down the stairs.

Clenching her teeth against the pain, Diana squeezed Madeline's hand. "How could this have happened?"

"It was the storm. It came up very suddenly."

"Storm? I don't remember a storm."

"It was raining. That's why you went into the barn."

Diana shook her head, refusing to believe what Madeline was telling her. "No, no, I don't remember that. I would never have gone out in the rain."

Madeline gazed helplessly at Diana, trying to jog her sister's memory, even though a barn collapsing on her was not something she would likely *want* to remember. "You went riding alone."

"Alone? Why would I do that?"

A shadow of alarm moved over Madeline. She spoke slowly, cautiously. "Don't you remember what happened yesterday?"

Diana's expression hardened as she concentrated. After a moment or two, she began to tremble. She shook her head. "I...I'm not sure. I know I had biscuits and apple butter for breakfast." She squeezed

Madeline's hand tighter. "I can't remember anything after that." Her face contorted with a sob. "Madeline, what's happening to me? I can't remember! I can't remember!"

Chapter Eighteen

Dr. Hudry sedated Diana and relieved her pain with an anodyne draft, after which she closed her eyes and quietly drifted into sleep. Madeline sank back in her chair, still feeling as if the world, just like the hay barn, had collapsed upon her shoulders.

"I don't understand. Why can't she remember anything beyond breakfast? The barn roof collapsing—I can conceive of forgetting that, but the whole day?"

Dr. Hudry packed his instruments into his bag. "It's not uncommon with a head injury to lose some short-term memory. I've seen it before."

"Will she ever regain it?"

"Difficult to say. She might remember later today, when she wakes up. Or she might never remember." The doctor closed his bag. "You should count yourselves lucky that's it's only one day she forgets. I've heard of patients being completely unable to remember anything. Not even their names or where they live. What's one day, after all?"

It was a very important day, Madeline thought anxiously.

The doctor moved toward the door. "The thing you must concentrate upon is helping Lady Thurston walk again. Try and be positive about things. She will be in pain for a time, but if she has loved ones here to support her and encourage her to get out of bed, she'll heal much faster. Give her something to occupy her mind, something to look forward to. Plan her wedding to Mr. Coates, for instance."

Madeline had to work hard to acknowledge the suggestion with a smile.

The doctor opened the bedchamber door and stopped to speak to Adam, who was pacing back and forth in the hall. "I gave Lady Thurston something to ease her pain. She should sleep for a while. I'll return this evening to check on her again."

"Thank you, Dr. Hudry. I appreciate your coming."

The doctor descended the stairs, and Madeline met Adam's gaze. He slowly entered the room.

"Are you all right?" he asked.

She nodded. "As well as can be expected under the circumstances. But we must talk, Adam. Alone."

He gestured toward the reading corner in the hall, where they had spoken the night before. They both sat down in the same chairs.

Madeline perched on the edge of her seat, not quite sure how to tell Adam about Diana's memory loss, or what they should do about it once she did tell him. She cleared her throat and decided to blurt it out quickly and go straight to the heart of the matter.

"I'm afraid Diana's head injury was rather serious. She cannot remember anything about what happened yesterday. She doesn't remember why she went riding alone, or anything about your conversation with her. The only thing she remembers is what she had for breakfast.''

Adam took in this news. It was difficult to imagine not being able to remember something that happened only yesterday, not to mention something as important as an engagement being broken. It took him a moment or two to comprehend it.

''Will there be any long term effects on the health of her mind?'' he asked.

Madeline answered him with a clear voice. ''The doctor assured me that a memory loss like this is common, and that we shouldn't concern ourselves with it, as it's only one day. As long as she remembers everything else, the important thing is to help her walk again.''

Adam pinched the bridge of his nose. ''She thinks we are still engaged.''

Madeline nodded. ''That seems to be the state of things at the moment.''

Adam stood up to pace the hall in front of the reading corner. ''Good God, I can't break with her *again*. At least not now.''

Madeline sat quietly for a moment. ''I'm relieved to hear you say that. What you decide to do in the long run is your decision, of course, but I must ask that you not tell her the truth right away. Please wait until she is feeling better. The doctor even suggested that we keep Diana occupied and lift her spirits by planning your wedding.''

"Our wedding! That will be taking things a little far, don't you think?"

Thank God, Madeline was reasonable about it, and nodded. "Yes, I think it would be a mistake to mislead her in that way, unless you think you might change your mind."

He gazed at her in the dim morning light shining in through the window. If only she knew how ridiculous such a notion was. Did she still not believe he truly loved her? If she thought he could forget about what he had said to her the night before, pretend it never happened and marry another, she underestimated his feelings, to be sure.

"Do you think I should?" he asked, testing her, for he had not been able to give up hope that she would one day accept his love.

On the other hand, if she pushed him to marry her sister, he would know for certain that Madeline was firmly resolved never to accept it. Ever. "Do you think I owe it to Diana?"

Madeline responded in a calm, indifferent tone that made him doubt she could ever care for him the way he cared for her.

"I think you owe it to yourself to do the right thing." She could not have been more cryptic.

"The right thing?" He heard the anger rising in his voice, but could do nothing to stop it. "What is the right thing, exactly? Marry Diana out of pity? Out of duty or guilt? I've already done that once in my life, and I promise you, it does not bode well for future happiness for either party involved. Besides, Diana already married a man who didn't love her. I doubt she would be happy with a repeat of that particular past.''

''But perhaps you might grow to love her again. It was not that long ago that you wanted to—''

Adam dropped to one knee at her feet, to stop her from saying anything more. ''This is difficult enough as it is, Madeline. What happened to Diana is killing me inside. I feel responsible, and yes, there is a part of me that thinks I should marry her, to try and make up for what happened. But I can't let pity rule my head and my heart, for I would not be doing Diana any favors. I can't change the fact that she was injured, no more than I can pretend to love her. She would know the truth, and it would chip away at her heart every day for the rest of her life until she knew nothing but misery. Diana may remain here as long as she wishes, and I will do everything in my power to give her all that she needs to get well—the best medical attention, the best food, the best entertainment to keep her spirits up. But I cannot marry her, Madeline. I will not make the same mistake twice in my life. It would be a disservice to both of us.''

He would have liked to add that he could not marry Diana—or anyone for that matter—because there was only one person in the world for him, and that person was Madeline. If circumstances were different, he would take her into his arms right now and never let her go.

Without revealing the slightest weakness or change of heart, Madeline simply nodded. ''I understand. We'll try to avoid the subject when we are with Diana, at least until she is stronger. We'll continue as we were when Lord Blackthorne was here, and pretend everything is fine. I can do that. Can you?''

"It is more than clear to me that you can do it, Madeline. You seem completely in control of your emotions.''

Why did that bother him so bloody much? Would he have preferred her to melt into a puddle of tears and tell him she loved him, too, and cry over what could never be? Or to leap into his arms and beg him to hold her, just for one single, glorious moment? Or kiss her, just once again, as he had the night before?

That was what *he* wanted to plead for, why he was on his knee in front of her now, wanting to pull her closer and make promises he knew she would never let him keep....

"I *am* in control of them,'' she said, her tone disturbingly controlled. Madeline stood. "I've learned to keep my feelings to myself, and deal with them in my own way.''

She made a move to return to Diana's room, but Adam stood and stopped her. He took hold of her arm and pulled her to face him. "Perhaps what you really need to learn is how to accept that you are worthy of love. Perhaps you need to learn how to open up to people.''

Her brow furrowed with incredulity, as if she could barely believe such a suggestion. "Why would I do that? It would be like opening a wound, when it's much less painful to close it up and keep it that way.''

"Feelings are not wounds, Madeline.''

"They are to me, because love has only ever been

painful. My feelings make me vulnerable, Adam, and lately, especially lately, I prefer to be impenetrable.''

She pulled away from him and he let her go. The door slammed closed behind her.

Later that morning, Jacob arrived to check on the family and inspect the marsh with Adam, who was still reeling with bewilderment over his conversation with Madeline. He was treading in strange territory, for Madeline was the complete opposite of Jane, who had wept and wailed over the smallest disappointment, or smashed things when she became frustrated or angry. He had always known where he stood with Jane, especially when he stood in the hall, locked out of their bedroom for the night.

Madeline's composure and unwillingness to express any of her feelings, on the other hand, was beyond reserved or constrained—it almost seemed as if she was denying the fact that she had a heart.

Yet, over the past few weeks, he'd come to believe he'd found his true mate. He had been certain that what lived beneath Madeline's polite exterior was perfection. They had everything in common. She always seemed so calm and levelheaded, which was one of the things he loved most about her.

How could his feelings have been real, if she had no heart and no affection for him in return? How could he feel so connected to her?

Perhaps it wasn't real, he thought soberly. Perhaps he had been dreaming again, wanting what he wanted—the perfect woman—instead of what was real.

He and Jacob rode their horses to the top of the

ridge to overlook the marsh below, and what they saw pulled Adam's attention back to where it presently belonged: on his land and his livelihood.

That, at least, was something he could be sure was all *too* real.

Speechless, Adam and Jacob stared at the inconceivable scene while they each contemplated the enormous losses.

By the hour of the day, Adam knew that the tide had already receded but was now on its way back in. The damage to the dykes must have been substantial, he thought, for most of the great marsh was still flooded with seawater. The lush green grasses, the clover, the goldenrod—all that once fluttered and swayed in the wind—it was gone, completely submerged, transformed into a muddy brown swamp that produced a sickening stench and a dismal fog. Carcasses of dead cattle dotted the area, and fence planks lay scattered about, floating and bobbing in dirty, shallow pools. A number of hay barns lay in disordered piles of lumber. Others had simply vanished from where they had once been.

My whole world is in ruins.

"It's a good thing we drove that herd to Halifax when we did," Jacob said with quiet resignation, "or we would have lost everything."

Adam clicked his tongue to urge his horse further along the top of the ridge. "It's going to be a long winter."

"What will we do for feed, Father?"

"We'll get what we can from the uplands, and purchase the rest. It'll be enough to get us through, though we won't see any profit. We'll all have to be frugal. No more pretty scarves for Mary, Jacob, or toys for the baby."

Jacob followed quietly behind. "What about next year? Will this drain off by then? Will we be able to start fresh?"

Adam wished he had better news for his son, but alas, he did not. Jacob, however, was a strong and bright young man, and Adam knew he would find a way to provide for his wife and child. They would all work together as a family.

"Even if we manage to repair the damage to the dykes," Adam said, "it will take a few years for the rain to rinse out the salt."

"A few years? What will we do in the meantime?"

"We'll farm the uplands. We've always had enough to meet our needs. We'll just have to forgo the luxuries."

They rode down the ridge road to the edge of the marsh, where the muddy floodwater was lapping up against the hill.

"I'm going to call a meeting of the dyke holders," Adam said, "and we'll vote on what should be rebuilt. I suggest you prepare yourself for a great deal of dirty work in the next few months, Jacob. We'll have to locate the breaks, repair them, then we'll be up to our elbows in marsh mud—digging ditches and trenches to drain it. And if we have to, we'll build new dykes, high enough and strong enough to hold back the sea, for we will not surrender to it, Jacob, even if it is determined to defeat us."

Jacob smiled at Adam with admiration. "Your confidence is contagious, Father."

Adam only wished he could be that confident about his future where Madeline was concerned.

Chapter Nineteen

The storm, they later learned, had caused the Fundy tides to rise to a level five feet higher than ever before, an unusual and extraordinary occurrence that no one had been able to predict. It took six days for the tides to return to normal levels, during which time Adam, Jacob and George, along with other local farmers, surveyed the dykes and searched for breaks and fractures.

To their surprise and relief, they found the damage minimal. Most of the dykes had held strong against the battering of the currents. It had been the extraordinary height of the tides that had caused a natural overflowing.

They also recovered a number of stray cows and goats, as well as Charlie's horse, Dante, who had managed to escape the flood farther down along the ridge.

During those days of investigation and decision making, Madeline learned that the dance at the Aikens' barn had been canceled, and to her own chagrin, she was relieved. She had not been looking forward to spending an evening with John Metcalf, trying to pretend that she was interested in him. That would have been too difficult, especially now after all that had happened.

So Madeline spent her days and nights nursing Diana's broken leg and keeping her company in her bedchamber.

Madeline also had hot soup dumped in her lap, had her hand slapped for checking for fevers, and had been hollered at for keeping the window open when Diana was too cold, or for keeping it closed when Diana was too hot.

Today Madeline found herself in the unfortunate position of having to give Diana a sponge bath. Cautiously, apprehensively, she approached the bed.

"Get that cold cloth out of my sight!" Diana shouted. "It must be your callused hands. You can't tell if the water is steaming hot or ice cold! I want another bucket of *hot* water brought up here! *Hilary!*"

Hilary came scurrying into the room.

"I'll get it," Madeline replied quickly, trying to quiet Diana. "You don't need to yell." She dropped the offending cloth into the basin on the washstand and left Hilary to baby-sit her ladyship.

Taking a few deep breaths to summon her necessary quota of daily patience, which was becoming more and more difficult to fill, Madeline ventured downstairs. She entered the kitchen and fetched a bucket, then went outside to fill it with water.

As she drew the bucket up out of the well, she thought about her relationship with her sister. It had been years since she and Diana had lived in the same house. Madeline had forgotten how demanding and vocal her sister could be about every little discomfort. It was one area where they differed greatly, for Madeline preferred to deal with her own discomforts quietly, by herself. Madeline wondered suddenly how it was possible they could have come from the same mother.

Madeline carried the heavy, sloshing bucket into the kitchen and poured it into the pot over the fire. She wiped a sleeve across her forehead and sank into a chair at the worktable.

Madeline then recalled the string of housekeepers they'd had when she was young. None had stayed more than a few months, until kind Mrs. Stapleton arrived and remained with them for ten years. Madeline had thought the woman simply had no other aspirations, for the others had always explained their reasons for leaving: a more profitable opportunity, a change of heart or a desire to take up a different profession.

Perhaps—as Madeline considered it now with a trifle more perspective—the only reason Mrs. Stapleton had been different from the others and had stayed with them was because Diana had left shortly after she was hired. Diana had gone away to live with their aunt in London and learn how to be a proper lady.

The house had become astonishingly quiet after that.

The sight of steam from the pot pulled Madeline from her thoughts, and she rose from her chair. As she carefully filled her bucket, she thought of Diana's many complaints that morning, and compared them to the number of complaints Diana had voiced the few times Adam had visited with her to read to her or play cards.

Whenever Adam walked into the room, Diana became perfectly demure and brave in the face of her pain. To be honest, it made Madeline angry enough to spit. Out of sheer agony, she would leave and hand her duties over to Hilary, for Madeline couldn't bear to watch Diana fluttering her lashes at Adam, using all her accomplished skills to bewitch him.

"Making soup?" said someone behind her.

No, not *someone*. She could not pretend to think it was anyone other than Adam.

Madeline straightened and faced him. His clothes were filthy with ground-in mud, his boots caked with it. He moved to the wash bucket to rinse his big, dirty hands.

Madeline set the heavy bucket on the floor. "I'm taking hot water upstairs for Diana."

His ebony hair, pulled back in a loose queue and tied with a leather string, gleamed in the late-morning light. Madeline watched him from behind as he rolled up his sleeves and washed his hands and forearms, then reached for a cloth to dry them.

He'd never looked stronger to her, more virile. She imagined him down on the marsh, thrusting a dyking spade into the tough earth with his big boot, using all his strength to haul sod.

His intense eyes cut through the distance between them. He dropped the towel onto the worktable and strode toward her.

She took an instinctive step back and realized uncomfortably that she had barely looked him in the eye since the morning after the accident, when she'd pulled away from him. They had hardly spoken a word to each other since. All they'd done was brush by each other on the way in and out of Diana's room, or avoid speaking to each other at the dinner table. Madeline had slammed the door in his face six days ago and driven a sharp wedge into their friendship.

Friendship? What kind of aberrant friendship was it? she wondered suddenly as he stopped before her, staring down at her in silence. Her heart was bouncing off her ribs!

Adam was so close she could smell his musky scent. She bent to pick up her bucket.

Adam touched her shoulder to stop her. "Don't go."

Her heart jolted at the feel of his strong hand upon her. She could feel the heat of it through her clothes, and it distressed her in every possible way. "I have to. Diana is waiting."

"She can wait a little longer. You've been caring for her continually around the clock. Stay and have some tea."

Reluctantly Madeline surrendered. She moved to the hearth and poured the hot water back into the pot on the fire to keep it warm, while Adam spooned tea leaves into the teapot.

The silence between them was excruciating.

Madeline sat down, fumbling and grasping for some casual conversation. Anything would do.

"Where is Penelope today?"

"She's at Jacob's place, helping Mary with the

baby. I believe that child is ready to be a mother, and she's only eight.''

"She's a wonderful girl, Adam. You should be proud.''

He gave her an appreciative look. Not that it mattered what kind of look it was. It was a *look*, an acknowledgment after days and days of disregard that she certainly deserved for being so cold and unfeeling toward him. Madeline felt her insides warm a little.

"Were you able to save any of your hay crop?'' Madeline asked.

"None. But the profits from the herd we just drove to Halifax will keep the animals from starving over the winter.''

"What about you and the children?''

He poured water into the teapot. "The crops in the high fields survived, so we'll have plenty to eat. We just won't be making any luxury purchases.''

"Thank goodness. What about the marsh? Will you be able to rebuild it?''

"With hard work, yes. All the farmers have been doing their share, and we've already begun the repairs. The floodwaters are draining off. Now, it's just a matter of maintenance over time.''

They talked more about the marsh and the flood and what the future held, and were so deep in conversation, they didn't hear Hilary descending the stairs. She walked into the kitchen and found Madeline and Adam sitting across from each other at the table.

Hilary hesitated awkwardly in the doorway. "Begging your pardon, Miss Oxley. I don't mean to interrupt, but Lady Thurston is waiting for her bathwater.''

Madeline cleared her throat and stood. ''Of course, it's ready now. I just have to—''

Adam interrupted. ''Hilary, please tell Lady Thurston that Madeline requires a cup of tea, and that she will be up with the water after she's had a moment to rest.''

Hilary gazed with bewilderment at the two of them. She looked uncomfortable with delivering the message.

Adam stood. ''I'll tell her myself if you like.''

Madeline gazed at him in horror. ''No, that's not necessary. Hilary, tell Lady Thurston I will be right there.''

She glanced back at Adam and saw his disappointment by the rise and fall of his chest. Hilary left the kitchen, and Madeline glared hotly at Adam. ''Just what did you intend to tell her?''

He sank back into his chair. ''Nothing, Madeline. I was only going to tell her you were having tea. She wouldn't have complained about it to *me*.''

Madeline sighed with relief. She sat down.

''Are you worried I'm going to tell her the truth before you think she's ready?'' Adam asked. ''I have to admit, I'm tempted.''

''Please, don't. Wait a little longer, until she's on her feet.''

''Fine. I will wait until then.'' His gaze lifted slowly to meet hers. ''But what about after that? If you return to Yorkshire with her, will you stay there?''

What was he getting at?

"Adam, I thought we weren't going to talk about this again."

"Why not? Have you no longings, Madeline? No desires? We've been ignoring each other for days now, and I've been forced to follow your lead, closing myself off to what I really feel and putting on a damn show for the rest of the world. What is it? Are you truly dead inside, or can I be optimistic and flatter myself by thinking that maybe someday, you might care for me just a little?"

An unwelcome tension wrapped tightly around Madeline. "There is no point in hoping. It only sets us up for disappointment."

"Is that a fact? Well, I can't help hoping. Nor can I stop wanting you."

She couldn't believe he was being so open after six days of complete silence.

He held the tea strainer over her cup and poured, then shoved her cup across the table toward her.

Madeline kept her eyes on her tea. Her heart was racing inside her chest like a runaway stallion. No one before Adam had ever spoken so candidly to her before, with such intense, pent-up anger. Nor had anyone ever told her that they actually *wanted* her.

Certainly not when Diana was within their grasp.

"Diana might be an invalid," she said, groping for words. "She might never walk again."

"She will *not* be an invalid. Those are excuses. I took you for more of an optimist than that."

Still Madeline would not look up. "I just want to be prepared for the worst."

He sat down. "Fine. I accept that. But if that's the worst, and you go back to Yorkshire with her and see that she is settled in your family home, you would not have to stay there forever. She'll have your father, and she has enough money to hire a nurse."

He shook his head. "It's ridiculous to hypothesize such a thing—she *will* walk again. I've seen her leg— it's still there. She'll have a limp at the very worst. She's still beautiful—she can move about in society and have a gripping story to entertain her acquaintances. It's my guess she'll have every unmarried gentleman within a hundred miles standing in line for hours, begging to hear her tell it in her own charming, melodramatic words."

For the next few minutes, they sat in stiff silence while Madeline drank her tea. When she finished, she stood up to leave, for she didn't know what else to say to Adam. She couldn't change the way things were. Diana still loved him and wanted him, and Madeline—no matter how angry she was at her sister for how she had been treating her—could not kick her when she was down.

Adam stood also. "Wait, you didn't answer my question."

"What question?" Whatever it was, she feared it.

"If Diana recovers and finds happiness—" his tone softened a bit "—will you consider returning to Cumberland?"

The very idea that he was asking her filled Madeline with such yearning her whole being came alive. All her life, she had smothered her emotions, kept them quietly still within, but at this moment, they were thrashing about inside her, leaping to life, fighting to get out! She slowly turned to face him.

Adam watched her briefly, then moved around the table that stood between them. He took her chin in his hand and lifted it, forcing her to look at him. "The other day, when you walked away from me, I was angry at you for shutting me out. I'm still angry at you for ignoring me every day since, but God help me, I burn for you and I can't stop it."

"I had no choice," she explained. "I'm sorry, Adam, but I can't betray Diana, not when she is still so in love with you."

"Yet you will not let me tell her the truth to end it."

She gazed up at him imploringly, wishing he would release her, but release her from what? She was not his prisoner. He was not holding her captive. Adam merely held her chin in his hand. She could leave if she wanted to.

Oh, but no...

She was locked in his gaze.

Suddenly he pulled her into his arms and pressed his mouth to hers. The feel of his moist, searing lips threw whiskey on the fire that had been simmering within her for weeks now. It burst into a roaring, raging blaze deep within. Her skin sizzled, and though she knew it was wrong, she couldn't stop herself from reaching her arms around Adam's neck and clutching him, finally allowing tears to spill over her cheeks.

He held her whole face in his hands and devoured her mouth. Madeline had fantasized what it would be like to kiss Adam passionately like this, but never could she have guessed it would be anything quite so astounding—white-hot and liquid, a luscious, pounding pleasure. It was unknown territory. Any physical sensation she had ever known before paled in comparison to this staggering, overwhelming attack.

She heard herself whimper, felt Adam's fingers caressing the wisps of hair surrounding her face. His mouth was warm and wet and insistent. Soon she was swaying with a debilitating desire that pulled her closer to him until she was pressing her body against his, wanting to melt into him until they were one single thing. Indivisible. Seamless.

The power of her emotions obliterated everything else. It was all so new to her.

The sound of a door opening and closing upstairs yanked Madeline back into the physical world. Heart pounding, she pulled away from Adam and listened for Hilary returning.

The house was quiet, though Madeline's blood was rushing noisily in her ears like a raging waterfall.

She gazed at Adam. His chest was heaving; he looked shaken. Agitated.

"We took this too far," she said.

He closed his eyes, then slowly opened them. "Will you always put Diana's feelings first, when she has never considered yours? You're not her maid. You're an independent woman. Don't disguise what you're doing as sisterly loyalty, Madeline. You're really just afraid of caring for me because you don't want to be hurt or rejected. You're trying to make me think that you feel nothing for me, to drive me away, so you can leave easily without any regrets. But you can't fool me. There *is* passion in you. I saw it just now, I felt it."

"Please, Adam, there is so much for me to work out." She heard Hilary's footsteps upstairs, returning to Diana's room. "You don't understand."

Madeline gazed up at the ceiling and thought of her sister and wished she could explain it to Adam. Yes, she and Diana had grown apart, but there was so much more to it than that.

"I know that Diana seems cruel sometimes, but she is still my sister. When I was very young, she used to read to me. And when you came calling, she would tell me all the romantic things you said to her. She would comb my hair and tell me that one day, I would marry my own prince charming. I cannot forget that, Adam. She was all I had. I cling to those memories. I'm sorry."

Not knowing what else to say, she turned away from him.

"Madeline," he called after her. She stopped in the doorway but would not face him. "You're wrong to cling to something that no longer exists. You're not a child anymore."

His words burrowed deep into her consciousness. Benumbed by their sharp effect, all she could do was turn and hurry up the stairs.

Adam stood in the kitchen doorway and watched Madeline wash the supper dishes with Penelope. He remembered all the things he and Madeline had said to each other earlier that day, and wished he had been able to say the one thing that would convince her to let go of the past. Maybe it was selfish of him, but what could he do? He wanted Madeline more than he'd ever wanted anyone, even Diana all those years ago. This was different. The need for Madeline was deeper. Truer. She was meant to be with him and he knew it as surely as he knew his own hand.

I tasted the passion in your kiss, Adam thought with solid, angry certainty as his whole body grew hard with tension. *You can't pretend you are in control of your heart. At least not to me.*

Suddenly he felt a great need to ascertain Diana's wellness, for so much depended upon her recovery. He quietly climbed the stairs and knocked on her door.

"Come in!" Diana replied in a singsong voice.

Adam entered. Hilary was seated at Diana's bedside, but as soon as the maid saw him, she lowered the book she had been reading aloud.

"Hilary, will you get us some tea please?" Diana asked in a polite voice.

"Yes, my lady." The young woman set the book on the tall chest of drawers and left the room.

Adam moved to pick it up. "*Clarissa, The History of a Young Lady.* Samuel Richardson."

He experienced the draining effects of melancholy, reading the title, remembering the night he and Madeline had discussed books in his study. She had wanted to read this, but she had never gotten the chance. She had been too busy caring for his children and making his house a home.

Diana shifted on the bed, sitting up straighter and fussing with her hair. "I sent Hilary downstairs for a book from your study. I hope you don't mind. I told her to get the fattest one she could find."

He set the book down again. "She chose well, then."

"If I had known, however, that Clarissa would be confined to her room for the first five hundred pages, I might have instructed Hilary to choose something else, something more descriptive of the outdoors." She smiled sweetly at him.

Adam moved toward the bed and sat in the rocking chair beside it. "How are you feeling today?"

"Much better, thank you. You are very kind to ask. My headaches have all but disappeared, and my leg—as long as I don't move it too much—is almost free of pain."

"Well, that is indeed good news. Do you think you would like to come downstairs tomorrow? Jacob and I could help you. It might do you good to sit in the parlor and—"

"Heavens, no. I'm not ready for that. My condition is still much too delicate."

He paused, feeling the effects of his hopes being cropped. "Well, I suppose that is to be expected. It's only been a week. But look how far you've come. This time next week, I'm sure you'll be ready to try and take a few steps."

"A few steps? Adam, you are much too confident. I can't imagine getting out of this bed for weeks yet! If I ever manage it at all! Quite frankly, I am afraid of it. I don't want you to see me fall or limp." She gazed morosely at the window. "What will become of me, Adam? I am no longer the beauty I once was."

They sat in uncomfortable silence for a few minutes. Adam wished Hilary would return with the tea.

"How are *you*, Adam?" she asked.

He knew with regret that she had expected him to hold her just then, or reassure her, tell her she was still as beautiful as ever. But he had not. He wondered what she was making of that.

"How is your work coming on the marshlands?" It was the first time she had ever asked him anything about "work." He was surprised she even managed to let the word pass her lips.

Thankful for a safe topic, Adam began to describe the situation. He explained the breaks in the dykes, the repairs necessary, and how it would be a few years before the land would be productive again.

"A few years? But that's your livelihood."

"Yes, it is, I'm afraid, but all is not lost. The uplands were untouched, and we will have more than enough food to see us through the winter. We'll simply have to forgo spending anything on luxuries."

He remembered telling Madeline the same thing that afternoon. Her reply had been a sigh of relief. She had said, "Thank goodness."

Diana was staring at him now, a look of bewilderment on her face. "You'll have no spending money at all? Nothing?"

"Nothing," he answered flatly.

She shifted uneasily on the bed again. "Well…I suppose there is my inheritance. That could tide us over, provide a cushion to meet our needs."

"We'll be able to meet our needs. As I said, the crops are quite substantial and—"

"People have other needs besides a full belly, Adam." Her tone was condescending. "We must be able to entertain, or to purchase the occasional trinket."

He cleared his throat. "Lavish entertaining is not exactly a common pastime here in Cumberland, Diana. The people here are farmers. This is not high society. Perhaps Viscount Blackthorne's visit gave you the wrong impression of how we live."

She laughed. "Oh, Adam, I don't expect to live like a queen. Besides, I'm sure the viscount will return. He seemed to enjoy himself very much."

Hilary entered with the tea.

"Will you read to me, Adam?" Diana asked, wincing with pain as she sat up to receive the tea Hilary was pouring. "I do so love the cadence of your deep voice. Perhaps it will help me relax, and I can get a good night's sleep. I've had such trouble sleeping the past few days."

"Certainly." He rose to retrieve the book, and realized with some discomfort that he could no more break her heart now than he could push her out of bed while she slept. It was that damned, irritating compassion again.

Yet tomorrow, he knew that Diana would again be treating Madeline like dirt under her fingernails. For a moment, he considered telling Diana the truth—the cold, hard truth, with nothing to spare—then he forced himself to just read.

Chapter Twenty

After nine sleepless nights and ten days full of abuse and unappreciated drudgery, Madeline's patience was reaching the end of its tether, and her compassion was almost completely dried up.

She stood over Diana's bed now—having just been called a lazy frump because she had insisted the wash water was *not* as cold as ice—all the while fighting hard against the urge to pour the whole bloody wash basin over her sister's infuriatingly pretty head!

"Diana, I have a dozen things to do before dinner, and I don't have time to boil another pot of water for you now. Perhaps Hilary could do it."

"Hilary is reading to me," Diana replied haughtily.

"Perhaps Hilary could set the book aside for a few minutes." *And perhaps I should ship you off to a hospital somewhere and let a bunch of cranky nurses take care of you!*

Diana glared frostily at Madeline. "Have you no pity? Do you have any idea what I would give to be able to boil that water for myself? To walk down those stairs and see the sun shining in the parlor windows? All I want is to feel clean and comfortable, for that is all I have, confined to this bed. But you…you have never thought of anyone but yourself. You were always so selfish, even as a child. You always wanted my hair ribbons and you took them, too, when I was away. I would come home from Auntie's to find you wearing them!''

Madeline swallowed over the fury that was rising like a tidal wave in her throat. ''I used your ribbons because Father wouldn't buy me any of my own.''

Diana gave her a disbelieving frown. ''That gave you no right to take what was mine.''

That's not all I want to take, Madeline thought, squeezing the washcloth in her hand.

She decided she needed to leave the room and be by herself for a little while, for her patience was dangerously close to breaking.

''I'm sorry, Diana, I really do have to tend to dinner. Hilary is going to have to look after your bath. I'll be up later with a tray.''

Diana simply huffed and waved a commanding hand to Hilary, who picked up the washcloth and proceeded to continue where Madeline had left off.

Madeline seized the opportunity to dash out of the room before Diana asked for anything else. She went down to the kitchen and met Adam just coming in the back door, wiping his boots on the mat.

He froze there and stared at her. ''You look exhausted, Madeline. When have you slept?''

She wiped her hands over her apron and tried to shrug casually. ''I've been sleeping when Diana sleeps.''

"From the sounds of it, she has you hopping all night long." His tone was contemptuous and stern.

"She's still very uncomfortable," Madeline explained. "She wakes during the night."

"And she wakes you, too. I hear you running up and down the stairs for things, and I hear her shouting, scolding you." He moved all the way into the kitchen, removed his coat and hung it on the back of a chair. "This is getting out of hand. She treats you like a slave, Madeline. You don't deserve to be spoken to in that manner. No one does." He ran a hand over the top of his hair and paused before adding, "Do you think she remembers?"

Madeline's heart lurched. "Remembers that you broke off the engagement?"

"Maybe she's lashing out at you."

Madeline considered it. "No, this is not Diana 'lashing out.' She would never be able to keep something like that to herself. She would come right out and say it, maybe throw a vase or two at my head."

He gave her a subtle smile, but it held some annoyance. "So this is just Diana's normal, everyday treatment of you?"

He raised an eyebrow. He seemed to be questioning her, pushing her to think about this.

Madeline didn't like to admit that it was normal for Diana to be cruel, not just because it seemed traitorous to her sister but because it forced Madeline to face the fact that she allowed herself to be treated that way, and always had.

I allow it. Why?

"Not entirely," she said in her own defense, skirting the issue that was now niggling at her brain. "The pain has made her personality a bit more...*intense* than normal."

"And no doubt, the doctor's pain medication has exacerbated it. You know what they say—*In vino veritas.*"

"There is truth in wine," Madeline repeated.

Adam's dark eyes softened. "The only reason I haven't said anything to her, Madeline, is because I know you would not wish me to. But I have been grinding my teeth so much lately, I fear I may be wearing them down to their roots."

Madeline stared at him in disbelief. She wasn't sure if she was flattered by his concern and pleased that, through the walls, he had heard the not-so-charming side of Diana's personality. Or if she was angry at him for making her question her own backbone.

He was right, though. This was getting out of hand.

Why had she always cowered to Diana?

"What would you have me do, then?" she asked, still not ready to admit that her obliging nature with Diana was anything more than an abnormally large sense of duty. "She's been through hell, Adam. It's natural that she should be bitter about—"

"She has a broken leg, Madeline. It will heal."

"But she'll have to walk with a cane, and she'll have a scar on her forehead."

"A cane and a scar? That won't be the end of the world."

"It will be to her. Her appearance matters to her."

He considered her point. "And I thought *I* was compassionate to a fault. It seems I've met my match.'' He moved toward her, close enough that she could smell his musky scent.

How long had it been since she'd been outside these walls with him? she wondered. How long had it been since she'd spent any time alone with him, talking easily, as they used to do? She promptly felt hungry and deprived of...of what? Of companionship? Of love?

Love.

''I don't believe that compassion is ever a shortcoming, Adam.''

''It is when it lays you out like a doormat.''

''I'm not anyone's doormat.''

''You are. Your guilt has made you into one, when you have done nothing wrong.''

''It's not guilt that makes me care for her, it's—'' She stopped.

''It's what, Madeline?'' He took a step forward. His eyes searched hers.

Madeline felt the air sail out of her lungs, taking with it her resolve to be strong and keep her emotions in a tight harness. She felt the rigid muscles in her neck and shoulders go slack.

''Diana needs me now. Maybe, if I'm there for her and help her, maybe she'll...maybe she'll...''

Adam's gaze narrowed. ''Maybe she'll love you?''

Madeline felt tears of realization filling her eyes. ''Neither she nor Father ever said a kind word to me, or made me feel important to them. I suppose...'' She paused for a breath. ''I suppose I just want to *matter* to someone. Is that so wrong?''

He held both her hands. ''You matter to *me*, Madeline. Why won't you let me love you? Why can't you let go of what Diana will never be?''

''She's my sister. My flesh and blood.'' Madeline could feel herself melting into him. ''I have to try and save us—as a *family*.''

Adam's gaze narrowed in on her. ''This is about your mother, isn't it?''

She shook her head. ''No, I—''

''Yes, that's it. You think it's your fault that Diana and your father were so miserable all your life. It's not your fault that she died, Madeline. God has His reasons for taking those we love from us, and we must accept that. If Diana and your father deprived you of love because of it, they hurt themselves as much as they hurt you, for look at your family now. You are spread out and distant from each other in your hearts.''

''But I don't want to be distant. I want us to love each other. I look at your family, Adam, and I long for what you have been able to create and nurture and sustain.''

He clenched his jaw in frustration. ''*Talk* to her, then. I know you've been afraid of opening your heart, but you must, if you are ever going to fix what is broken in your life. Tell Diana how much she means to you, for love is as much about what you say and do and what you show, as it is about what you feel inside. Perhaps Diana needs to learn that as well.''

Madeline felt a spark of recollection flicker inside her. ''Mary said those words to me once—about how important it is to *show* your love.''

"I've said those words to Jacob many times."

So the lesson she had learned from Mary and Jacob had really come from Adam, for it was he who had passed that knowledge on to them.

She stood in the warmth of the kitchen, gazing up at the man who had come riding into her childhood on a big black horse looking like her very own prince charming, coming to rescue her from her locked prison in the tower. She hadn't known how long it would take, or how he would do it. Scale the walls perhaps? Fight off a dragon? Who would have thought that he would simply hand her a key made of hope, to open her heart?

Her voice quivered with a flood of emotions. "Adam, I have pushed you away, tried to *drive* you away, yet you continue to be a friend to me."

He smiled down at her, but she knew he was not entirely pleased about this. He was sending her to reconcile with her sister, knowing that a reconciliation might bring them closer together but leave him standing outside in the cold.

With nervous apprehension, Madeline returned to Diana's room to find her quietly reclining on the pillows while Hilary read aloud to her. Madeline moved fully into the room. "I'm sorry to interrupt, but I would like to talk to you, Diana. In private."

Diana nodded at Hilary, who closed the book and left the room.

Madeline sat on the bed. Diana held her head high, her chin slightly elevated, and Madeline knew that look all too well. She was still angry at Madeline for having walked out on her earlier, disobeying her orders and leaving Hilary to finish the sponge bath Madeline had started.

This was going to be exceedingly difficult.

She reached for Diana's hand. "I...I want to talk to you about us."

"About *us?* What *us?* Are you going to propose marriage to me, Madeline?"

Madeline tried to smile and make light of the joke that was meant to distance her. "Us, as sisters. I...I want to apologize for some things."

Diana's expression relaxed visibly, and Madeline was glad she had been able to wrestle with her pride long enough to break the ice. Perhaps, this way, Diana would open her ears and actually listen.

"Do you remember when I was six years old, you taught me how to walk with a book on my head?"

"Yes, what does that have to do with anything?"

Madeline tried again. "Do you remember putting me to bed at night? Climbing under the covers with me, lying beside me and reading, then stroking my forehead before saying good-night?"

"Goodness, Madeline, I don't remember."

"Well, I do. I also remember that when you packed up to leave for Auntie's house to live in London, I did not say goodbye. While you waited in the front hall for the carriage to arrive, I complained to Father and accused him of loving you more than me, and I said you were spoiled. Tell me you remember *that.*"

Diana pursed her lips indignantly. "How could I forget? You ran off down the lane and then my carriage came. *You,* as always, were the one who was spoiled that day, Madeline, not me. Don't think for a minute I was hurt."

Madeline sighed deeply. "I said I was here to apologize. I'm sorry for that. I...I was angry that you were leaving, and I knew I was going to miss you. I had no mother to hold me and console me after you were gone, and I was afraid." *Lord, this was difficult.*

Diana was not moved. "I had no mother, either. Do you think it was easy for *me*? You never even knew her. I had to watch them put the mother that *I* loved into the ground."

Swallowing uneasily, Madeline continued. "I'm sorry for that, too. It was hard for all of us."

For a long time they sat in silence. Madeline felt her courage faltering and feared that she would not be brave enough to say what she had come here to say. She squeezed her hands together on her lap, then looked at Diana and saw the pain in her own eyes, the memories of a distressing time in her life.

"I didn't want to say goodbye to you that day, Diana, because I *loved* you. More than anyone in the world."

There was a long silence. Diana's brows drew together in a frown. "Why are you telling me this now?"

Madeline's stomach began to churn. "Because I want you to know it, and because I want...I want us to be close again."

The color rose in Diana's cheeks. "You think I'm going to be an invalid, don't you? You feel sorry for me, that's why you're saying all this."

"No, Diana—"

"How can you expect us to be close when you will not do the smallest favor for me, like warming the water when I ask? We are nothing alike. You walk around like the living dead, keeping your thoughts to yourself, looking at me as if I am silly and frivolous for wanting to keep my hands soft or my dress clean while you bounce about in the barnyard, taking pleasure in feeding the hogs!"

Madeline felt she'd been slapped across the face. But there was more....

"You judge me," Diana said, "with that look on your face. I never know what you are thinking because you never tell me. At least when you were a child you expressed yourself by disobeying Father and running off somewhere. You were such a difficult child."

"I believe I did it for attention," Madeline replied. "At least, that's what the housekeepers used to say."

"Well, thank heavens you gave up trying."

I did give up, Madeline thought sadly. Just as she was going to give up now, for nothing was worth this torment. She rose from the bed.

"I should go downstairs and start dinner," Madeline said. "I'll summon Hilary for you."

There would be no more apologies. No more attempts to reconcile with her sister. She fluffed up Diana's pillows, quite secure in the knowledge that she had been right to keep her heart closed at least toward her sister. Her father had deceived her and shipped her off without a second thought, and Diana blamed her for their mother's death, and clearly still despised her. Madeline had been burdened with that guilt for her entire life.

The key Adam had given her hadn't worked, after he'd made it sound so simple.

Just then, the noise of a coach driving into the yard interrupted her thoughts. Madeline went to the window and pulled the lace curtain aside.

"Who is it?" Diana asked.

"Good heavens, it's the lieutenant-governor, Lord Blackthorne. He's returned." With unsteady fingers, Madeline quickly untied her apron.

Diana shouted at her. "Wait! You can't leave now. I look terrible!"

"You have a maid, Diana, and I have work to do."

With that, she hurried downstairs to greet the viscount, thankful to have something to keep her mind occupied. For she was damned if she was going to think about her heart, or ever try to awaken it again.

Chapter Twenty-One

"You don't say." Lord Blackthorne lowered his quizzing glass and followed Adam and Madeline into the parlor. "My word, Coates, what an abominable turn of events."

"Shall I get tea?" Madeline asked.

Adam gestured for the lieutenant-governor to take a seat. "No, Madeline. Please stay. I'm sure Lord Blackthorne would like to hear your story as well as mine."

"Yes, yes," the viscount replied, raising his quizzing glass again and shifting his attention toward Madeline. "I understand you were the one to find Lady Thurston. Heavens, you did well, Miss Oxley. It must have been a terrifying night for you."

For the next half hour, Adam and Madeline described the events of the flood, as well as the current condition of the marsh and what the future held for Cumberland. Lord Blackthorne was both sympathetic and optimistic, and promised to do all he could at Government House, to attend to the matter.

"And what about Lady Thurston?" he asked. "How is she faring?"

Adam and Madeline glanced at each other. After an awkward pause, Adam answered. "Her spirits are rather low, I'm afraid."

"Ah. That is to be expected. I presume she is still in some pain."

"Yes, my lord."

"And what does the doctor have to say? Is he a dependable fellow?"

"Yes, he's very capable," Madeline said. "I have complete faith in him. He did his best for Diana the night of the accident, and he saved her leg."

Lord Blackthorne gestured toward his own wooden leg. "I wish he had been on the battlefield in '42."

Madeline smiled in understanding.

The viscount waved a dismissive hand through the air. "But that was so long ago, now. I rarely think of it. Perspective," he said, raising an authoritative finger. "Lady Thurston must look to the future and see her life as a whole, and know that this is just a small piece of it. These difficult weeks will pass, and she'll be up and around before she knows it. Soon, everything will seem normal again. It's just a matter of acceptance and determination, and perhaps a little reassurance from those who care about her."

Quite unable to mask the despair in her voice, Madeline lowered her gaze to her hands on her lap. "I wish she had your vision, my lord."

Madeline did care about Diana, she truly did. Even though Madeline was angry at her for all the cruel things she had said in their lifetime together, Madeline still wanted her sister to rise from this setback. She wanted her to find joy in life again, no matter what became of their sisterly relationship.

There was a moment of grief-filled silence, then Lord Blackthorne pushed himself to his feet. He squeezed the polished brass handle of his cane. "May I see her? I might be of some assistance. I have personal experience with this sort of thing after all."

Madeline rose. "I will go and tell her, my lord. I'm certain she would be grateful for your concern and your generous regard for her welfare. I'll need just a moment."

She calmly left the parlor, but Adam followed and took hold of her arm. "What happened with Diana?" he whispered. "Did you talk to her?"

She saw the hope in his eyes again, and couldn't bear to look at him. She lowered her own gaze. "Yes, I did, Adam. Nothing has changed."

Adam let go of her arm and dropped his hand to the side. His dark eyes narrowed and hardened. She felt she had failed him. She *had* failed him.

"Right. That's it, then," he said flatly. "I see I was wrong to have thought there was more to you than what you have shown me. Go now. Go and be with your sister."

He turned on his heel and went to join the lieutenant-governor again in the parlor.

Fighting tears, Madeline picked up her skirts and walked slowly up the stairs to Diana's bedchamber.

Two days later, after Lord Blackthorne had spent the better part of each one talking to Diana, she surprised everyone by asking to take supper downstairs at the dining table.

Hilary spared nothing in preparing her ladyship for dinner. She washed her hair and swept it into a spectacular twist on top of her head, helped her into her best silk gown and draped her in her most exquisite jewels.

Adam carried Diana down, and she sat across from Lord Blackthorne while Madeline and Penelope served the meal. The whole family was present except for Mary and Jacob, who were now living in their own home, and the conversation was light and full of laughter.

"You still remember *nothing* from the flood?" Lord Blackthorne asked over dessert, leaning forward with fascination. "Even after Madeline described it all to you again today? What a remarkable situation. Does it trouble you greatly, Lady Thurston?"

Diana raised her wineglass. "No, it is truly the least of my troubles. How can one regret what one cannot remember? To put it simply, I really don't know what I am missing."

Lord Blackthorne laughed uproariously. "Oh, what a wit you have, Lady Thurston, and after such an ordeal. I am both dazzled and moved by your courage and fortitude."

Madeline glanced across the table at Adam. He was watching her. Studying her. She felt exposed, as if he knew every thought she was having, even though for the past two days they had not spoken a word to each other.

In many respects, she was an open book to him

now, no matter how hard she tried to keep herself closed off to the world. He knew she was aching from a botched attempt to reconcile with her sister. He knew she loved him, but was afraid to give in to it.

She hated that open feeling. It was strange and unfamiliar to her.

Adam slowly blinked and turned his cool gaze away from her. She could see how angry he was in the set of his jaw, the way he squeezed his spoon. He did not even want to look at her now. He had finally accepted that she was not the person he thought she was, and he could not change her.

Her entire being flooded with sadness at that moment, and a profound sense of loss. The loss of hope.

Was it too late to become that person? she wondered suddenly, knowing that he was right about so many things. She *was* afraid, and she was clinging to something that no longer existed. She had tried to reconcile with Diana, and Diana had rejected her.

Was Madeline going to allow that rejection to destroy her and stop her from finding happiness somewhere else? It was true: Madeline was using duty as an excuse to run from what could be the best thing that ever happened to her.

She gazed with fresh eyes at her sister, and felt she was seeing her for the first time.

Diana giggled and gave the viscount a sweet, humble smile.

Madeline felt her own courage and fortitude rising. Perhaps there was still a chance.

After dinner, Adam carried Diana into the parlor and she entertained everyone with her talents at the pianoforte. Madeline turned the sheet music for her, while Diana sang a ballad and a few old English folk songs, bowing her head appreciatively at the applause after each piece.

Adam then carried her to the sofa, where she sat with Lord Blackthorne, telling him more about her life in England as Lady Thurston, and how she had spent her days there.

From her chair in the corner of the parlor, Madeline noticed Penelope yawn and knew she should take the children upstairs. She collected them, they said good-night, then she escorted them to the stairs. She stopped, however, when she heard Adam address her from the parlor door.

"You'll return?" he said in a cool, formal tone.

She hesitated a moment, staring into the intense blue eyes that never failed to set her insides afire.

Adam continued to gaze at her, waiting for her answer. Now was the time to act, if she was ever to find her own happiness. Yes. She would act. She would talk to him tonight. Try to fix things.

A knock rapped at the door. Madeline jumped. Adam seemed startled, too. He turned to answer it.

Madeline waited at the bottom of the stairs to see who had come calling at this hour. As Adam opened the door, the bright pink of the final rays of the sunset momentarily blinded her before she could ascertain that the man at the door was John Metcalf.

Adam cleared his throat. "Hello, John."

John removed his tricorn hat. "Evening, Mr. Coates. I know it's late, but I wonder if I might have a word with Miss Oxley."

"This isn't really the best time, John. As you can see, Lord Blackthorne is here, and—"

"I know you have visitors, sir, and I'm sorry for intruding, but I just couldn't wait."

For a long, tense moment, Adam stood in the doorway, barring John from entering, then he finally stepped aside. John nodded gratefully and entered. His gaze fell upon Madeline at the other end of the hall, and she froze there, not sure what she was feeling.

Part of her was annoyed at John for interrupting her moment with Adam, when she was so close to finding her courage. Another part of her was thankful that John had interrupted, for she was not yet as brave as she wanted to be.

Diana and Lord Blackthorne laughed from the parlor, seemingly unaware that anyone had even knocked on the door.

"Miss Oxley, may I have a moment of your time?" John asked.

Madeline looked at Adam questioningly. He gave her a nod that told her she was free to do as she wished.

She whispered to the children to go upstairs and get ready for bed, and that she would be up shortly to say good-night. Then Madeline put one foot in front of the other, slowly moving down the hall to where Adam and John stood side by side, watching her.

"Shall we go sit on the veranda, John? The sunset is quite lovely."

She noticed Adam's shoulders rise and fall, and knew that he was worried.

* * *

John sat on the bench outside on the veranda. "Thank you for seeing me, Madeline. I know it's not the usual time to call, but I needed to come and say my piece, before it was too late."

"Too late?" she replied. "What is it, John, that holds such urgency?"

He squeezed his hat in his callused hands, took a deep breath and blurted out, "I've come to ask you to marry me."

Lively music from the pianoforte inside began again, lending a clumsy quality to the already awkward moment.

Madeline cleared her throat. "You surprise me, John. Why do you feel you must be rushed?"

"Because I can see what's going on with Mr. Coates."

Madeline stiffened. "I beg your pardon?"

"Maybe you don't see it, but he's fallen in love with you. I saw it in his eyes the night he came to my house, searching for you. I saw it when he looked at you when you came out of Lady Thurston's room, after the doctor tended to her, and I saw it in his eyes, just now. He didn't want me to speak to you. I can't in good conscience let you go on living here, especially when Mr. Coates is engaged to your sister. I've had a mind to propose for a while, and I decided I ought to do it now, before something terrible happens."

"Something terrible…such as?"

"Before he...you'll pardon me if I don't say it, miss."

Madeline sat very still. "I have a will of my own, John. You need not worry about anything like that." She recalled the day she'd punched a Yorkshire vicar between the eyes.

He leaned back, only somewhat appeased. "My proposal still stands, Miss Oxley. I...I want to marry you."

John did care for her; she knew it with certainty. It wasn't exactly the most romantic or heartfelt proposal she'd imagined—considering he made it appear that he was doing her a favor—but he was a decent man. She knew that, too.

But did she love him?

No.

Could she *ever* love him?

No, she could not. She loved only one man.

She had to admit, however, there was something safe about being with John Metcalf. She noticed that her heart was not racing, and she felt no anxieties. There was nothing confusing about him.

The truth of it was that he was not a danger to her, for there was no intimate connection between them. Nothing fragile. She could marry John and simply live a comfortable life in his house, farming the land, gardening, and fearing nothing, for essentially, she would continue to live alone.

At least, her heart would. She could retreat into her own thoughts most of the time and make casual conversation with John when he was at home, and he would not even know that she was keeping anything from him, for he had never seen the real Madeline. He had never even suspected that there *was* a real Madeline beneath what she showed to the world.

Adam knew it, and he made her feel so vulnerable.

Yes, John would be safe.

Still, she could not marry him. She would be making the same mistake Adam did not want to make— marrying someone he did not love. He said it would be a disservice to both parties involved. John deserved more.

Besides that, she suspected John didn't really love her either. At least not passionately. He was proposing to her because she was the only single woman in Cumberland, and he was afraid someone else was going to snatch her up before he had the chance to.

Madeline reached for his hand. "I'm sorry, John, I can't marry you."

He blinked a few times. "But why?"

"Because I'm not in love with you, and you deserve to be adored by the woman you marry. I'm not the right one for you."

"But you're the *only* one," he replied.

Madeline smiled gently. "That's because I'm the only unmarried woman in Cumberland above the age of twelve."

He managed a laugh. For a moment, they both sat on the bench without saying anything.

Madeline stood and hugged John. "I'm sorry. I hope we can still be friends."

"I guess that'll have to do," he replied.

She took some comfort in the fact that she had not broken his heart. She could see it in his eyes.

She said good-night to him and turned to go back inside. Stepping into the front hall, she peered into the parlor.

There was Diana, all smiles and laughter, playing her heart out on the pianoforte while Lord Blackthorne turned the pages for her and sang along. What a silly little ditty it was that they played. Madeline had never heard it before.

Contrarily, Adam sat in the chair by the fire with one leg crossed over the other, gazing dolefully into the flames.

Madeline's knees went weak at the sight of him in the firelight, looking so handsome and elegant. So somber. She longed to throw all her foolish caution to the wind and go to him. Pull him to his feet and tell him nothing mattered more to her than he did, for no one in her life had ever treated her better, or managed to open her eyes to what real love truly was.

It wasn't about loyalty or duty, she realized. It was about tenderness and affection and kindness. It was about how you treated someone.

Madeline took a deep breath and slowly approached her sister. She didn't even wait for the song she was playing to come to an end. Madeline tapped Diana on the shoulder.

"I need to talk to you, Diana. It's very important. Would you gentlemen excuse us, please?"

Chapter Twenty-Two

The men retreated to Adam's study for brandy, and Diana glared up at Madeline from the piano bench. "That was very rude, Madeline! What did you think you were doing? Lord Blackthorne is an important man."

Madeline sat down beside her. "Yes, and I like him very much, but this could not wait."

"What could not wait? La, you'd think the house was on fire."

"It is, in a way."

"What in the world are you trying to say? As usual, you're making no sense at all. Selfish, selfish, selfish."

Madeline held up her hand. "Diana, stop."

To Madeline's surprise, Diana *did* stop. She gazed at Madeline with surprise, waiting for her to say what she wanted to say.

Madeline tried to speak clearly and confidently. "I know that you've been through a difficult time, and you're still not entirely better yet, but there is something you need to know about the day of your accident. Something happened, and there was a reason you went riding onto the marsh alone. This may come as a shock to you, but you were looking for me to tell me something, and—''

Diana wiggled on the bench to face Madeline. ''Wait, wait. Since we're being honest with each other, I have something to tell you, too. I was afraid to tell you, because we have been growing so close lately…''

Growing so close lately?

''…and I know that you stayed here with Adam all this time to wait for me to finally arrive to marry him.''

Distracted by the interruption, and losing her concentration, Madeline stared blankly at her sister.

Diana continued. ''The truth is, I need your help. I don't know what to do.''

''What kind of help?''

Diana clasped both Madeline's hands in hers. ''Oh, my dearest sister. I am suffering.''

''Why? What's—''

''Madeline, I can't marry Adam! And I don't know how to tell him.''

Madeline slowly swallowed. ''I beg your pardon?''

''I can't marry him!'' She glanced over her shoulder and lowered her voice to a whisper. ''I thought I wanted to when I arrived, but life here is just not what I thought it would be. *Adam* is not what I thought he would be. He always…oh, heavens Madeline, he smells like the *outdoors*.''

''He's a farmer,'' Madeline said dryly.

''I know! That's exactly it!''

Madeline tried to keep herself from physically shaking her sister.

"All that aside, the real problem now is that I'm afraid I've fallen in love with someone else."

Trying to focus on Diana's lips moving, Madeline shook her head. "Who? You mean..."

"Yes, the viscount. He adores me, Madeline, but he respects Adam and does not wish to do anything dishonorable."

"Are you sure? Has he confessed his feelings to you?"

She whispered even more quietly. "Yes. He told me tonight, while you were outside with Mr. Metcalf. Incidentally, what happened out there?"

Madeline's reply came out light and airy, as if her words were floating languidly on her disbelief. "He proposed to me."

"Heavens. What did you say?"

"I said no."

"But why?"

"Because I don't love him."

She waved a dismissive hand. "Well, you could do better anyway." Then she shifted the topic back to herself faster than Madeline could say *pox on you.*

"As I was saying, Adam left us alone for a few minutes, and Lord Blackthorne told me how he felt. He said I was the most beautiful creature in the world, and that he wished I were free, and that if I were, he would take me to Government House and make me his viscountess. Imagine—a viscountess!"

Madeline felt the color drain from her cheeks. "But you barely know each other."

Diana sighed dreamily. "Sometimes, you *just know.*"

Madeline stood up and paced the room. "I don't know what to say, Diana."

"You don't have to say anything. Just help me."

"You want me to *help* you? After the way you've treated me? After the way you treated Adam fifteen years ago, leading him on only to cast him aside?"

"Please, that is precisely why I need you—to lessen the blow. You must try to convince Adam that I am all wrong for him. Perhaps you can prepare him. I feel beastly about it, Madeline, honestly I do, for I remember how I shattered his heart all those years ago and ruined his life, and here I am, about to do it again. I am such a cruel, cruel person! Why do marriage proposals keep coming at me like this? From all directions so that I am forced to break hearts?"

Clearing her throat, Madeline continued to pace. Her anger at her self-centered sister was rising up in her again, and she was beginning to form words and sentences in her mind—nasty, insulting, biting ways to tell Diana the truth: that Adam didn't want to marry her in the first place! The only reason he hadn't broken it off with her before was because Madeline had begged him not to!

She took a breath to say it, but Diana interrupted her again. "Oh, Madeline, you must help Adam get over me. Will you take care of him? Will you stay here and try to mend his broken heart? I know he enjoys your company and you share an interest in gardening. Perhaps you could encourage a union between the two of you? He's a good man, Madeline, and you deserve to be happy. Do you think...do you think you could ever love him?''

Madeline stared dumbfounded at her sister. The look in her eyes...Madeline had never seen it before. She wasn't even sure what it was. Pleading? Remorse? Desperation?

"Diana, I—"

Diana reached for her hand and pulled her down to sit beside her again. "Madeline, I am a dreadful sister. I know it. But I've been doing a lot of thinking lately—I haven't been able to do much of anything else—and I *do* want you to be happy. I want things to be right.''

Right? Could it be that Diana remembered that Adam had broken off their engagement? Or did she just *suspect* that there were feelings between Madeline and Adam, and this was her way of holding on to her dignity and pride?

Madeline treaded cautiously into her next question. "What makes you think I could love Adam?''

Diana tilted her head and grinned. "Honestly, Madeline, you're my sister. You've always loved him, ever since you were a child following Adam and I around everywhere.''

Feeling an odd mixture of embarrassment for having her secret known, and tenderness for her sister in the wake of what seemed like a backward attempt to make up for her behavior lately, Madeline took in a deep, cleansing breath. She squeezed her sister's hand. "I *am* in love with him.''

Diana slowly absorbed her confession. She laid a gentle hand on Madeline's cheek. "Yet, when you thought I loved him, you kept it to yourself. How you must have suffered. Your loyalty and your sacrifice makes me feel so ashamed."

Madeline gazed into her sister's beautiful blue eyes, glistening with sentimental tears, something Madeline had never seen in Diana before. *Ashamed?*

Diana stroked a lock of hair back off Madeline's forehead. The gesture was familiar, for Diana had always done that when Madeline was a child, snuggling into bed at night.

"I'm sorry for the way things have turned out between us," Diana said. "I have been positively wretched to you. When I found out what Father had done, I came on the first ship out of Scarborough because I...I didn't want you to have what I considered mine. Just as I didn't want you to wear my ribbons, even though I wasn't wearing them anymore. And I had unrealistic fantasies about Adam. I wanted to be young and innocent again. I wanted to go back to those days when he came calling and all I knew was that he adored me. But he was never right for me. He talked about farming all the time, and as you know, I didn't have the slightest interest in anything to do with dirt. But you...my little sister, the gardener."

Warm, tender emotions rose up in Madeline like a swift tide; her eyes filled with tears. Diana pulled her close and hugged her.

"Adam was never meant to be mine, Madeline. He

was meant for you. You're the one he loves. He told me so.''

Madeline squeezed her eyes shut against the tears. ''You remember.''

''Yes. I might as well admit it now. I remembered everything the second day after the accident. And I'm sorry for the way I've treated you. I wanted to punish you and push you away so that I could take back what I considered mine. But then you came the other day to apologize to *me!* I was angry at first because you made me feel like such a cruel monster—which I am!—but then I realized how horribly I had always treated you, and I am desperate to make up for it, Madeline. I want to be a better person. I want to be more like you. Can you ever forgive me? Can we be close, as you wanted us to be?''

Madeline threw her arms around Diana. ''Of course we can. It's all I've ever wanted. I was just afraid to open up to you.''

''But you did, and I am so glad. At least one of us had the courage.''

Madeline knew she had Adam to thank for that.

''But are you sure you want to go with Lord Blackthorne?'' Madeline asked. ''He's not just an escape for you, is he? A way to give Adam to me, because I won't let you make that kind of sacrifice. There are other ways—''

''I know the viscount is not the most handsome man in the world, Madeline, but it may surprise you to know that looks are not that important to me. He adores me, truly and passionately, and I am in heaven.''

Madeline smiled knowingly. "And he will make you a viscountess."

"There is that, yes," Diana replied with a wickedly satisfied glint in her eye. "And when he completes his term here, we will return to his estate in England, and I will live out my days there, moving about society with him, for he is a very popular man."

It was the perfect life for Diana, that was certain.

Madeline hugged her sister again. "You have made me very happy." She sat back and gazed at the fire in the hearth. "But all is not yet perfect. I have been unfeeling and distant toward Adam. I can only hope that he will be able to forgive me for shutting him out, and believe that I am capable of love."

"*I* know that you are, Madeline. You have proven it to me beyond a shadow of a doubt. And if you believe it yourself," Diana said gently, "he will believe it, too."

Madeline paced back and forth along the oval rug in her candlelit room, wearing only her white nightdress, nothing else. Diana had giddily informed her that she would be leaving the following day with Lord Blackthorne, and they would be married in Halifax as soon as possible. She planned to speak to Adam after breakfast to officially end their betrothal, and to apologize for leaving so soon, with so little notice.

Should Madeline simply stand back and wait for the events to unfold? she wondered, as she continued to pace. Diana would drive away tomorrow, and Madeline would be left behind, standing beside Adam in the yard, waving goodbye. Everything, if she was lucky, would simply fall into place after that.

Or should she go to Adam now and be the one to tell him what was transpiring? Diana had wanted Madeline to seize the opportunity to take him for her own.

But how was she to tell him?

Should she begin by informing him that he was free, that Diana did not wish to marry him after all, and see where it went from there?

Or should Madeline begin by telling Adam that she had gone to Diana first to tell her the truth—that she had intended to betray her sister and choose a life with him—whether Diana liked it or not?

Would he even believe that?

A part of her was tempted to go with the first option and act only as messenger. She could deliver Diana's news and leave the rest to Adam. Perhaps he would be relieved to know that he would not have to go through the ordeal of breaking with Diana again, and he would take Madeline into his arms and propose.

If only it could be that easy. She would not have to risk pouring out her heart. All she would have to do was say yes.

Oh, but what a cowardly thing—to sit back and simply watch the tide turn.

Madeline blew out her candles and climbed onto the bed. There was a chill in the air, she noticed, wrapping her arms around herself. Her feet were as cold as a couple of frosty turnips. She hopped out of bed again and pulled on a pair of stockings, then made her way back to the bed and snuggled down, thinking.

The clock ticked. Madeline stared at the ceiling.

Something made her sit up. With a strange quivering feeling, she swept her feet off the bed to the floor again.

Hadn't Adam taught her that love was as much about what you said and did as what you felt inside? She loved him, didn't she? And the key he had given her *had* worked. Diana had proven that to her tonight.

Would it work if Madeline used it on Adam?

With trembling fingers, she lit her candelabra and carried it to her door. She paused there to take a breath. She had to do this. If she didn't, Adam would never know how much he meant to her. He would never know how much she truly loved him.

Madeline reached for the door latch, let herself out into the hall and walked apprehensively toward his door.

Chapter Twenty-Three

It was the fullest, roundest, brightest moon Adam could recall seeing in a dog's age. Hands clasped behind his back, he stood on the ridge, overlooking the marsh where moonbeams gleamed on the glossy dales below and stars glimmered brilliantly in the night sky overhead. There was a chill in the air—a sign of late summer—yet not a hint of wind off the bay. He closed his eyes and breathed in the fresh scents of chamomile and spruce, and thought of Madeline.

What was it that made him think he could fall in love with women he knew nothing about? Was he somehow daft in the head? At the very least, he was a severely poor judge of character. All his life he had thought he'd loved Diana, only to discover she was not at all the woman he remembered. Why hadn't he seen her true nature all those years ago? Had he been that blinded by her beauty? He supposed he had.

Jane had seemed like a rational woman when he'd met her, and he'd not had any serious doubts about marrying her when it became a necessity. Perhaps again, he had blinded himself to her deeper person, for what could he do but close his eyes and hold his breath and leap, hoping that it would all turn out right.

It hadn't. She'd been a difficult woman to live with, but he had survived.

Now Madeline. What had happened there? Everything had been fine, things were progressing as they should. They were becoming friends and he'd fallen in love with her gradually and sensibly, he'd thought. The friction only began after he had confessed his feelings to her. She had retreated from him, like a spooked rabbit in the forest.

Now he was wondering what John Metcalf had said to her. Surely he had proposed.

Adam truly had no idea what Madeline was going to do.

He really did not know her.

He watched the moon shadows drift eerily over the land as a few lone clouds passed across the dark sky. It was too late to be out here in the dark, analyzing his mistakes. He buried his hands in his pockets and headed back to the house.

An owl hooted somewhere nearby. He stopped at the end of the tree-lined driveway to look up at the tall pines and spot the owl, but heard the sound of his front door open and close.

His attention darted to the house and then to Madeline on the stoop, wearing only her white nightdress and a shawl, holding flickering candles over her head.

Was she looking for him? he wondered, feeling startled and shaken by her unexpected appearance. He'd thought everyone was asleep.

Observing a slight change in his body—a tightness,

a squeezing apprehension—he approached and climbed the steps. "Is something wrong?"

"Yes. I mean, no, nothing's wrong. I...I want to speak with you."

Her hair was down. How curly it was. He hadn't known it would be so full around her face, so soft looking. God, she was lovely in the candlelight, so natural and unaffected. He could feel the overwhelming shock of her beauty in his bones.

He forced himself to look down, to try and block his body's response, but found himself staring at her stockinged feet, her toes peeking out from under the hem of her nightdress. With an irritating surge of arousal, he pulled his gaze back up to her face. "Let's go inside, then."

Not knowing what to expect—perhaps she wanted to announce her engagement to John Metcalf—he held the door open for her. He would not be surprised if she wanted to marry the man. Nothing would surprise him now.

She led the way into his study rather than the parlor, then she boldly closed the door behind them.

Adam stood motionless in the center of the room, trying to subdue the dread that was spreading through him like a climbing vine. Following closely behind that dread was an unhealthy dose of dangerously frustrated lust.

For heaven's sake! He should not be in this room alone with her with the door closed, facing the prospect of losing her to another man, while the entire household slept upstairs. It was too much to ask of himself. He did not think he could resist the hunger to devour her and demand that she finally open herself to him, give herself to him, body and soul. She was meant for him, and no other!

Madeline walked to the desk and lit a few more candles from the flame of the one she held. The room brightened.

"First," she said, "I'm going to tell you what I had intended to do tonight. What I *tried* to do."

Adam strode to the window, working hard to speak with aplomb. "I'm listening."

Her voice was shaky, as if she were holding too much air in her lungs and could not let it out. "Tonight when I asked you and Lord Blackthorne to excuse Diana and I, I was acting on an impulse that came over me very suddenly. I wanted…or rather I *needed* to talk to Diana about everything that had happened."

He held up a hand. "Wait, you didn't want to talk to her about John Metcalf?"

Madeline shook her head. "No, this has nothing to do with John."

He contemplated that for a moment. "He didn't propose?"

"Yes, he did," she said uncertainly, "but I turned him down. Did you think…?"

"It doesn't matter what I thought." He swallowed uncomfortably. His legs seemed to be made of butter. "I thought nothing."

Madeline wandered to the bookcase and ran a finger over the spines. He wished she would just spit it out, for his patience was all gone.

She faced him. "I tried to tell her what she had

forgotten the day of the flood—that you had broken off your engagement."

Had he heard her correctly? Adam stepped away from the dark window. "You tried. You did not succeed?"

"I did, eventually. You may relax now, Adam. Diana will not be holding you to your proposal. She plans to leave tomorrow."

The muscles in his back and shoulders relaxed in one great sweep of comprehension. The secrets were out.

"How? What did you say? Was she shocked? Angry?"

Madeline tilted her head, as if she were considering how to describe it. "Neither shocked nor angry. When I tried to tell her, she informed me that she already knew. She said she remembered everything the day after the accident but kept it to herself, because she...she didn't want me to have you."

Adam fought to check his anger. "She knew, and she didn't want you to have me? What I really want to say to you now is that I told you so, but I will not because I know how ridiculously loyal you are to her, and that nothing I say will make you choose happiness for yourself over hers."

Madeline walked to him. She took his hands in hers, pressed them to her soft cheek.

Caught off guard and instantly flustered, he looked into her eyes for the first time, searching them. What was this?

"Please, let me finish," she said. "I must say everything I came to say before I lose my mettle.

When you convinced me the other day to talk to Diana, I did, but I failed. At least I thought I did. She turned me away and made me more certain than ever that I was doing the right thing to keep my heart closed off to the world. But Adam, somehow I managed to open her heart with all the things I said, and afterward, she began to regret what had become of our relationship. You were right. I did need to open my heart, and I want to open it now. Again. To you. Diana is leaving, and I want to stay.''

She kissed his hands and pressed them to her cheek again, and he tried to focus on what she was telling him rather than the feel of her moist, hot lips on his skin and the fires kindling in his veins.

Yet, even through it all, he still had questions. ''You said she is leaving tomorrow. Why so quickly?''

''Diana is going to leave with Lord Blackthorne. She is going to marry him.''

The fires within began to cool slightly. ''She is leaving to marry Lord Blackthorne? When did this transpire?''

''Over the past few days, and I suppose it began when they met on the ship.''

He shook his head. ''This seems all too familiar.''

He pulled his hands from hers and crossed to the other side of the room where the candlelight did not reach. He stood in the darkness, his pulse pounding in his ears. ''She handed me over to you, did she? On a silver platter with her happy blessing?''

Madeline's voice was quiet. ''Yes, but—''

''But what? How can I be sure that if Diana had

not met Lord Blackthorne, you would not be packing your bags right now to return with her to Yorkshire? I do not wish to be your second choice, Madeline.''

She took a step toward him. ''How can you speak of second choices, when I was not even as good as that when I came here? For weeks I had to live with the heartbreak of discovering that you did not want me, when I wanted you more than anything. I was rejected in the worst way, and now you fault me for being afraid! You broke my heart, Adam. Everyone in my life had broken my heart, and if you could only know how much courage I had to scrape together to come here and talk to you tonight.''

''But you have stumbled backward into the necessity of acting upon your feelings. How can I be sure you even know what you want?''

''Stumbled backward?'' She crossed to him and dropped to her knees again, wrapping her arms around him and resting her cheek on his hip. Adam sucked in a breath. She was squeezing him so tightly he doubted he could pry her off if he tried. Then he heard her sob and the sound of it brought his own heart into his throat.

''I am not stumbling backward now. I will *not* let go of you! Not until you believe that I love you, and that I would have thrown Diana out of here myself if she had tried to keep me from you one more day.''

He stood in shocked silence, his hands floating in the air over her head.

''I am on my knees, Adam, weeping for you. I don't know how else to show you that I do have a heart. You were right about me from the beginning.

You knew *everything*. You saw inside to the real me, where no one had ever bothered to look before. I don't care what brought us to this moment—all the mix-ups and the backward stumbling and tripping and falling. All I care about is you, and what I know is true. My heart—my frightened, reluctant heart—beats only for you."

She gazed up at him, her cheeks stained with tears, her eyes repeating everything she had just said to him. They were pleading with him.

God! She was right! Nothing mattered but this moment of pure openness! Madeline, his beautiful, timid Madeline, was wearing her heart on her sleeve. How could he even think of turning her away?

With aching, jubilant surrender, he dropped to his knees before her and took her delicate face in his big hands, tilted it up toward his. The room was dim, but he could still see the faint luster of her eyes, smell the sweetness of her breath, feel the silky texture of her skin. He needed her, dear God, he needed her. And he would show her just how much.

Gently, cautiously, he lowered his mouth to hers.

She rose to meet his kiss, wrapped her arms around his neck and pulled him fast against her soft, heaving breasts. She parted her lips for him, and he plunged eagerly into the warmth she offered. He kissed her deeply and passionately, stopping only to say, "I'm so sorry, Madeline."

She laughed out loud—a happy, joyful release. "*You* are sorry? For what? You have done nothing but force me out of myself. You've made me feel beautiful."

He pulled her into him and kissed her again, this time with an abandon that almost knocked him off his knees. For too long he had shouldered what was forbidden, and now it burned in him like red-hot flames licking over his flesh.

A brief second of panic ensued, when he wasn't sure he could restrain his desire for her and keep from taking her here on the cold, hard floor, but it passed when she gazed lovingly into his eyes and touched his face. He knew he could do anything for her. He had waited this long. He could wait a little longer.....

"Marry me, Madeline."

She smiled. "Oh Adam, I have dreamed of this moment all my life. That day when I stepped off the boat and you did not want me, I thought I was doomed to live without you forever. And when you still wanted Diana..."

He touched a finger to her lips. "Forget about dreams, Madeline. No more of that. We are real, you and I. No more idealizing. Love me for the man that I am, as I love you for the woman you are. You, my darling, are the one I want to spend the rest of my life with."

"Oh, Adam." She wrapped her arms around his neck and kissed him deeply. "I've waited so long for this. Please don't send me back to my room to sleep alone tonight. Take me to your bed."

He gazed into her sweet, dark eyes. "You ask the impossible if you expect me to sleep next to you and not love you as I intend to when I am your husband."

"I would not ask that of you. I want you, Adam. Tonight. If all had been right with the world, you would have been my husband ages ago. Let us make up for lost time.''

It took no more to convince him. Rising to his feet, he gathered her into his arms and carried her up the stairs as quietly as possible. By the time he reached his bed and laid her down upon the soft covers, his entire being was pulsing with need.

He stood over her, loosening his neckcloth. The moonlight shone in the window, illuminating Madeline's white nightdress. She looked like a goddess, lying back upon the pillows, waiting for him. Her beauty was breathtaking, her innocence intoxicating. He had not known he could ever love a woman as fiercely as he loved the one before him.

Adam pulled off his shirt and came down gently upon her. His lips found hers in the darkness and he reveled in their delicious flavor. She wrapped her long legs around his hips and he held her tightly in his arms, pressing his body against hers. He wanted all of her. He had waited so long.

He kissed the smooth, warm skin at her neck and unbuttoned her gown, then let his lips trace a path down to her luscious breasts. Gently his hands slid from her hips down to her legs, sliding the gown up and up until he found the warm center of her womanhood where she was delightfully damp with desire.

Feeling the warmth of Adam's hand caressing her in her most private place, Madeline's heart quickened with both anticipation and anxiety. She had no experience with any of this. She wanted Adam more than she'd ever wanted anything, but she had no idea what to do.

"You're shaking, Madeline," he whispered softly, sounding surprised but charmed as he gazed into her eyes.

"I'm sorry. I want to please you, but this is all so new and I don't know what to do."

His hands caressed her thigh up under her gown. "Don't apologize for being adorable."

She laid a hand on his cheek. "Tell me what to do, Adam."

He smiled. "We could start by removing this." He glanced down at her gown.

She sat up and pulled the linen garment off over her head. She should have felt self-conscious, for no man had ever seen her in such a bared state before, but nervousness faded away with the oncoming wave of arousal when Adam's face revealed his wonderment and his desire.

"You are the most beautiful creature I have ever seen."

She gloried in the awe in his eyes and the sound of sexual hunger in his voice. He wanted her. It was a dream come true to see him this way.

He came down upon her again, but this time she felt the heat of his bare skin against her own and shuddered with inconceivable pleasure. She met his open mouth with eagerness and delighted in the rhapsody of his kiss. Instinctively, Madeline parted her legs and thrust her hips upward, astounded by the feel of his firm arousal pressing against her. Still devouring his mouth with her own, she gave in to her burning curiosity and reached down to touch him over the thick fabric of his breeches. The rigid feel of him was wondrous. She felt so blessed to be intimate with him at last.

Adam moaned and kissed her more deeply. He leaned on one elbow and unbuttoned his breeches, then slid them off. He took her hand in his and showed her how to touch him. Never taking her eyes off his, Madeline carefully observed what pleased him.

"Yes, like that." He closed his eyes for a moment, then opened them again and lowered his mouth to her breasts, kissing and sucking, thrilling her with his fervid tongue. She began to ache and tingle all over.

He kissed down her belly and around her navel, then went lower until he reached the center of her womanhood, where her desires both began and culminated.

An urgent response blazed through her at the exquisite feel of his mouth. Shocked at the intensity of her body's sweet, throbbing ache, she clutched Adam's shoulders until the pleasure became too potent to bear. The tension that was coursing through her body like out-of-control floodwaters surged to a forceful peak, then everything exploded within.

All her muscles squeezed tightly, held fast for a moment, then relented with a titillating, debilitating release. Euphoria filled her, and for the first time in her life, she experienced pure and absolute physical contentment.

"Oh, Adam." Her voice was a breathy whisper. "I had no idea."

He rose up to settle himself between her thighs and gently thrust into her opening. Though she was tight and virginal, she was also relaxed, and the pain seemed insignificant compared to the spiritual bliss of his entry as he broke through her maidenhood. Tears of joy sprang to her eyes.

Adam touched his forehead to hers while he moved within her, their bodies mating in pure, primitive harmony. It was everything she had dreamed it would be—intimate, pleasurable, loving. She had never known anything could be so beautiful.

Adam's pace intensified and she recognized his mounting need. He rose up on both arms and drove into her again and again until he pulsed within. "I love you," he whispered hotly in her ear, his breath sending a torrent of gooseflesh down her satiated body. "And I promise I will never stop telling you that, Madeline, for as long as I live."

The love she felt brought tears to her eyes again. "Then I am yours. For as long as you'll have me."

"That will be forever, my love. Forever."

The following afternoon, all the family gathered on the veranda to say goodbye to Lord Blackthorne and Lady Thurston and their entourage. Penelope had picked wildflowers to give to Diana, to wish her well and to celebrate her betrothal to the viscount, and Mary had baked biscuits to send with her for the long journey to Halifax.

Adam felt a surge of warmth and gratitude for the people and blessings around him. His family was together; Madeline would soon be his wife. Everything seemed true and proper. Idealistic dreams were gone now, replaced by what was real, and there was a certain security in that.

"Will you come back to visit us, Lady Thurston?" Penelope asked. "You'll be my auntie, after all."

"I will indeed be your auntie, Penelope, and I will be happy to visit, as long as you promise to make your father bring you to Halifax to visit me as well." She tapped Penelope lightly on the nose, and a smile spread across her sweet cherub face.

Adam escorted Diana to the lieutenant-governor's coach and swept her up into his arms to lift her in. She squirmed on the leather seat to try and sit naturally, fumbling with her skirts to cover her injured leg.

"You'll be all right?" he asked her, closing the door and standing at the window. "There's no hurry, you know. You can stay here if you like, until you're fully recovered. Madeline and I would gladly take you to Halifax in a week or two."

She waved her gloved hand through the air. "Don't be such a silly worrywart, Adam. I'm fine. You're just looking for an excuse to go to Halifax for a honeymoon."

He smiled warmly at her.

"Goodbye, Adam," she said. "My future brother-in-law. I am trusting you with my baby sister. You had best not disappoint me."

"You know I won't. I intend to make her happy, Diana. I promise you that."

"You don't have to promise. You are a good man, Adam. I've always known that. I'm sorry for how things were between us, but it has all turned out for the best. We are all where we are meant to be.''

''Indeed we are.'' He squeezed her hand one last time. ''Goodbye, Diana.''

As he turned away from her, he spotted Lord Blackthorne. The viscount was the last guest to leave the house, leaning on his cane and limping down the steps on his wooden leg, following his valet, who carried a leather satchel.

''My word, Coates, Mary has just given me enough blueberry tarts to turn me into one! What a perfectly delightful family you have.''

Adam met the viscount in the middle of the yard and pumped his hand. ''Have a safe journey, my lord.''

''I most certainly will, and I will take up the case of your marshlands at Government House and see what can be done.''

Their handshake continued. The viscount seemed reluctant to leave. He nervously cleared his throat and lowered his voice. ''And do accept my apologies, man, for what occurred between Lady Thurston and me. I must thank you for not challenging me to a duel or something of that nature, Coates. You certainly had the right.''

Adam smiled at Lord Blackthorne. ''Nonsense. Diana was free to do as she chose. Life here in Cumberland could never have been right for her, and I think we all knew it.''

''Yes, yes, well, I'm glad things worked out.'' He peered over Adam's shoulder at Diana, waiting in the coach. ''By God, but she is a lovely creature, is she not? More charm than a sparkling jewel. What were the chances that a man like me could ever *dream* of marrying a woman like her?'' He whistled in disbelief.

"You are a lucky man, my lord," Adam replied dutifully.

"And so are you, Coates. Miss Oxley is a lovely young woman in her own right. Quite ravishing, actually. She seems to belong here. I always thought so, from the first moment I saw her. She'll be a good mother to your children, and with God's blessings, give you many more."

"I have no doubt." They said goodbye again, and the viscount limped off to his coach.

Madeline went to say goodbye to her sister. Adam watched them hold hands and kiss each other on the cheek. It was a fine thing to see sisters reunited with each other after so many years apart. Or perhaps they had found each other for the first time, here in a new land.

Penelope and Charlie appeared on either side of him, and he wrapped his arms around his children.

The coach lurched forward and Madeline waved goodbye. As soon as the convoy turned into the lane, she faced Adam, a glow of true happiness lighting up her face.

Adam moved toward her and held out his hands. The children giggled and dashed for the house, leaving Adam and Madeline alone in the yard, facing each other with the sun raining down on their faces. Adam raised both of Madeline's hands and pressed his lips to her soft knuckles.

"Shall we go and find the reverend?" he asked, with a seductive grin.

Madeline giggled. "Now?"

"Yes, now. I would have preferred it to be yesterday, or the day before, or the day before that, but I will settle for today."

Her voice was silky and flirtatious. "Why the hurry?"

"You know why, love."

"Because you're afraid I'll change my mind?"

"No."

"Because you're afraid John Metcalf will come back and propose to me again?"

"No."

"Because…hmm. You have dykes to build and fields to drain, and today is your only free day?"

Adam covered her mouth with his own, tasting the sweet honey of her kiss, consuming the light that had finally begun to shine from her soul.

"Does that give you a hint?" he asked, rubbing his nose against hers. "If not, just wait until tonight, my Yorkshire bride—and I will show you exactly why."

Madeline smiled enticingly and kissed him again. "Then take me to the reverend, and let me tell him that 'I do.'"

*   *   *   *   *

JULIANNE MacLEAN

Before embarking on the wonderful challenge of writing romance, Julianne earned degrees in both English literature and business administration. She spent some time as a financial statement auditor, but is now wildly happy to be a full-time mom and romance writer. She lives in Nova Scotia, Canada, with her husband and five-year-old daughter. Julianne loves to hear from readers, and invites you to visit her Web site at www.juliannemaclean.com.

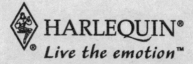

Can't get enough of
our riveting Regencies
and evocative Victorians?
Then check out these enchanting
tales from harlequin historicals®

On sale May 2003

BEAUTY AND THE BARON by Deborah Hale

Will a former ugly duckling and an embittered
Waterloo war hero defy the odds in the name of love?

SCOUNDREL'S DAUGHTER by Margo Maguire

A feisty beauty encounters a ruggedly handsome
archaeologist who is intent on whisking her away
on the adventure of a lifetime!

On sale June 2003

THE NOTORIOUS MARRIAGE by Nicola Cornick
(sequel to LADY ALLERTON'S WAGER)

Eleanor Trevithick's hasty marriage to Kit Mostyn
is scandalous in itself. But then her husband
mysteriously disappears the next day....

SAVING SARAH by Gail Ranstrom

Can a jaded hero accused of treason and a
privileged lady hiding a dark secret save
each other—and discover everlasting love?

Visit us at www.eHarlequin.com

HARLEQUIN HISTORICALS®

HHMED30

COOPER'S CORNER

Welcome to Cooper's Corner....
Some come for pleasure,
others for passion—
and one to set things straight....

Coming in May 2003...
FOR BETTER OR FOR WORSE
by Debbi Rawlins

Check-in: Veterinarian Alex McAllister is the man to go to in
Cooper's Corner for sound advice. But since his wife's death
eight years ago, his closest relationship has been with his dog...
until he insists on "helping" Jenny Taylor by marrying her!

Checkout: Jenny has a rare illness, and as Alex's wife her
medical costs would be covered. But Jenny doesn't want a
marriage based on gratitude...she wants Alex's love!

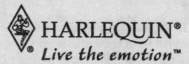

HARLEQUIN®
Live the emotion™

Visit us at www.eHarlequin.com

CC-CNM10

eHARLEQUIN.com

Sit back, relax and enhance your romance
with our great magazine reading!

- **Sex and Romance!** Like your romance
hot? Then you'll *love* the sensual reading
in this area.

- **Quizzes!** Curious about your lovestyle?
His commitment to you? Get the
answers here!

- **Romantic Guides and Features!**
Unravel the mysteries of love with
informative articles and advice!

- **Fun Games!** Play to your heart's content….

**Plus…romantic recipes,
top ten lists,
Lovescopes…and more!**

**Enjoy our online magazine today—
visit www.eHarlequin.com!**

COMING NEXT MONTH FROM

HARLEQUIN HISTORICALS®